D0285788

Down Home Blues
A Novel

Phyllis R. Dixon
New Generation Press

Down Home Blues

A Novel

Phyllis R. Dixon
New Generation Press

Cover design by HPP Design
Cover photography by Corrine Wells

Grateful acknowledgment is made for permission to reprint lyrics from *I'm Smilin Again* by Grady Champion, GSM Music Group LLC.

Printed in the United States of America

ISBN 978-0-9749540-0-4
ISBN 978-0-9749540-2-8 (eBook)

Happiness is having a large, loving, caring, close-knit family... *in another city.* George Burns

For Maggie Jean
My first teacher, my role model, and my best friend.

Acknowledgements

At last. It's been a minute since the Washingtons have told their story. A lot has happened to them and to me since *Forty Acres*. Two of my biggest cheerleaders have made their transition, Fitzgerald 'Fitz' Dixon and Clovice Wilder. In the words of James Taylor, "I always thought I'd see you again." My babies Trey, Candace and Lee are all grown up now and I am proud of each of you. Keep moving forward and keep your head to the sky. I've got some new angels, Braylon, Erica and Brenton – what a precious gift. A shout-out to some more new people who have come into my life, Arlender Jones and Michael Stewart, seems like I've known you forever. And a shout-out to Tanya Beckley, Tujuana Britton, Karen and Sheryl Dean, who I have known forever. Special acknowledgement to Sharon Williams and Linda Campbell, my extra-special sorors (Delta Sigma Theta of course). Thanks to Shelia (yes, she spells it like that) Bell, and Written Word Editorial. I am eternally indebted to Evelyn Palfrey and Miss Mary. I thank the Jacksons and the Lees, my OCC friends (you know who you are) and my St. Andrew family for your support. And a special thank you to YOU for taking the time to read what I write. I hope you enjoy.

Phyllis R. Dixon

"...the winter'll soon be over, children.
And when we get on Canaan's shore,
We'll shout, and sing forever more.
Oh, the winter'll soon be over, children." Negro Spiritual

Chapter 1
WINTER SOON BE OVER

Just five more hours left in this year and I say good riddance. I lost my mother nine months ago. I never imagined my world without Lois Washington in it, and not a day goes by that I don't think about her. I miss hearing her call me by my full name, Beverly Ann. Of course, that name is as country as a gravel road, and I always wanted something sexier like my sisters Carolyn and Cecelia. Now I'd give anything to hear her say it again. They say it gets easier with time. I'm still waiting. That's how my year started, and the bad news kept coming.

My sisters and I didn't speak for three months due to a silly dispute over my mother's jewelry. I was in a car accident and couldn't work for six weeks (although that could have been a blessing in disguise since that's when my sisters and I started speaking again). My son enlisted in the military and is fighting some ridiculous war on the other side of the world. In July, my dog, Money, got loose. He usually finds his way home, but this is the longest he's ever been gone. And my husband, Anthony, moved out after breaking his promise to be faithful – again. Not that I really believed him. After more than twenty years of marriage, I had gotten used to his roaming eye and other body parts.

We've been together since high school, and even though we're separated, and I've been dating, he's still the measuring stick — in more ways than one. But when his latest hussy posted pictures of the two of them online, I couldn't keep looking the other way. My sisters said it's about time, although Cecelia controlled her husband, and I didn't want a docile man. Apparently, my brother-in-law didn't want to be controlled anymore, since they just got divorced. And my little sister Carolyn is a newlywed. She beat the odds and actually found a keeper. It took her twenty years to find him, but he looks like he was worth the wait.

Anthony and I have been separated more than a year — although I still see him every week. We own The Oasis, a beauty salon and barber shop. A few years ago, we bought the house next door to our house and transformed the corner lot into The Oasis. Anthony still comes by to check on the barbers and keep up with handyman projects. Aunt Belle says he keeps sniffing around just enough to keep a claim on me, like a dog guarding a bone. He's not going to gnaw on it, but doesn't want anyone else to either. I know she's right, and my New Year's resolution was going to be to see a lawyer and start divorce proceedings. Then, our son Tony came home for Thanksgiving. That was the good news. The bad news was that he was being deployed to Afghanistan. Why should my baby put his life on the line trying to settle a dispute that's been going on since Bible days? He was leaving the Tuesday after Thanksgiving, and he wanted to spend the holiday with both of us, so his father came home and the three of us spent the holiday weekend together. It was like old

2

times, maybe even better. Anthony didn't have to lie and I didn't have to question everything he said and did.

Other than him not being able to keep his thing in his pants, he was a great husband. We rarely argued. He didn't drink or do drugs. He was generous with his money and kept up with the house and salon repairs. We both enjoyed bowling, dancing, and the blues. He remembered all holidays and anniversaries. He wasn't abusive and there were no complaints about our sex life. Even with all those positives, I know they don't outweigh the scales of his messing around. When I decide I've finally had enough, he'll do something to rekindle the flame I keep trying to stamp out.

I don't know how I would have made it through Christmas without him. I hadn't heard from Anthony since we took Tony to the airport. Then, he showed up the day before Christmas Eve and said he knew the holidays would be hard for me. He took me down home to see my father early on Christmas Eve. We came back that evening, and he hasn't left since. My sisters will berate me for taking him back again, but this was the longest we'd ever been apart, and I really thought he had changed.

Anthony and I had planned to bring in the New Year on Beale Street with twenty thousand other partyers, then come home for private festivities. I've lived in Memphis twenty years, but had never been to Beale Street for the midnight guitar drop. As part of our vow to rekindle our marriage, we said we'd start doing new things together, and the guitar drop was one of them. We usually spent the days around the New Year down home in Eden, Arkansas. It's just sixty miles from Memphis, though it seems like a world away.

Eden is a refuge and my daddy still farms and lives in the house he and Mama built fifty years ago. Every New Year's Eve, I attended Watch Night service with Mama, while Anthony played cards and dominoes with his relatives. Daddy loved to play cards, so when Mama and I got home, we would all go to Anthony's folk's house for all night rise and fly bid whist. At dawn, we'd go home, sleep a few hours, then eat black-eyed peas for good luck, cabbage for money, and fried chicken because Mama's was the best and it was everyone's favorite. This is the first New Year since Mama's death. I feel like I'm abandoning Daddy, but I couldn't face that ride knowing she wouldn't be there. My brothers said they would stay with Daddy so he wouldn't be alone.

Anthony was making a daytrip to Eden to see his relatives from Chicago. His truck needed an oil change, so he took my car. I wasn't going anywhere and he was coming right back to Memphis in time for us to go to Beale Street. That was the plan – until he called and said his brother from Chicago had just gotten there and would I be terribly upset if he stayed longer. I told him to stay put, since the roads were supposed to turn icy. I asked Anthony to check on Daddy for me, and to promise not to try to surprise me by coming back to Memphis. He promised, and said he would leave first thing the following morning.

With the change in plans, I decided to bring in the New Year with a pampering session. I lit jasmine candles, found my Etta James playlist, and opened the Moscato wine I had been saving. I texted all my siblings to wish them a Happy New Year, then called Daddy.

"Hey, Big Sis," Carl said, answering on the first ring.

"I know I'm early, I just called to wish you guys a Happy New Year."

"Same to you, but you'll have to wait until next year to talk to Daddy."

"Is he sleep?"

"He isn't here."

"Oh. Did he go with Aunt Belle to the rehabilitation center?" Aunt Belle volunteers at the Dwight County Rehabilitation Center. She says too many times people her age are just thrown away, and she wants them to know someone still cares. She planned a full itinerary that would culminate with Jell-O and line dancing at midnight. She made sure she had tapes for the electric slide, cupid shuffle, and the wobble, and invited Daddy to the party.

"He said that was for old people. He's visiting his lady friend."

"Which one?" I asked. Daddy is in his eighties, and other than a skin cancer scare a few years ago, he's in pretty good health. He still drives and we had to make him promise not to go hunting alone anymore (we also hid his shotguns just to make sure). He's got hair, most of his teeth, and his right mind. At that age, men with those traits are in short supply. My brothers think Daddy's eligible bachelor status is cool and hope his stamina is hereditary. My sisters and I have been amazed at the women who swarmed around Daddy like flies on you-know-what before Mama was even cold in the ground. Even more amazing, Daddy seemed to enjoy the attention.

"Miss Emma. She looks like the front-runner."

"Are you serious? Miss Emma Davis, our high school English teacher?"

"That's her," Carl replied.

"She doesn't seem like Daddy's type. She's nothing like Mama. He shouldn't be out driving on New Year's Eve anyway. There are too many drunk drivers out and the roads are supposed to turn bad. Plus, folks will be shooting guns all night. It's not safe."

"I guess he forgot to ask your permission," Carl said.

"Here I was thinking Daddy would be missing Mama but instead he's hanging out. I asked Anthony to check on him, but looks like there's no need for that."

"He did come over this morning. He said we were his last stop, and he was heading back to Memphis. It was good seeing you guys together for Christmas. Maybe the New Year will bring you two back together. It just doesn't make sense to break up after all these years."

"Now you sound like Mama."

"You should listen to her. I wish I had," Carl said.

"Well, tell Daddy I called and you take care," I said. I called Anthony's phone and it went straight to voicemail. In days past, I would have immediately called his folks and asked to speak to one of his relatives. I enjoyed talking with them and they treated me like a daughter. While I was interested in their welfare, my real motive for calling was usually to make sure Anthony was where he said he would be. I thought we had moved beyond those days. *I should have known better*, I thought, as I scrolled through my cell phone apps.

I traded in my Navigator and got a new Lexus last summer after my car accident. I even dated my salesman a few weeks. He showed me how to use all the bells and whistles, including syncing the GPS system to my phone. It was supposed to help if the car was stolen or if you wanted to monitor a teen driver. Tracking

6

down lying husbands wasn't listed as one of the uses, but over the years I've had enough experience that I should patent an app for it. Although I have mellowed over the years, especially since the shooting incident a few years ago. I missed on purpose and wasn't really trying to shoot that skank, but Carolyn said I'm lucky she didn't press charges. Even Daddy, who usually stays out of his children's marriage drama, said I went too far. Women are always flirting with Anthony, but to have a so-called friend betray me was too much.

I don't know why women won't leave my husband alone. Then again — I do. Anthony is fine with a capital F. He was good looking in high school and he's good looking now. Most of our classmates have potbellies, bald heads (not the good Michael Jordan kind), or an inside out Mohawk. Those that do have hair are gray. Anthony looks better with age. Women talk boldly among themselves and proclaim what they will and won't take. My response was, "Look at Jesse Jackson and Bill Clinton. They had affairs and got caught. Do you see Hillary swiveling her neck and moving on? She's sitting right there reaping the benefits she has worked for, and I plan to do the same. Why should I let some other woman step in after I put in all these years? I drive a new car every two years, have a three thousand square foot house and an eight-hundred credit score. I work, but only because I want to. Running the beauty shop doesn't feel like work because it's what I've always wanted to do. Anthony has always worked one and sometimes two jobs and gives me his checks. So, no I'm not leaving."

That was my mantra for years, but losing Mama made me realize how short life is and I don't want to look back and see I wasted half of it chasing Anthony Townsend. The address *5909 Elm,* popped up on my screen. Anthony was less than ten miles from the house. Usually my New Year's resolution was to lose weight. Grieving over Mama and my marriage had been the catalyst for a thirty-pound weight loss, so that wasn't my goal for the coming year. This time I vow not to be seduced by Anthony's lies anymore. That had also been my resolution in other years. But this time, I mean it. Aunt Belle says the only time you can change a man is when he's a baby in diapers. The time and energy I spend snooping, plotting, and stressing over him are better used on something else. Before I set Anthony aside for good, I have one more plan to carry out. I looked through the drawer and found my license plate number, then got my AAA card to call for towing service. This is going to be Anthony's nightmare on Elm Street.

CAROLYN

New Year's Eve is the worst holiday to be single. No other day is it more obvious that you are alone. Christmas and Thanksgiving are for family and you can go solo. Valentine's Day is for sweethearts, but it's usually a work day, so you can get through it by treating it like any other work day. You can spend your birthday with your girls, go to church on Easter, and find a barbeque for the Fourth. But New Year's Eve is different. No one wants to go to a party alone. And if you stay home, you feel like you're missing something. I've spent more than my share of New Year's Eves alone, or babysitting my nieces and nephews, or with someone I wasn't that crazy about just so I wouldn't be alone. And though I'm ashamed to admit it, I've spent New Year's Eves alone, while my man spent the holiday with his wife. Not this year. To quote Sophia, "I's married now." Mrs. Derrick Roberts. It will be a year tomorrow, and I'm still getting used to the sound of it.

I had given up looking for Mr. Right. By the time I turned forty, I would have settled for Mr. Suitable, but Derrick had all the qualities I was looking for. He seemed perfect, except for the fact that he lived in Eden, Arkansas. But he wouldn't let six hundred miles stand between us. We racked up frequent flyer miles and Amtrak points and spent as much time together as I had with some guys I dated that live right here in Chicago. In the beginning, I kept trying to figure out what was wrong with him. How could this thoughtful, good looking, financially secure man be unattached? I figured he would show his true colors eventually, so I'd just enjoy the attention while it lasted. Instead of disappointments piling up as they usually did, this relationship only got better. We had only been dating six months and when he got on his knee to propose, I thought he was bending over to tie his shoe. He quoted romantic Smokey Robinson lyrics and presented me with a stunning two-carat diamond engagement ring. You'll hear women say it doesn't matter if a man marries them; it's only a piece of paper. Just like when they say size doesn't matter, don't believe them. I said yes before he finished the 'e' in me. Even though I was next in line for a promotion at work, I applied for a transfer to Memphis and quickly planned a wedding. If I had known Southern men were so gracious, I would have set my sites below the Mason-Dixon Line a long time ago.

Derrick and I reconnected during a family reunion when he came to my parents' house to visit. I remembered him as Bucky, the annoying buck-toothed kid who played with my younger brothers. That kid had turned into a good-looking, lean, six-foot tall man, with a warm smile full of straight teeth. He remembered me as Chubby, his friends' dismissive big sister. Let the record reflect, I was given the nickname after the singer, (they said I did the twist like Chubby Checker when I was small) not for being fat. Anyway, it was supposed to be time with my family, but I spent more time with Derrick as it became obvious he was interested in me. We stayed in touch and he courted me old-school style. He sent flowers just because. When we went out he paid, and he ordered for me. On the weekend, he would drive to Chicago like he was driving around the corner. He made me feel like he was glad to be with me and not just sexually. When we announced our engagement, I don't know who was happier, me or my parents. They were proud when I got my law degree. I work for the IRS, and to hear them tell it, I run the agency. Despite my success, Mama never really embraced my career woman lifestyle and always inquired about marriage prospects.

Daddy described Derrick as a hard worker — his ultimate compliment. Derrick is the first black Field Agent for the State Agricultural Commission in Dwight County and Daddy adores him. Daddy said Derrick didn't just focus on the large farmers like the others had. To us, his farm is huge. But he said his is considered a small family farm and most of his peers are selling out because it is hard to compete with the bigger farms. Derrick helped him file a claim in the Black Farmer's lawsuit and told him how to apply for crop insurance. Mama said he doted on his grandmother who raised him, and that was a sign of thoughtfulness. When she got sick, he moved back to Eden from West Memphis to take care of her. My parents couldn't stop singing his praises, although they would have been happy to see me date any man with a job.

My sisters had a slightly different opinion. Cecelia said he was a mama's boy, and besides it was too soon. She even paid for a background check. My oldest sister, Beverly, said he and Karen Jones had an on-again off-again relationship and would probably get back together. I dismissed their negative predictions as sour grapes since their own marriages were disintegrating. My brother Raymond's only comment was that we were contributing to the global exploitation of Africa by buying diamonds.

Tomorrow will be our first anniversary. We got married on New Year's Eve in Key West. My sisters, two of my brothers and sisters-in-law, two of Derrick's fraternity brothers and their wives came. I casually mentioned our plans to Mama and was shocked when she said she wanted to go.

"You and Daddy haven't slept apart in years. Someone has to be dead or at death's door for him to agree to you traveling, and you know he's not getting on a plane."

"You let me worry about your father," she said.

To my surprise, not only did Daddy agree to let Mama come, he came with her. My brother, Paul, is a big time corporate attorney in Dubai and he and his wife made the trip. So my wedding turned into a mini-family vacation. I had never seen my parents so happy. Derrick's grandmother came too. And leave it to my brother, H. Rap Raymond, to find a black history angle. He got us front row seats for the Junkanoo parade which was a New Year's day tradition started by former Bahamian slaves who were given three holidays during the Christmas season. The trip was perfect and I started the new year with a new name.

Phyllis R. Dixon

Unfortunately, the new year also brought new problems. Derrick's grandmother was telling everyone that I was already wasting her boy's money on trips. Going away had actually been Derrick's idea. I didn't want a church wedding, although I did want to do something special. After watching the Travel Channel, Derrick is the one that suggested a destination wedding in Jamaica. We settled on Key West so anyone that wanted to join us wouldn't have to deal with passports. We divided the bills in half, and I charged my portion. I planned to pay off the bills right after the wedding, once I was sure everything was in order. But Derrick didn't want any debt and insisted on paying off my cards - although that really wasn't any of Mother Roberts' business.

Then, the cold we thought Mama had caught from the change in temperature wouldn't go away, and within six weeks she was dead.

Mother Roberts was in and out of hospitals all summer, until the doctors figured out her medicines were interacting poorly and changed her prescriptions. She spent weeks in a rehabilitation center so she could regain her strength, then stayed with Derrick until she was well enough to go home. Then my division at the IRS office in Memphis was restructuring, and my transfer was delayed twice.

We're going to live in Eden initially, and I will commute to work. I grew up on a farm on Route 4, next to the highway, and I had enough of country living. Chicago is my kind of town. But living in Eden is a small price to pay to be with my husband. I've put so many things on hold, hoping I'd find someone to share my life with. I want to go on a cruise. The last cruise I went on with some girlfriends was fun, but seeing the couples there made me yearn for my own special someone. I hated waiting for someone to ask me to dance, and I vowed not to go on another one until I had someone of my own. I can finally get a real house. I love my condo, but I've always wanted my own walls, yard, and porch. This situation was supposed to be a short phase, unfortunately, the four month transition period has been a year, and instead of living with my husband, we're still nursing a long distance relationship.

In the beginning of our long-distance romance, we always went out when he came to town. I loved being a couple and not waiting to be asked to dance. Lately we've settled into a routine and seldom leave my condo. Derrick doesn't like cold weather and is content to stay in. I'm not complaining, but I am a little tired of my life revolving around work and Derrick's phone calls and texts. We do Facechat, but that's getting old too. Even though we're married, I'd like our time together to revolve around more than food, sleep, and sex. We're starting to act like an old married couple.

We last saw each other three weeks ago and that visit was disastrous. I flew to Memphis, rented a car, and went straight to the rehabilitation center where Derrick was with his grandmother. She hadn't been taking her medicine properly and suffered a setback. We spent half the day sitting with her. When we went back to Derrick's house, it was a wreck. He had been spending most of his time at work and with his grandmother. He was keeping her dog, Poochie, and the house smelled like it. The sink was full of dirty dishes and clothes were everywhere. I told him I couldn't function in a dirty, smelly kitchen and didn't plan to spend my weekend cleaning, so we went out to dinner – which in Eden meant we ate inside the KFC rather than going to the drive-thru. What Derrick did during our fine dining experience shocked me so much,

I really don't remember what started the next argument. He raised his voice to me - in public. This upset me even more than whatever started the initial argument. I didn't speak to him the rest of the evening and took the first flight home the next day.

We had even argued about where to spend the holidays. Derrick wanted me to come to Eden. Eden, Arkansas is my hometown. It's the county seat of Dwight County, sixty miles west of Memphis. It's the kind of town where six degrees of separation is five too many. High school sports is the primary entertainment and Walmart is the primary (make that only) shopping. Of course there are good points too. Costs are low and there's no rush hour. People are friendly, and the front porch is more than just the entrance to the house. When I got to Chicago, I learned hanging out on the front porch is considered ghetto. But down home, the porch is a place to greet your neighbors and watch the world go by. Evergreen magnolias line the streets, and there are no homeless people. Despite these good points, there's one thing Eden doesn't have, jobs, making it the kind of town that people move from, not to. Many residents commute to Memphis for work, taking advantage of small town living, with big, make that medium, city access. I hope soon to be one of them. I'm not looking forward to trading my easy twenty minute trip for a sixty plus minute commute. But I'll be joining my man and a brief stay in Eden is a minor price to pay.

Derrick wanted me to come home for Christmas. I told him the tickets were too expensive and I had to get back to work. That was true, but I think the real reason was that I wasn't ready to spend a holiday without Mama. And he didn't want to leave his grandmother. I guess I should have given in – I haven't yet mastered the art of being submissive. It seems unnatural to me, like trying to write with my left hand. So neither of us budged and we spent our first Christmas as husband and wife in two different states. We realized this was silly and a waste of precious time so Derrick agreed to come to Chicago for New Year's.

This will be my last New Year's Eve in Chicago and I plan to enjoy all the attractions I've grown to take for granted. In Eden, to celebrate New Year's Eve, people either shoot their gun at midnight or go to Watch Night service. I've planned a full schedule for our anniversary weekend – which will culminate with the Navy Pier fireworks over Lake Michigan. Derrick wasn't enthusiastic when I told him and could only think of cold, snow, and crowds. What happened to the man that would follow me to the mall, a chick flick, or the nail shop, without complaint?

Mama said it was years before she and Daddy came to an understanding about a lot of things and sometimes the worse comes before the better. It's no coincidence that we got married shortly before Mama died. The Lord sent Derrick to me, not to replace Mama, but to give me a new kind of happiness. I know marriage isn't all wine and roses, and I'm willing to put in the work. I'm going to make an extra effort to get to know Mother Roberts, or Mamalil as he calls her. I'm going to work on this being submissive thing. And I'm going to pressure Human Resources to speed up my transfer. Having a baby is a long shot at my age, but it definitely won't happen with me living in another state.

The eight introductory notes of my *Rock Me Baby* ringtone means Derrick sent me a text. His train just left Kankakee, so he should arrive downtown within the hour. A light snow is floating from the sky like in a snow globe, covering the sidewalk with a thin feathery layer of powder. This light snow is supposed to taper off, meaning there will be no weather obstacles to our night on the town. So I'm heading to the train station to pick up my man. Change that, anybody can claim a man—make that my husband.

CECELIA

Cecelia stepped aside as the paramedics rolled the moaning woman covered with blood soaked sheets through the glass doors. After the stretcher rolled by, Cecelia dashed in front and led the way down the brightly lit hall. She swiped her badge on the keypad and the double doors parted. Two nurses met them when the doors opened and joined her at the front of the stretcher.

"I thought you were gone," one of the nurses said as they trotted to the emergency room."

"Haven't you already done a double?" the other one said.

"I don't mind staying," Cecelia said. "You guys are going to be swamped."

"So what else is new? Go get some rest so you can get back here tonight. I have plans for New Year's Eve that don't include Chicago Central General Hospital," the first nurse said.

Cecelia stopped, as a doctor and two more nurses rushed past her to the room. The second nurse waved her off then closed the curtain. Cecelia turned around and headed toward the employee exit. The woman looked like she had lost a lot of blood, but she was still conscious. Cecelia surmised it was a domestic situation. Car accident cases rarely came to General, and gunshot victims were usually accompanied by a police officer.

Home accidents or illnesses were usually accompanied by a family member. Her nineteen years of nursing, with seven years in the emergency room, had trained her to recognize trauma cases. If someone would have told her the high prevalence of domestic violence, she would not have believed them. Her father was never coarse with their mother, at least not that she had ever seen, and she had gotten her brothers in trouble plenty of times just by saying they had hit her, whether they had or not. Michael rarely raised his voice during their twenty-year marriage. Not that he had been a pushover. He had other ways to get his message across. The one time he raised his hand, he drew it back and left. That was the confirmation that their marriage was over. Like the George Jones song, he stopped loving her that day.

Cecelia had planned to go home, cook breakfast, and hope something decent was on television before going to bed and trying to get enough rest to do this all over again. The combination of alcohol, family, high expectations, and close quarters were lethal. Combined with staff wanting to take off for their own revelry made holidays, the busiest time in the emergency room. The trauma, drama, and short staff was a recipe for stress. But at least the time went fast and kept Cecelia from feeling lonely. Her ex-husband had taken her daughter and granddaughter to visit his parents for the holidays, and her son was working. Her brothers had lost their minds and moved back to Arkansas. Her friends were all married or coupled up. Even her sister had finally met and married her Prince Charming. So with no family around, she scheduled herself to work every day. Triple time pay didn't hurt either.

She had planned to go home, but the steering wheel seemed to have other plans. Instead of taking the Dan Ryan Expressway to her house, the car headed east to Indiana. Working in the emergency room was more stimulating than any drug, so she was wide awake. Rather than go home and watch reruns or unreal reality shows, she decided to visit Lady Luck.

When most people go on a diet, they restrict calories and change their eating habits. Cecelia was on a casino diet. She even changed her wireless plan so she couldn't go to online video poker sites. She hadn't been since the summer and had accumulated free play points, complimentary meals, and hotel nights on her Players' Card. There was a time when she spent endless hours and unmentionable amounts of money at the casino. Some people vegetated in front of the television or had wine to relax. Cecelia played slot machines and black jack. And even though she didn't have a problem, she decided to take a break, and hadn't been since summer. She didn't freak out, so it was obvious she wasn't an addict like her sister and ex-husband said.

She didn't see what the big deal was anyway. The whole country was built on gambling, they just called it something else. Christopher Columbus thought he was going to Japan but ended up in the Caribbean. That was a gamble he actually lost, but it worked out. The gambling term is miracle bet. Wall Street and the stock market are just legalized gambling. They use fancy words like arbitrage, options, and stock splits. In reality, a stockbroker is nothing more than a bookie and the Federal Reserve is the ultimate pit boss. Folks that buy stocks are called savvy investors, but they're playing the odds just like the folks at a craps table. A real estate developer takes a chance that he can spend a little money turning a plot of dirt into houses, office buildings or shopping centers and make big money. They're admired as astute businessmen yet that's pure speculation. Even her conservative father gambled.

What could be riskier than relying on the sun and rain to feed and clothe your family? At least at the casino, she could pick which game to play and she could walk away if the cards weren't going her way or the machine was cold. With farming, it was all or nothing. Her father had more good years than bad, and no one focused on his losses. So why not treat herself. She could afford to "invest" a few dollars and if it didn't work out, she'd just call it entertainment. To be on the safe side, she would stick with cash and leave her debit and credit cards in her car. Taking a chance was the American way. After all, it was a holiday. What could it hurt?

CARL

Carl checked one more time that the alarm was set, then gingerly tiptoed across the parking lot. The sleet and rain mixture that had been falling all day was turning to ice, so his manager called and told Carl to close early. His coworkers cheered when he made the announcement, but Carl wanted to work. He needed the money. Besides, he didn't have any exciting New Year's Eve plans. The only thing on his agenda when he got home was to take a hot bath. He was helping his brother coach the high school basketball team and they had practiced that morning. He had gotten out of shape since coming home, so even though he was just standing under the goal returning balls, as the boys practiced their free throws, his muscles ached. He would rather have been working, although he was looking forward to soaking them in a hot tub. That saying *you don't miss your water until your well runs dry* is really true. He didn't know if he fantasized more about women or bathing while he was locked up.

19

His father was putting on his coat as Carl entered the house. "You're heading out in this weather?"

"I'm just going 'round to Emma's," C.W. said.

"It's icy out there, Dad."

"I'll be fine. You forget I taught you to drive. I'm taking my old truck. That bad boy can get through anything. I'll stay over there and come home in the morning. So you'll have the house to yourself."

"All right. I'm going to soak in the tub then go to bed."

"That's it?"

"Afraid so," Carl said as he draped his coat on the back of the dining room chair.

"I'm glad you've settled down son, but I hate to see you spend so much time alone."

"I've been working twelve hour shifts and I'm tired."

"Isn't there some young lady you want to invite over?"

"No."

"It's New Year's Eve. Don't seem right for you to be alone. Whatever happened to you and that Taylor girl your mama liked?"

"She was too clingy. I don't need anybody checking my phone and coming up to my job."

"What about the girl Beverly introduced you to?"

"I love my sister, but matchmaking is not her strong suit. The last thing I need is a woman with three kids. I'm still trying to get to know my own kids."

"Okay, but like I said, I won't be home until morning..."

"Dad, I get the hint. Times sure have changed. I can remember when you and Mama warned us not to have girls in the house. Now you're practically setting me up."

"Well, you're grown now, and I need to ask you something," C.W. said as he put his cap on his head.

"What is it?" Carl asked.

"Did you turn into a gay? You do still like women, don't you?"

"I can't believe you're asking me that. Yes, I still like women and no, I'm not gay. I would just rather be alone than waste time with the wrong person."

"Okay," C.W. said with a sigh. "I've heard lots of stories from the guys at the barber shop. That Ferguson boy came home and never was the same."

"Well, prison does change you. But that wasn't one of the things that changed about me. The only new thing I picked up was cigarettes, and I plan to quit soon."

"Okay, son. I was just wondering," C.W. said as he put on his coat. "Guess I'll see you next year. Don't wait up," he said and walked out the door.

Carl smiled and shook his head, as he watched his father pull out of the driveway. There was a time when Carl divided holidays between his wife, his girlfriend, and whatever new woman he was trying to talk to. Those days were history. Although, not due to lack of opportunity. When he first came home, he tried to make up for lost time and had no trouble finding ladies willing to help him. There weren't too many stray men in his age group in Eden. He was drug-free and everyone knew his family had land. But they all wanted to claim him and Carl just wanted to have a good time.

He had been locked up four years, but it was more like a five or six year drought. Everyone knows crack addicts lose weight, steal, don't sleep, and lie. No one talks about what it does to you sexually. There were times where his mind was ready but his body wasn't and after a while his mind wasn't even ready. He had

21

vowed to give Wilt Chamberlain a run for his money when he got out.

The first time Carl stayed out all night, he returned home to find his mother and father sitting in the living room on the plastic covered couch just as they had when he was a teenager. He reassured them that he was all right and they didn't have to wait up for him. The next time he stayed out all night, they weren't in the living room, but he saw their bedroom light turn off, so he knew they had been awake. The next time he came home, the living room light was on, but it was Beverly in the living room instead of his parents.

"Hey, what are you doing here?" Carl asked as he closed the door behind him.

"Daddy has an appointment tomorrow in Memphis with his specialist. I came on over after I closed the salon and we'll leave early in the morning. Although with him worrying about you, his blood pressure will probably be sky high."

"What are you talking about?" Carl asked.

"I know you are grown, but considering everything you've put our parents through, I would think you'd show some respect and come in their house at a decent hour."

"Why are you tripping?" Carl said as he went to the kitchen.

"Because you are being selfish as usual and only thinking about yourself," Beverly said, as she followed him.

"I already talked to Mama and Daddy. They gave me the usual speech about being careful, but otherwise everything is cool."

"Everything is not cool. Do you know how much you worried them while you were on your crack odyssey? They worried when the phone rang, and they worried when it didn't ring. They're not going to give you a curfew like a child, but you should be considerate enough not to put them through any more stress. Can't you get your groove on before midnight?"

He resented Beverly being so bossy, yet she was right. He did not want to cause his parents any more pain, stress, or worry. After that, he never came in after midnight. He figured abiding by his self-imposed curfew wasn't a big sacrifice, especially since it would only be for a few months. He naively thought he would find a job and have his own place within a few months. Thirteen months later and he was still calling his parents' house home and rushing like Cinderella to get in before the clock struck twelve.

His father had just been glad that he still liked women. "I know some guys start liking men once they go to prison," he had said.

"You don't have to worry about that Dad."

"Good," Lois said. "Although you know we'd still love you. Some of them boys can fix themselves up pretty good."

"I don't care how good they fix themselves up, some things they can't change, if you know what I mean," C.W. said.

"Well, actually, these days they can. I remember watching on Oprah some girls that had operations to be men and men had operations to be women. They're called trans something or other," Lois said.

"That's why this world is so messed up. Can't even tell the boys from the girls," C.W. said.

"This is nothing new. Folks just used to cover it up. Remember that Franklin boy that went to school with us? You know what they said about him."

Carl smiled when he remembered those times. His parents were the perfect example of hard work and commitment. C.W.'s father cobbled together forty acres after working as a sharecropper for most of his life. He left the land to his sons, C.W. and Beau. They worked the land together and added to it after their father died. C.W. left for a few years and went to Detroit just like millions of other African Americans during the first half of the twentieth century. He came back when his father had a stroke while plowing one of the fields. Two years later, his brother fell off a tractor and died. Since his brother didn't have any children, there was no controversy with the title or heirs property, which is how a lot of black people lost their land. C.W. felt his father and brother gave their lives for the land and he had a responsibility to make the farm a success.

C.W. and Lois worked from sunup to sundown and bought more land whenever they could. C.W. did the visible work, but their mother was just as integral to his success. She was a seamstress and was tighter with a dollar than bark on a tree. It had been a fifty-year marriage and business partnership and both were successful. They had endured the loss of two sons, weathered economic cycles, and nursed each other through various illnesses – partners in every sense of the word.

Carl's ex-wife had been a loyal partner and he knew he had messed it up. He hoped for a second chance to have a family, but that wasn't a priority right now. All he wanted to do was make and save money. He had done a few plumbing jobs and helped on the farm when he first came home. He actually had a long list of plumbing customers, which looked lucrative on paper. But he learned that family, friends, and business don't mix. They always had a story about why they could only pay half of what they owed – if that much. After buying supplies and paying on his restitution debt and child support, his earnings were gone before he got them. He had gone with Aunt Belle's senior group on the bus to the casino, figuring he would try his luck. He lost his money so quickly, he spent most of his time people watching in the lobby. He had even been suckered into sending money to an envelope stuffing scam. His cousin, Perry, kept trying to talk him into joining his "business." Carl knew his cousin always took the quick money route, and he said he would clean toilets before he'd risk going back to jail. Then it looked like he couldn't even get a job cleaning toilets. Finally, Burger Barn called. Carl had been there almost a year and had already been promoted three times. He started as an intermittent environmental engineer. In other words, a part-time janitor. His parents couldn't have been happier if he had been elected President. Unfortunately, just three weeks after starting the job his mother died. He had planned to take his parents to dinner when he got his first paycheck. Instead, he bought a black suit.

Rather than sit around the house, he worked as many hours as he could. He didn't just cut the lawn around the store, he manicured it. He brought fertilizer from the farm and revived the scraggly bushes. The manager noticed his work ethic and moved him from janitor to the grill. Now he could do any job in the restaurant and was a shift leader. Many of the teens scheduled to work during the holiday were nowhere to be found and Carl was taking up their slack. The managers tried to avoid people working more than forty hours, but inevitably he was asked to stay late or come in on his off day because someone didn't show. Carl didn't mind. He was going to see his sons next weekend and planned to take them shopping at after Christmas sales. He hadn't touched his last check and this one should be almost double his regular pay. He earned just above minimum wage, and working extra hours increased his check from pitiful to meager. He didn't see how people made it that actually had to pay bills. He lived with his parents and drove his mom's old car. He had offered to pay them, but of course they refused. He used that money to pay extra on his child support. He was so far behind, he had no illusions of ever catching up, but he was determined to do as much as he could. He knew he could never make up for the years that he was gone, though he was determined to try.

CAROLYN

One of my husband's favorite things about Chicago is pizza. It used to be mine too, but I rarely eat it anymore. I lost sixty pounds four years ago. Derrick hasn't seen me fat and I intend to keep it that way. I did an extra forty minutes on the treadmill this morning, since I knew Derrick would want pizza for dinner. I ordered the four-cheese Mediterranean special and prepared a spinach salad. Judging by my husband's heavy eyelids, he enjoyed dinner. But the nap will have to wait.

"Oh, no you don't," I said and clapped my hands in front of his face. "I see you nodding off. Let's get ready to go."

"Babe, after completing Mamalil's 'to do' list, then riding on a train for eleven hours, I really don't feel like going out. I could use one more nap, except this time you should join me," he said as he pulled me to his lap.

"You promised," I said, struggling to get up. "Tomorrow is New Year's Eve and we're staying in. It's supposed to get even colder New Year's day, so I know you won't want to go anywhere then."

"All right. But it's already below zero, I don't see how it can get much colder," he said as he stood and followed me to the master bedroom closet. "Where in the world are you going to put all this stuff when you move? My closets are half this size. You've got boxes packed and your closets are still full."

"Well, hopefully we won't be in your house too long. I've been looking at houses online and the prices are unbelievable. We can live like royalty compared to the prices here," I said as I opened my jewelry box and switched watches.

"That jewelry box looks like you've already been living like royalty," Derrick said as he picked through my jewelry. "Mamalil has one ring she always wears, some pearls, and about five pair of earrings."

"I am not your grandmother," I said and pecked him on the cheek.

"Is this full of cash?" Derrick said as he picked up an envelope at the bottom of my jewelry box and thumbed through it. "You know this is the first place a thief will look. Why do you have so much cash in the house anyway?"

"Cecelia paid me part of what she owes me. She's trying to use a cash only basis to control her spending, and she doesn't have checks for her new bank account. I was going to deposit it, but Sheree called and her grants didn't come in yet, so I told her I'd give her this money for tuition and she can pay me back when her financial aid comes in."

"Whoa, whoa. I thought you agreed to close the Bank of Carolyn."

"What are you talking about?"

"I thought you weren't loaning your sister any more money."

"We have a clear understanding. Cecelia doesn't ask like she used to and she knows she must pay me back. Her taxes went up last year because it was the first year she filed as single. She got an extension but October was the deadline. She paid me back from her bonus."

"So she borrowed this money since we've been married?"

"Yeah, it was the beginning of the semester, and she's paid me back in full already. She's been keeping her word."

"Well, I'm glad someone is."

"What is that supposed to mean?"

"You told me about the money you loaned her last year for your niece's tuition. I thought we agreed that was it."

"She didn't get as much financial aid this year."

"She is not our responsibility. She's not just borrowing from you. We're a couple, remember? How can you dish out thousands of dollars without asking me?"

"I didn't realize I had to ask for permission."

"Well, at least discuss it with me. Sheree can work like I did. And your sister could have gotten on a payment plan. They need to learn to stand on their own."

"I don't mind helping my niece finish her education. And, why should Cecelia pay penalties and interest? You didn't discuss moving your grandmother into the house with me or paying for renovations to her house."

"That's different."

"Not from where I sit."

"It was just a few days while they installed a ramp and a walk-in tub in her house. That's the only way she could move back into her house. She could never afford anything like that. What was I supposed to do?"

"Exactly what you did. You helped your grandmother just like I helped my sister and niece."

"It's not the same at all, and the fact that you didn't mention it, tells me you know you were wrong."

I didn't mention it because discussing my money is one of those things about being married I haven't quite gotten used to. We opened a joint saving account and have both been depositing to it. We both got a raise when we changed our filing status from single to married, so we deposit that money to the account. Otherwise, we haven't combined our finances since we both still have our own bills.

"That is not the case, but I don't want us to argue. I paid too much for these tickets for us not to enjoy the evening."

"If you want me to enjoy the evening, let's stay in. It is too cold for words out there. I'm ready for my dessert," he said as he squeezed my behind.

"We can't let these tickets go to waste. Do you know how hard it was to get them? This August Wilson play won all kinds of awards."

"Well, I don't feel like it. You should have asked me first."

"I was trying to do something nice."

"Something nice for you. You know I don't care about August or July or whoever he is. We already don't spend much time together, so the last thing I want us to do is go sit up somewhere and watch other people play make-believe on stage."

"And the last thing I want to do is to watch you snore."

"Most women would be glad their man wants to make love. If I didn't want to go to bed with you, I guess then you'd be happy?"

"I'm not saying that. I just wanted to do something different."

"You haven't forgotten that you're my wife have you? That means you should consult with me on everything from spending money to how we spend our anniversary."

"I cannot believe you are being this petty."

"And I can't believe you don't get it," Derrick said as he slammed the jewelry box shut and laid across the bed.

"We're going to be late. Let's go," I said.

"Now you even want to decide when the conversation is over. I'm not going."

"I paid almost three hundred dollars for these tickets."

"Then you go. I'm staying here," Derrick said as he grabbed the remote control and found a football game.

I picked up my purse, keys, coat, scarf, gloves, hat, and earmuffs, and left for our anniversary date. I knew marriage would have ups and downs, but I hadn't expected to see the downs so soon. The honeymoon is definitely over.

CECELIA

Cecelia heard the ringing, but wasn't sure if it was the clock, the phone or a dream. The answering machine clicked on and she heard her sister's voice, "Happy New Year!" Cecelia reached for the phone and knocked over the half full glass of Merlot.

"Yeah, Happy New Year," she said as she tried to clear her throat.

"So you're screening your calls now?" Carolyn asked.

"No, the house phone is usually some telemarketer, so I rarely answer it." Telemarketers weren't the only ones calling. Bill collectors seemed to have her number on speed dial. She had thought about canceling her house phone, but the hospital required her to have a house phone for emergencies. One of the last things she and her ex-husband, Michael, had done together was file for bankruptcy, again. They each kept their car and car payment, and discharged all other loans and credit cards. The house was in foreclosure, but the bank didn't seem to be in a hurry to take over the property, so Cecelia was living rent free. Just when she thought she would be able to save a little, her daughter's transmission went out. Cecelia used her car payment money to fix Sheree's car and now the finance company was calling relentlessly. Then the garage door broke and she had to get it fixed, and she had to use cash. Living without credit cards was tough. She wasn't accumulating debt, but now she was broke. She was broke before, but it didn't feel like it when she could select from her deck of plastic to pay bills, shop, and eat out. She had made a brief visit to Lady Luck, but it was too crowded. Her favorite machines were taken and the dealers seemed to be rushing the games so she had come home, poured a glass of wine, toasted to herself, and climbed under her Mont Blanc comforter. It seemed like that was just five minutes ago. The bright sun peeking through the blinds told her different.

"What time is it?" Cecelia asked as she put on her glasses.

"It's almost ten o'clock. You must have gone to a wild party last night."

Phyllis R. Dixon

"Not quite. I rang in the New Year knee deep in blood, IV bags, and paperwork. I was supposed to get off yesterday afternoon and ended up working a double. We had six trauma cases and then we had three nurses who called in. I don't know why folks think the holiday is a license to act a fool."

"You have a lot of seniority. You shouldn't even have to work on a holiday."

"I didn't have any grand plans and we're always short this time of year. I don't mind. I'd rather use my vacation days during warm weather."

"I thought that guy from the billing department invited you to a party."

"Girl, please. I am not trying to date anybody with four young children. My baby just turned eighteen."

"It's only a party. Nobody says you have to marry him."

"I know. I'm just not interested in that whole getting to know you ordeal."

"Then try online dating. You can specify all the criteria you want and don't want. Then when you meet the person, you can skip all that preliminary getting to know you stuff. My administrative assistant just married a guy she met on a dating website."

"That sounds like shopping, and I'm not in the market. If I do get with someone, they'll have to find me. I'm not looking."

"I guess it's too soon. Your divorce hasn't been final that long."

"That was only a formality. Our marriage was over a long time ago, although Michael has been calling me lately. He even called me at midnight to wish me Happy New Year."

"See, maybe you'll get back together," Carolyn said. "Maybe you just needed a break."

"I do miss him. Despite everything, we had some good times. But I don't want to talk about that. What did you guys do to bring in the holiday?"

"I wanted Derrick to come to Chicago so we could go out, but we haven't gone anywhere. He says it's too cold. If I had known we were just going to stay in and watch football, I would have gone to Eden. This is Daddy's first New Year's without Mama and I'm sure he misses her. I called at midnight and didn't get an answer. I guess he just went to bed."

"It does seem strange for Mama not to be here. She always called when she got home from Watch Night service," Cecelia said. Their mother's death had been unexpected. She had been losing weight, but they all thought it was from grieving. Their oldest brother, Charles, had died a year earlier. His diabetes had gotten out of control and while having his foot amputated, he had a stroke and died. Charles was the only child that never left Eden, and he and his wife, Brenda, lived right next to the farm. Their mother took his passing hard. Their father had a stroke and was diagnosed with skin cancer a few years ago. He made a full recovery from the stroke and his doctors had declared him cancer free, but their mother still kept a close watch on his condition and treatment. While she was caring for everyone else, she neglected her own check-ups. When Cecelia saw her mother at Carolyn's wedding, she was alarmed at how much weight she had lost and changed her return flight so she could accompany her mother home and to a doctor in Little Rock. Her mother had protested, said she preferred to go to her regular doctor. Cecelia insisted and after numerous tests, her mother was diagnosed with an endocrine disease. It was very aggressive and within two months, their mother was gone.

"I think about all the times she wanted me to visit and I didn't. When I do finally move, I plan to spend a lot of time with Daddy," Carolyn said.

"When are you moving? I know Derrick is tired of having a long distance wife."

"They moved my transfer date back again. Now it will be the first of May. Not thrilled about the delay, although it does give me more time to sell my condo. I've only had three showings. Hopefully things will pick up in the spring. Did you make any resolutions for the new year?"

"Only to reclaim my life." Carolyn wasn't the only one looking for things to pick up in the spring. Cecelia had been living like a hermit the past six months. Part of her self-imposed exile was a way of grieving for her mother, and the other part was her way of proving to herself that the casino was a hobby, not a habit. One other small issue was the fact that she was broke. Withdrawal from plastic hadn't been easy, but she had learned to live within her means. The bankruptcy had given her a clean slate and she was getting her finances in order. With the new year, she was ready to get back to her life.

"I'm going to apply for the nurse practitioner program. I'm doing the work anyway, so why not be compensated. I'm going to spend more time with Daddy, and I'm finally going to the Essence Festival. The girls at work invite me every year, but Michael wouldn't go. He said he didn't like crowds, like fifty thousand people at a Bears game isn't a crowd. Anyway, Michael's preferences are no longer my concern. I've already started saving for the trip. Want to go?"

"I doubt if Derrick will want to go. He doesn't like crowds either."

"I forgot, you're an old married lady now. I know you're ready to move with Derrick, but let me warn you, you guys actually have the best of both worlds right now. There's still the excitement of dating without the drudgery of laundry, bills, and the daily what-to-cook-for-dinner dilemma. Enjoy it."

The tables had changed. For almost twenty years, Cecelia had been the married sister, fitting activities around her husband and children. Now her children were grown and her husband was an ex.

"You just say that because you're still reeling from your divorce. Now that you're back in circulation, I'm sure you'll meet some hot guy who will make your toes curl and have you giggling like a teenager."

A hot slot machine would be more like it, Cecelia thought.

"I'm always making a comeback, but nobody ever tells me where I've been."

Chapter 2
MAKING A COMEBACK

"**B**everly, how many times have I told you to keep this door locked?" Anthony said as he walked in.

"First of all, you don't *tell* me anything," I said.

"Don't go getting all huffy. I'm just concerned about your safety. You wouldn't sit in the house with the door unlocked. Why do it here? A shop full of women – you're just asking to be robbed."

"I'm so used to Money standing guard, and I had planned to be gone by the time it got dark, so I forgot about the door." Actually, I hadn't planned to be here at all. Everyone in the world knows beauty shops are closed on Mondays — everyone except Aunt Belle. She seems to pick the busiest day of the month or a Monday to come to Memphis to get her hair done. Most women her age wear a wig, a short afro, or braids. Not Mae Belle Washington-Parker-White-Johnson-Roy. She still gets her wash, press and curl, and her auburn rinse.

Aunt Belle is our father's aunt. She's just seven years older than Daddy, but she practically raised him and his siblings when their mother died in childbirth, so she's more like our grandmother. She's always been on the thick side with big legs and a set of breasts that she uses like most women use a purse. I used to do Aunt Belle's hair in Mama's kitchen. I haven't been to Eden as regularly since Mama passed and I referred Aunt Belle to a shop in Eden. But she claimed the younger beauticians don't know how to press hair anymore. She said I've been doing her hair for the last twenty years and she saw no reason to stop now, unless I was too busy. I couldn't say no. Aunt Belle and Mama were my practice heads when I was growing up and while I attended cosmetology school. I loved listening to Aunt Belle's stories about her days as an entertainer on Beale Street and back-up singer at Stax Records. They didn't call it gossip, but they knew who was cheating, lying or breaking up in Eden. They both had sage advice about men. Mama, because she had a long marriage, and Aunt Belle because she had a few husbands and a few almost husbands. They were the ones that told me I should open my own shop and not just work for someone else. Aunt Belle even thought of the name, The Oasis. And they were the ones that counseled me on keeping Anthony in line, or at least trying.

Aunt Belle is a walking history book with a story for any situation. And watching Mama manage our household while working occasionally as a seamstress was better than any business school lesson on time management. I left high school with a diploma, a baby, and a husband (thanks in part to Daddy's shotgun). I didn't go to college like my sisters, but I got an education in life from those special times with Mama and Aunt Belle.

"Locking the door is something you can't afford to forget. This new breed of thugs doesn't care about the time of day. They rob a bank in broad daylight, so you know they'll rob a beauty shop," Anthony said. "Aunt Belle, did Beverly tell you the Lexus was stolen a few weeks ago?"

"No, she didn't mention it. So did they find it? Isn't that the same one in the driveway?"

"Yes, it was recovered," I said.

"Well, that was lucky. Them poleece in Dwight County never find anything," Aunt Belle said.

"Yes, very lucky," Anthony said.

"I'm told it was at some ugly woman's house not far from here," I said.

"As usual, you got the story all wrong," Anthony said as he looked through the stack of mail on the counter.

"I don't need stories when I have the facts. GPS is a great invention."

"Sounds like there's more to this story," Aunt Belle said.

"Nothing more. I've got to run," Anthony said as he handed me an envelope. "I'll come by tomorrow. Remember to keep the door locked."

We had worked out our own separation agreement. Anthony kept the money from the rental houses and from the barbers' booth rent. I kept the money from the salon and paid the bills. Anthony paid half the mortgage and kept up with maintenance. The only disagreement we had was over, Money, our dog. She was a salt and pepper German shepherd and I couldn't imagine staying alone in the house without her. Anthony said he found and trained Money, and she was his dog. We both lost when Money got out of the back yard and never came back.

"We'll be fine. Don't let the cane fool you," Aunt Belle said as she patted her chest. "Anybody come in here for something other than getting their hair done is going to get a little surprise."

"And I have my own peacekeeper in the drawer," I said. Mama protested when Daddy would take me hunting. She said it wasn't lady-like. But I always wanted to go with Daddy and Charles, and turned out, I had a pretty good aim. My eyesight may not be what it used to be, but I pity the fool that puts me to the test.

"I'll install a doorbell tomorrow. I can't have my wife and favorite aunt going to jail," Anthony said then planted a kiss on Aunt Belle's forehead.

"Don't be wasting your kisses on me. That's the one you should be kissing," she said, pointing to me.

"I've been trying to tell her the same thing. Talk to her Aunt Belle," Anthony said as he doubled checked the lock on his way out.

"I always liked that boy," Aunt Belle said.

"You said he was a dog." Aunt Belle had warned me about a pretty man, and she was right. Anthony turned out to be the slick, philandering rogue that she predicted. But he was also funny, kind, generous, easy on the eyes, and still the best kisser.

"He's a dog, but that doesn't mean he's not likeable. He came by it honest. He's just like his daddy and granddaddy. You know, I don't like getting in your business, but you need to either break up or stay together. This limbo you got going on can be dangerous and basically just lets him do what he wants to do and still claim you as his territory."

"We're both grown. He can do what he wants and so can I."

"Baby, it's not the same for women. A man with a lot of women is a player. A woman with a lot of men is called a ho."

"Times have changed, Aunt Belle."

"They ain't changed that much. These men is just telling you things is changed so they can get what they want. I see all that mess on the television. Such a shame, girls don't even know who they baby's daddy is. It's pitiful."

"Getting pregnant is one thing I don't have to worry about."

"It ain't just about getting pregnant. It's about keeping yourself. I know I had me a few husbands, but that's because I let them jokers know there would be no laying, playing, or staying without a ring. Course, every now and then I let one slip through, but that was the exception, not the rule."

"But I don't want to get married. I'm not even divorced."

"My point exactly. That's why you need to you-know-what or get off the pot. You'll never find anyone while you're still tied to Anthony."

"I've been dating."

"Is that what you call it? Men don't like to share. They can have fifty women, but their feelings get hurt when a woman steps out. They can't stand another man having what's supposed to be theirs. So these men you fooling around with is just passing time with you. A woman will spend years being a mistress, have kids for him and everything, on a promise of him getting a divorce. You ever heard of an 'other man'?"

"I guess I never thought of it like that," I said. "I'm not looking for a relationship, but I don't want to be somebody's sidepiece either."

"Your mama isn't here to tell you these things. You're good and grown, but you haven't had much experience with men. If you and Anthony are through, there will be somebody else – when and where you least expect it. But seems to me anytime you see somebody more than a few times, Anthony pops back up for another chance to break your heart. "

"No more chances. He knows it's over."

"But do you know it's over? It's like being a little bit pregnant. Menfolk love to string you along, but either you're married or you're not. My third husband kept coming around after I put him out. Then his girlfriend come up pregnant. I knew he was seeing her, that's why I put him out in the first place. But it still hurt to know he wasn't seriously trying to get back together. For years me and Libby Douglas didn't speak. Then he did her the same way and she begged my pardon."

"Sister Douglas at Mama's church?"

"They didn't always wear white missionary dresses down to their ankles. There's nothing new under the sun. It's just that now people advertise their mess on the television. Folks used to try to hide it back in the day."

The older I get, the more I realize that drama isn't a new invention. A few years ago, I got the shock of my life when I learned that Daddy isn't my biological father. Apparently, Mama and Daddy had their own on again off again thing going on back in the day. I am the darkest in the family, and my siblings would tease me when we were younger. I know James Brown said we were supposed to be 'black and proud', but light skin and long hair was still the beauty standard. Now, I love my cocoa brown skin, and my sisters are jealous of my smooth skin and even tone. I was taller and bigger than most of the boys and envied my sisters' compact frames. But most black family histories are an unknown gumbo of genes, so it never occurred to me that we had different fathers. I did meet my biological father, but felt no connection to him and didn't pursue the relationship. I saw no need to pursue someone who hadn't shown any interest in me. I guess I need to transfer that philosophy to Anthony. It's time to quit holding on to the past and embrace the next phase of my life.

"You're right, Aunt Belle. It's time for me to let the brother go. That New Year's Eve stunt was the last straw."

"I didn't say let him go. I just said make up your mind."

"It's not easy to let go of someone I've spent the majority of my life with. But I promise you, I'm going to do it," I said.

Aunt Belle turned around and said, "I'm not the one you have to convince."

CARL

Today was Carl's two-year anniversary. He had spent one thousand four hundred eighty three days locked up and each hour crawled by. Now it seemed that time had sprouted wings. He was grateful to be home, but nothing had gone as he planned. The joyful reunion he had envisioned with his boys had been more of a tepid introduction. His older son tolerated him and his younger son didn't know him. He was still living in his parents' house. He was broke and since his plumber's license had expired while he was in prison, he couldn't get a contractor's job.

Despite these obstacles, he had faith that the situation was temporary. But one thing that wasn't temporary, his mother was gone. A few months after his return, his ex-wife, Pat, agreed to let Carlton and Terrell spend spring break in Eden. He didn't know who had more fun, him, the boys, or C.W. He and his oldest son, Carlton, weren't best pals, but at least they weren't strangers anymore. There was no internet or video games, but they went fishing, played cards, and watched basketball. He and his father played baseball with the boys, which was déjà vu, as he remembered C.W. pitching to him and his brothers. He was shocked to learn his boys had never even played baseball. Lois complained about the boys running over her periwinkles and about cooking for an army, but she was in her element. She said it reminded her of the days when she had a house full of children. In a matter of months, she was gone and Carl was glad his sons had gotten to know their grandmother.

He smiled when he remembered the expression on his mother's face when she saw him walk through the door, two years ago today. She ran toward him, grabbed his hands, and just looked at him with tears in her eyes.

"Thank you, Jesus! Oh, thank you, Lord! Praise God! Why didn't you tell me?" she said looking at Raymond, who walked in behind Carl.

"We didn't want to get your hopes up," Raymond said as he put the olive green prison issued duffel bag on the floor. Carl served four years of a six-year sentence. He was released early due to a combination of good behavior and prison overcrowding. He had been convicted of aggravated robbery. But his real crime was stupidity. He wasn't raised in a ghetto by a poor single parent. His parents weren't drug addicts or alcoholics and his mother had raised him in Sunday School. He had never been hungry or without a roof over his head. He had been a star athlete in high school, which meant celebrity status in a town like Eden. He started smoking marijuana, like all the other so-called cool kids in high school, and by college was dabbling in cocaine. But when everyone else was dabbling, Carl did cocaine the way he did everything else—full speed ahead. He left college without a degree, or the NBA contract he just knew he was going to get. He was able to function for several years, but eventually he went from cocaine to crack, lost his family, and forgot the solid values he had been raised with. He was with some guys he barely knew, and even though he waited in the car while they robbed a convenience store, because one of them shot the owner, he was charged with aggravated robbery. If the owner had died he could have gotten even more time. Once he came back to himself, he realized how much time he had wasted and how many people he had hurt. But there was nothing he could do but stay out of trouble and try his best to get out as soon as he could. He had been devastated when the parole board denied his first application. So this time, he didn't tell anyone until he was sure he was approved.

"We didn't find out until last week, but we didn't want you wearing yourself out trying to prepare something," C.W. said as he entered the room.

"You mean you knew too?" she said wagging her finger at her husband. "I thought it strange that Cecelia announced she was coming for a quick visit. I should take all of you over my knee. But I'm just so happy," she said, while still holding Carl's hand. "What time is it in Dubai? Is it too late to call Paul? Let me call the girls."

"They're on their way," Raymond said. "And we called Paul on the ride home."

"Well what about Aunt Belle and your cousin—"

"Mama, I told Raymond not to contact anyone other than you guys. I didn't want this to be a big deal."

"Boy, you must be crazy. My son coming home is a big deal. I'm so happy I could burst," she said, finally letting his hand go.

"I haven't been able to sleep all week. We're both glad to see you son," C.W. said.

"I'm glad to be seen. Sometimes I wondered if this day would ever come."

"I knew it would. I had faith and knew my prayers would be answered," Lois said, as she put her arms around her son's waist.

"Okay, Mama, don't monopolize all the hugs," Carolyn said as she and her sisters entered the room.

"Look at you," Carl said as he spun his big sister around. "Old age is agreeing with you."

"What old age? Forty is the new thirty," Beverly said.

"And, Carolyn, I heard Bucky's put a ring on it. Congratulations. Cecelia, I'm even glad to scc you," Carl said. "You dyed your hair."

"Hey, big head," Cecelia said as she hugged her brother.

"She's trying to hide her gray. I told her gray hair is a sign of wisdom and a blessing from God," Lois said.

"Well, I'm not ready to show my wisdom yet," Cecelia said.

"That's because you've been brainwashed by this materialistic Western culture that doesn't value its elders. Most African cultures revere older women," Raymond said.

"Last time I checked we were in the USA, not Africa."

"I see you two are still at it," Carl said, as he put his arm around his mother's shoulders.

"Sometimes I wonder how I could have given birth to two people so different. But I know one thing, all my children love my peach cobbler. You all can help us finish it off. Neither me or your daddy need to be eating it."

Not only did his mother have peach cobbler, but between leftovers in the refrigerator and unthawing frozen concoctions, she magically prepared a feast that Martha Stewart couldn't match. They even used the dining room. Carl's request for a quiet homecoming was ignored. But he didn't care. There were platters of chicken, corn on the cob, and fresh sliced tomatoes. He was happy and he was happy that they were happy. He had caused them so much heartache and expense that he wasn't sure what their reaction would be. But the atmosphere was as festive as for any returning war hero or winning election night.

News travels fast in Eden and visitors were in and out all evening. His cousin, Perry, came to the back door while Carl was in the kitchen. "Carl, welcome home! I heard you'd be home this evening. I know you're glad to get some real food. Aunt Lois is still the best cook in town. After we eat, I want to take you out. I know you want to celebrate on your first night home. I got a fine little *something something* waiting to meet you. I figured we can go to the casino, go to Beale Street for a little bit, then see where the night leads us. My treat."

"I'll take a rain check. All I want to do is stay home, eat some of my Mama's cooking, and sit on the porch looking as far as I can see with no concrete or barbed wires in my view."

"You're kidding, right? When I got out, I couldn't wait to get to a woman."

"I don't want to be out late. Raymond's taking me to Little Rock to see my boys tomorrow. I want to be at my best."

"Cool. Just call me when you're ready. As far as money, I got some prospects lined up for you. I've been putting in a good word for you."

"Perry, I don't even want to hear about none of that old stuff."

"It's nothing like that. We leave that to them young dudes. But you'd be surprised what you can do with a computer."

"Thanks, but I don't think I'm going that route. I'm going to get a job."

"A job?"

"Yes, a job. I took programming classes while I was inside and got a certificate of completion. Plus I'm going to see if I can get my plumber's license reinstated."

"Let me school you," Perry said as he patted his cousin on the back. "You're back in the real world now. And people in the real world don't give jobs to ex-convicts. You'll be lucky to get hired to wash dishes or flip burgers."

"Well, I'm not trying to get locked up again. So if I have to wash dishes or flip burgers, so be it."

"I thought that too. But it's not just hard out here for a pimp. It's hard for everybody."

"Carl! Come on out here," Lois called. "I thought you were bringing the ice."

"I'll handle this," Perry said as he took glasses full of ice from Carl. "Since you plan on working, you'll probably be spending a lot of time in a kitchen. Tonight, let us wait on you," Perry said. "A job," he said, shaking his head and laughing.

"Well, look what the cat drug in," Beverly said when she saw Perry. "We need to put a deadbolt on that back door."

"So nice to see you too, cuz."

"Carl is not supposed to associate with felons."

"Beverly, that's not nice. Perry has turned his life around. Maybe he can help Carl."

"Mama, I don't think we want Perry's help," Beverly said as she rolled her eyes.

"We are not to judge. The Bible says judge not, or you too will be judged," Lois said.

"The Bible also says, the companion of fools will suffer harm. I hope you're not planning on going out with him," Cecelia said as Carl came in the dining room. "That's just asking for trouble."

"Cecelia, that's enough."

"Yes, ma'am," Cecelia said as she stuck her tongue out at her cousin.

"I invited him, but he said he wants to stay home with his loving sisters."

"Derrick is expecting me in thirty minutes," Carolyn said.

"And I have a dinner date," Beverly said as she pulled a chicken leg off the platter. "I just stopped by to greet my baby brother and then I'm heading back to Memphis."

"If you're going out to eat, why are you stuffing your face?" Raymond asked.

"So I can play over my food and look cute."

"You women and your games," Raymond said.

"And I have Bible study tonight. I thought about not going, but God has been so good, I want to remain faithful. Why don't you come with me?" Lois said as she grabbed her son's hands.

"Not tonight, Mama. I'm going to do something I've been dreaming about for four years."

"So you changed your mind? That's what I'm talking about," Perry said as he rubbed his hands together. "Glad I didn't cancel. When you see her, you'll be glad too."

"That's not it," Carl said.

"Good. You don't want to mess with any hoochies that Perry lines up," Beverly said.

"No, man, that's not it. All I want to do is take a long bath. I can't remember the last time I took a bath."

Now it seemed like yesterday, but two years had passed. In six months, he'd be off parole. Maybe he would go to North Dakota. There were supposed to be plenty of good-paying jobs up there. Carl stepped on the back porch and lit a cigarette – something else that hadn't gone as he had planned. He had always been an athlete and never smoked. Even when he was doing drugs he considered cigarettes unhealthy. Carl had started smoking out of boredom, and said it was just something to help him do his time. Despite being contraband, they weren't hard to get. It was kind of hard to worry about getting cancer years in the future, when all your future looked like was prison. He said he would quit as soon as he got out. Two years later he was still puffing. His mother found his lighter when she washed his clothes. She left it on his dresser, her way of letting him know she found it. He knew what was going through her mind – that he was smoking crack again.

"I never knew I could be so relieved to hear that my child smoked cigarettes," she said when he told her. "Although promise me that you'll quit. It's bad for you."

Carl thought about his mother and vowed this would be his last pack. He finished his coffee and headed to work. Burger Barn was closed for the holiday, but he had volunteered to come in and work with the cleaning crew. They would sanitize all equipment and surfaces, and strip and wax the floors. Carl wasn't interested in watching football or parades and he could use the extra money. It took him all day to make what he used to make in one hour. But after months of searching, he was glad to have a job. His boss said Carl had what it takes to be a manager and this was just a stepping-stone. He may have taken the detour, but at least he was back on the road.

CAROLYN

"I got your check today, Cecelia. What a pleasant surprise."

"I came by on my way home from the hospital. I didn't want to wake you at that time of night, so I stuck it in your mailbox. I met my repayment date like I promised. Thanks again, Carolyn."

"I must admit, I wasn't expecting you to repay it in one payment."

I know folks say family and money don't mix, but Cecelia always pays me back, though it's usually in dribs and drabs. Getting five hundred dollars over an eight or ten month time frame always seems like less money than getting it all at once. But I don't mind helping her. I don't have any kids and my niece and nephew deserve the best. She usually gives me cash, but this was a larger amount so she wrote a check. Not that I don't trust her, but I will be at her bank first thing in the morning to cash it, and she remembered to make it out to Carolyn *Roberts*.

"No one changes their last name anymore," she said when I complained about spending six hours at the Department of Motor Vehicles getting a new license.

Initially I agreed with her, and had planned to hyphenate my name. Then Derrick pouted for a week. He said of course it was up to me, but he had waited so long to share his life with someone, it never occurred to him that I wouldn't want to share his name. He was so sweet about it, that I gave in. Seeing my married name on the bank account that we opened was a proud moment. I had finally found someone to love me all the way. The flip side, is that I have to do more explaining about my finances. So even though I don't need the money that desperately, I am glad I'll be able to tell Derrick that she paid me back.

"I really appreciate you hanging in there with me through all of this," Cecelia said. "Now I understand the saying cheaper to keep her. Only in my case it's the reverse. I can't thank you enough."

"It's too early for a tax refund. Did you get a bonus?" I asked.

"Isn't that a personal question?"

"Well, I think I have a right to ask personal questions when you borrow two thousand dollars."

"Remember, you offered. I didn't ask you for it."

"I know, but I couldn't have you chained to those loan sharks. Those payday loan places should be outlawed. They only put them in our neighborhoods, and they charge obscene rates of interest. I can't believe you even went there." I found a receipt from Chicago Title and Loan in a Michael Kors clutch I borrowed from her. "Cece, tell me this isn't yours," I asked her when I opened the purse.

"Then I won't tell you."

"So it is yours?"

"You said not to tell you."

"Okay, very funny. Those places are just legal robbery. You know better."

"I needed the money quick. All of Sheree's financial aid hadn't come in and they were going to drop her. I'm going to withdraw from my 401k to pay it back, but then I figured she will need money next semester. So I'll just wait until next semester and make one withdrawal," Cecelia said.

Phyllis R. Dixon

"Then how about I loan you the money now? When you get your 401k money, you can pay me back and avoid the sky high interest and fees."

I conduct financial literacy seminars as part of my outreach at work. I couldn't very well have my own sister going to those shady places. Sheree was in school. Cecelia wasn't running up a ridiculous bill. Problem solved. But according to my husband (stills sounds funny to say that), there was a problem.

"You gave your sister how much?" Derrick asked, when I said how sweet it was of Sheree to call and thank me.

"I loaned her two thousand dollars."

"Doesn't she have a gambling problem?"

"She's doing better. And this money was for Sheree's tuition. I couldn't let my niece get put out of school."

"But she wasn't getting put out. They had already found a way to pay her tuition."

"At an exorbitant rate of interest."

"If I remember my finance class, high risk equals high interest. I would say your sister is a high risk. But that's not the point. You should have asked me first."

"Asked you?"

"Yes. We're supposed to make major financial decisions together. Two thousand dollars is a major financial decision in my book. What if I spent two thousand dollars on my boat?"

"That's different."

"Why? Because you make more money than I do?"

"That has nothing to do with it. Your boat is not a necessity and there's no plan to replace that money. Cecelia will pay me back and you should trust my judgment. I wouldn't have done it if I didn't think it was important." This turned into our first big argument and we didn't speak for days. Since we weren't in the same city, that meant neither one of us called the other. After four days, I decided to apologize and was going to call him and to my surprise, he was parked in my parking space when I got home from work. He had taken off work and driven from Eden. We both apologized, spent eighteen hours making up, and he went home the next evening.

"I thought you weren't going to be able to repay me until next semester," I said.

"You sure do ask a lot of questions. Seems like you would be happy to get the money back early."

"I am. I just hope this doesn't mean you're still going to the casino." I know it's not my fault, but I do feel a twinge of guilt, as though I was the person to give an alcoholic his first drink. A few years ago, I won a trip for two to Las Vegas from the radio station. Me and my boyfriend at the time, broke up, well actually, he went back to his wife. I was too depressed to go alone and was going to forfeit the trip. Cecelia went with me and we had a ball. It was cold in Chicago and eighty degrees there. We saw Toni Braxton and Sinbad. The food and shopping were great. We played the slots and took craps lessons. Unfortunately, what happened in Vegas didn't stay in Vegas. Cecelia brought a new pastime back with her – gambling.

"What difference does it make? Why can't anyone ever just be happy for me? Yes, I occasionally go to the casino. I didn't see you complaining when I got us those complimentary tickets to see Patti LaBelle or New Edition. My marriage is over. My daughter has her own life, and I rarely see my son. My job is frenetic from the time I get there to the time I leave, which is usually at least two hours later than the time I'm scheduled to leave. We have two nurses out on some humanitarian trip to Haiti for three weeks. So I'm sorry if sitting in a corner reading a book doesn't relax me like it does you. Forgive me for wanting to have a life."

"But don't you see – going to the casino, blowing your paycheck isn't a life. And your marriage didn't just fall apart. You and Neiman Marcus gave it a big shove." I guess I had a little hand in that too. One of our favorite things to do together was to shop. We turned it into a sport. We would start with breakfast, then make the rounds of stores on Michigan Avenue, have a late lunch, then go to one of the outlet malls and stay until closing. We pursued sales like experienced safari game hunters. I didn't have a husband and children and could afford to indulge my shopping binges. And I figured Cece had two incomes so she could afford it too. I was shocked the first time she filed for bankruptcy. I felt guilty and started declining Cecelia's shopping invitations. Unfortunately, she replaced our shopping sprees with casino trips.

"Again, thanks for the support. I'm not blowing my paycheck. Give me a little credit," Cecelia said.

"Then why did you need to borrow money and why was your mortgage past due?"

"It's called strategic default. Even Suze Orman recommends it. The house isn't worth what we paid for it. Why keep throwing money down a rat hole?"

"How about so you have somewhere to live?" I said.

"Since the money is so tainted, you can give it back to me."

"I'm disappointed, not stupid."

"I didn't think so. I've got things under control, so quit worrying. If it makes you feel better, I received a bonus for a project I worked on last year. Now, let's talk about something else," Cecelia said. "Didn't you go to

Eden last weekend? How's Daddy doing? It's getting close to the anniversary of Mama's death."

"He's gained a few pounds and he stays on the go, so I guess that means he's doing fine."

"Last time I talked to Carl, Daddy was staying out all night. Sometimes people express grief by acting totally out of character."

"I think it's just a case of him trying to get away from the house and memories," I said.

"More like a case of Viagra," Cecelia said. "I just hope he doesn't give himself a heart attack trying to be Grandpa Player. We have at least one patient a week come in with a heart attack associated with so called male enhancement pills."

"Uggh, let's change the subject. Daddy getting his freak on is not a topic I ever thought I would be discussing. So what about you? I haven't heard you mention any men lately."

"I haven't met any worth mentioning lately. I may have to cross to the other side. I see no brothers on the horizon. But you found Derrick. I guess I was wrong about him. Hopefully I'll meet a great guy just like him."

"That money talks, I'll not deny, I heard it once: It said, 'Goodbye'."

Richard Armour

Chapter 3
MONEY BLUES

Carl wiped his debit card on his pants and reinserted it into the ATM machine a third time. He got the same insufficient funds message. *This can't be*, he thought, as he looked in the rearview mirror at the line of cars stacking up behind him. He had transferred five hundred dollars to his prepaid credit card in anticipation of this weekend. Yesterday was payday and he paid his phone bill and planned to withdraw the rest for the trip. Stopping at the ATM was the last item on his 'to do' list before leaving town.

He left the drive-thru lane, parked, and went inside. When he made it to the front of the line, the teller said the majority of his direct deposit cleared up the overdraft and his balance was less than ninety dollars. He had worked overtime, so this had to be a mistake. Working fifty hours a week, at nine dollars an hour, wasn't anything to brag about. He used to spend that much in one day on coffee. But he wasn't complaining. He was just happy to have a job.

Carl was filling in for the assistant manager who was on maternity leave. This weekend, he finally had two consecutive days off and he had reserved two nights at a hotel. He was taking the boys shopping, to the movie, and for pizza. He planned to be in Little Rock by the time they got out of school, and this was putting him behind schedule. He called his ex-wife, Pat, to let her know he was running late, then called his manager, Wayne, to straighten out his pay.

"Let me do a little more digging and call you back," Wayne said.

Carl lit a cigarette and paced the bank parking lot while waiting for Wayne to call him back. After ten minutes that seemed like an hour, his phone rang. "So did you get it fixed?" Carl said when he answered.

"Your check was for fifty-two hours, but the state garnished half of it."

"What do you mean?"

"There are no details, but usually when I see this, it's for child support. Do you owe back child support?"

"I do, but I've been paying. They never said anything about garnishing my check."

"They don't warn you because a lot of guys quit working or change jobs to keep from paying. Tough break," Wayne said. "Let me know if I can do anything."

After leaving the bank, Carl went home. He threw the overnight bag he had packed on the floor, then went to the back porch and lit a cigarette. He had a job, but was still broke. What good did it do to work if he couldn't support himself?

"Hey, son," C.W. said as he opened the screen door. "I thought you'd be gone by now."

"I'm not going," Carl said as he hurriedly put the cigarette out. "They took half of my paycheck for back child support."

"That's no reason not to go," C.W. said.

"I can't afford the hotel or any of the other stuff I planned."

"So change your plans, but you still need to go. The most important thing is to show up."

Carl felt two inches tall when he called to tell his sons he wouldn't be able to spend the night and was just coming on Saturday. He and his father left at dawn with plans to take the boys to breakfast. Then they were going to go to the zoo (free before noon) and to a movie. C.W. gave him two hundred dollars and wouldn't take 'no' for an answer. Carl hated borrowing money from his father. But he would have hated not keeping his word even more. He didn't want to disappoint his sons, not that they would be that upset. It had been two years and sometimes he still felt like they were strangers.

Little Rock to Eden was a ninety-minute ride, but today felt like nine hours. "Brinkley, Arkansas is the last place I expected to be in a traffic jam," Carl said.

"Someone must be getting a kickback based on dragging out the completion date. I haven't been to Little Rock since before your mama passed and they were working on the road then," C.W. said.

"Sorry to waste your Saturday, Daddy, spending all day on the highway."

"Anytime I get to see my grandsons is not a waste. I'm proud of the way you've stepped up for those boys. They need to spend time with their father. That's what's wrong with a lot of kids today."

"Most times they seem like they would rather play video games. They would probably be happier if I sent a check and didn't bother to visit."

"They'll appreciate it one day. You just keep doing what you're doing, son."

Carl's first order of business after being released from prison was to visit his sons. Even though their mother had sent him pictures, in his mind they were still his little boys, riding tricycles and mesmerized by cartoons. He was not prepared to find that his oldest son, Carlton was almost looking him eye to eye, and Terrell wasn't far behind. For his first visit, Raymond and his wife Geneva drove him to Little Rock and they visited the Clinton Library while Carl took the car to see his sons. He easily slipped into a relationship with Terrell, but Carlton wasn't as easy. Lois had told him that it was just a normal teen phase, but Carl had missed so much time already. He didn't want to waste more time with attitudes and sullenness.

Carl had slacked off on his visits in the last three months. It was hard to get a weekend off, but his boss told him he was in line to get his own store, so he needed to keep showing high energy. The first step was to get promoted to Assistant Store Manager. Right now, he was doing the job without the extra pay. But he was next in line to be promoted. No longer than eighteen months after that he should have his own store. He was going to need two jobs if the state was going to keep taking his money, but he wasn't going to worry about that today. Today the Washington men were hanging out.

"Dad, I'm starving," Terrell said as Carl and C.W. walked in the door.

"Me too. Get dressed and let's go," Carl said.

"I'm afraid Terrell's not going anywhere," Pat said. "He had a sore throat yesterday and now he has a fever. I'm glad to see his appetite is coming back. But I think he needs to stay in. I'm going to give him some Tylenol and send him to bed."

"Then I'm not going either," Carlton said.

"Do you feel bad?" his mother asked.

"No, I just don't want to go. I never wanted to go in the first place."

Carl walked over to him and put his hand on his son's shoulder. "Would you rather do something else?"

"Granddaddy, I'm glad to see you, but I don't feel like pretending with him," Carlton said as he jerked away from Carl. "I go along for Terrell's sake. But if he's not going, I'm not either."

"They have come all the way from Eden. You should—"

"Mom, I wish you'd stop acting like he's some great man who's come back from the war. He was a sorry, lying, crackhead. Now he's out and has a big time job at Burger Barn. Pathetic. And I'm not going."

"Don't turn your nose up at honest work, son," C.W. said.

"Well, I'm not going."

"Carlton, do not be disrespectful. That's no way to talk about your father, and you are not going to tell me what you will and won't do."

"Fine," he said and jerked his jacket from the hanger. "You tell us to choose our friends wisely. Too bad you didn't follow your own advice."

"Don't speak to your mother like that," Carl said.

"You can't come in here and tell me what to do."

"He is still your father," Pat said. "I've taught you better than this. Where is all this coming from?"

"He's not my father; he's your baby's daddy."

His mother raised her hand to slap him, but C.W. grabbed it.

"Let the boy speak his mind," Carl said. "I'm not condoning him being disrespectful, but after all this time, he has a right to speak his piece."

"Terrell was a kid. He doesn't remember, but I do. I remember you telling me we were going to the park or to get pizza and you not showing up. I saw you take money out of mom's purse and I know you took the envelope I had underneath my mattress. Mom, I heard you crying when he didn't come home. So I'm sorry if I don't feel like sitting around with him acting like none of that happened. You treated us like dirt, then just pop back up and expect to be treated like father-of-the-year. That's not going to work with me. I've done okay so far without you. You're just trying to ease your conscience."

"I can't argue with anything you've said. All I can do is try to be the best father I can be now and hope one day you'll feel differently."

"Whatever," Carlton said and left the room.

"Don't feel bad, Daddy," Terrell said in a raspy whisper. "He's just mad that he didn't make the baseball team."

"Okay, I'll keep trying. But sounds like you need to go lay back down," Carl said.

"You drove all the way over here. Let me fix breakfast for you," Pat said.

"Thanks, at least I'll get to spend a little more time with Terrell," Carl said.

"You got some cards?" C.W. asked. "We had a good gin rummy rivalry going last summer. Let's see what he remembers."

The game and Tylenol made Terrell sleepy and their card rematch only lasted thirty minutes. Pat's biscuits, eggs, rice, bacon, and fig preserves stimulated memories that Carl hadn't thought of for years. She had been a good wife, he just wasn't ready. He didn't know if she was just being polite since C.W. was there or if she was actually mellowing, but this was the first relaxed conversation they had had since he got out. He gave her one hundred dollars and she promised to keep working on Carlton.

"I know things didn't go as planned, but just be patient," C.W. said as they walked to the car. "Carlton will come around eventually."

"Most of the guys I was locked up with barely knew their fathers. They grew up acting tough to make up for that void. I vowed that my sons would not carry that burden. I may not be able to give them much, or spend as much time with them as I would like, but one thing they can't say is that I don't care about them," Carl said as he buckled his seatbelt.

Fortunately, the construction was only on the east side of the freeway, so they had a smooth ride back to Eden. "Daddy, I'm going to run into the store a minute and see how things are going," Carl said as he pulled in the Burger Barn parking lot.

"Carl, I didn't expect to see you," Wayne said as Carl walked in the office.

"My youngest son had a fever and needed to stay in, so I cut my visit short. I can work tonight if you need me."

"We have a little problem," Wayne said as he closed the door. "I thought you were out of town, so I wasn't going to bother you until tomorrow."

"So what's the problem?" Carl asked.

"I'm just sick about this, but I'm going to have to let you go."

"Let me go?"

"Believe me, it's not what I want to do. You're my best worker. I submitted the paperwork for your promotion and when they did the background check, your felony record came up."

"I told you about that up front."

"I know, but an assistant manager has to be able to be bonded, and the insurance company rejected the application."

"Fine, then don't promote me."

"It's not that simple. Apparently we can hire people with a record, but it can't be for a financial crime. I knew about the robbery, but you had some bad check convictions before that. Passing bad checks is considered a financial crime."

"So if I had murdered somebody that would be okay, but since I passed bad checks, I'm a bad risk?"

"Carl, I don't know what to say."

"It's not your fault. Thanks for giving me a chance." As Carl exited the store, he noticed a new BMW pulled up beside his car. As he got closer, he saw Perry walking away from the car.

"Hey, cuz. I was stopping to get my burger fix and saw Uncle C.W. sitting out here. Can you get me a hook up on a free combo?"

"No, not today. Nice car though."

"Thanks. I know you're doing the fast food thing now, but my offer still stands. Give me a call sometime."

"I just might do that," Carl said.

CAROLYN

I can't believe I've accumulated so much stuff. When I first moved in the condo, I wondered how I would fill two thousand square feet. Now I've got to figure out what to do with all this stuff. I have a keep stack, a discard stack, and a donate stack. But so far, the keep stack dwarfs the other two. Derrick agreed that I can have the larger closet, but I have three closets full of clothes to condense into his one. I won't need all of my winter coats, so I'll only keep two and I'll give Cecelia the lynx. I rarely wear suits since the dress code changed to business casual. But Memphis may be different, so I'd better keep the suits. I definitely won't be needing my 'fat' clothes. I've managed to keep off the forty pounds that I lost a few years ago, but they would make stylish maternity clothes. I know pregnancy is considered high risk at my age, but I'm healthy and still have regular periods. Everyone says forty is the new thirty, and Mama always said to claim what you want. The fat clothes go in the keep stack. I've got enough books to start a library, but I can't bear to part with them either.

My realtor says the condo has been getting more hits on the website and we should have lots of traffic at the upcoming open house. I'm glad I followed her advice and lowered the listing price. I'll clear less profit, but at least I won't have to worry about being a long distance owner. My job is paying for the move and the moving company will pack everything, but I need to purge first. Derrick's house is half the size of my condo. But that's just temporary. As soon as the condo sells, we can move closer to Memphis. I've been looking online and we can get a huge house and land for half what I paid for the condo. And the taxes are super low. My commute time will be longer, but more relaxing. Instead of driving through gang-infested neighborhoods and stop and go freeway traffic, I'll be driving through soybean fields and catfish farms. Derrick's ride will be a little longer, but he'll still be able to get anywhere in his territory within forty-five minutes.

In three weeks, I'll be a wife in more than name only. I applied for a transfer when we got engaged. My boss said he was sorry to lose me, but if I waited six months, I could probably move with a promotion. I felt like a prisoner applying for parole, where the date keeps getting moved back, as the six months turned into nine and now twelve. With the New Year, I decided not to wait for a promotion or a lateral and took a demotion. My pay will be saved for three years and with a lower mortgage and taxes, I'll actually have more money left after bills and less stress. Management isn't all it's cracked up to be and sometimes I feel more like a babysitter than a supervisor. I'll just do my work and collect my paycheck like everybody else. Plus, there's Derrick's salary. There was a time when rising at work meant everything. But I'm ready to move in with my husband. These last few months haven't been easy, but I'm sure once we're actually living together things will be better.

Timing has never been my forte, and the ten years that I've owned the condo coincided with the peak and bust of the real estate boom. At one point, my equity was over two hundred thousand dollars. Now it's declined by almost half. But I won't complain. Cecelia and Michael lived in their house almost twenty years. Rather than celebrating a mortgage burning, they're losing it to foreclosure. If there ever was a poster child for being overextended, they were it. They bought the best of everything, or at least Cecelia did. They borrowed against their equity for trips, private schools, and furniture. Cecelia's trips to Lady Luck and Treasure Palace over in East Chicago didn't help. In most divorces, couples fight over the house. In theirs, neither of them wanted it, or at least could afford it. The last thing they did as a couple was file for bankruptcy. They had filed for divorce first, but their attorneys told them it would be more advantageous to file bankruptcy first. I do feel a little bad. My life is beginning an exciting new chapter, and Cecelia's is in shambles. But she made the shambles.

A knock on the front door startled me as I taped a box of books. "Why do you have the chain on?" Cecelia asked when I peeked through the crack.

"Just habit," I said as I unlocked the door. "I forgot you were on your way."

"Whew. You need to open some windows in here. That smell is strong," Cecelia said as she turned on the ceiling fan.

"They finished painting the kitchen yesterday but the smell is still strong."

"You just did your kitchen a couple years ago. Why are you painting again?"

"The realtor said the colors in here were too personal."

"Well, beige is boring," Cecelia said.

"That may be true, but apparently beige sells better than blue. I'm also putting hardwood floors in the bedrooms and hall. Everything should be done in time for the open house."

"That's crazy. She must be getting a kickback from the painters and the floor guy."

"I prefer sinking my toes in plush carpet during cold Chicago winters, but she says carpet dates the property and it will sell faster with hardwood floors. I had a few more repairs done like fixing the hole behind the bedroom doorknob and the leaky tub faucet."

"I guess she knows what she's talking about. You're not ready to move yet anyway. I still see way too much stuff here. I thought you were purging your closets," Cecelia said as she picked through the piles.

"I know. At this rate, I'll be here until Christmas. For every item I decide to throw or give away, I put six in the keep pile."

"Let me help. You know, this reminds me of us going through Mama's things. It's hard to believe it's been a year already."

My sisters and I spent a week going through Mama's closets and drawers after the funeral. Daddy said he couldn't bear to do it. Mama had saved all of our cards and many of the gifts we'd sent were still in their boxes. She had a trunk full of sheets and towels. Mama used white sheets and towels and saved the colored linens for company. I sent her a beautiful seven hundred thread floral sheet set and it hadn't even been opened. We shipped most of her clothes and hats to our aunt in Detroit. Beverly took her wedding ring, the cake pans, roaster and cast iron skillets. Cecelia and I both claimed the same china set. Mama had promised it to me as a wedding gift. I hadn't taken it out of the house since I hadn't moved yet. But Cecelia said since I was getting the quilts and porcelain ashtray set, she should get the china. Daddy, in his Solomon wisdom, split the china set.

"I hope this is the throw away pile," Cecelia said as she picked up my red velvet skirt.

"Can you believe that was in style? I wore it when we went to the Oprah show."

"That's no reason to keep it. Where is your phone?" Cecelia said looking around. She picked it up off the dining room table and handed the skirt to me.

"Hold it up."

I obeyed and held it up. She took two pictures, then tossed it in the giveaway pile. "Now you'll have the memory without the clutter."

"You need a television show," I said. "It wouldn't take you long to straighten out those hoarders."

"I have an even better idea on how to help you. Why don't you sell me your condo?"

"Well, I hadn't thought of that. Can you get a loan approved?"

"Not right now. The divorce ruined my credit. But I can take over your payments. I have to wait ten more months before I can take out another loan from my retirement account. Then I'll get the money to pay you your equity and just keep making the payments until my score improves and I can get a loan."

"I don't think that would be a good idea."

"Why not? You have a condo you can't sell and a husband waiting to live with his wife. The redemption period on my house will be up soon and I'll need a place to live. You won't have to paint or make any repairs, and you can just pack whatever you want to take and leave the rest here. And this is so much closer to the hospital. It's a win-win for both of us."

"I should probably discuss it with Derrick first."

"He's the one pressuring you to move. Why would he be opposed?"

"Cecelia, don't take this wrong, but remember my job. I work in collections for the IRS. One of the main reasons people run into money problems is cosigning for a boyfriend or a relative. You know money and family don't mix."

"You wouldn't be cosigning."

"Right, it's in my name. That's even worse."

"You think I wouldn't pay you?"

"You already owe me three hundred dollars from last month."

"I know, but this is different and you save the broker sales fee by finding your own buyer."

"We're going to buy a house in Arkansas so I need this one off my credit."

"Then, if you don't want to sell it to me, rent it to me. I have to pay rent somewhere. Why not pay you? I can put my things in storage and stay here while your place is for sale," Cecelia said. "That gives me a little more time to find an apartment."

"Your house is in foreclosure. You don't exactly have a pristine payment history."

"That's different. We had one of those crazy loans where the interest rate jumped after the first two years."

"Which I told you not to get."

"I know, I know. Anyway, our house payment jumped right when Michael decided he didn't want to be married anymore. I wasn't going to pay all of that by myself. I could have paid it, but I figured why struggle when we didn't have any equity? Sheree had moved out and Junior wanted to stay with his dad. I didn't lose the house; it was a decision not to keep it. I made a monthly mortgage payment for almost twenty years, so you will get your money."

"What you say makes sense, but something still tells me this isn't a good idea."

"Girl, please. We can do it all legal and I'll sign a lease and give you a deposit and whatever else you require. At least the property won't be vacant and you can finally move."

"The realtor will need access to the unit at a moment's notice. You're always at the hospital."

"We can work something out. I'd prefer they not have a key. You can give them the number to the nurse's station and I can break away. I can even post notices at the hospital. Doctors and interns are always looking for properties in this area. I'm not going to lose my job or disappear. You'll get your money. I'm your blood. If you can't trust your blood, who can you trust?"

Phyllis R. Dixon

BEVERLY

What is Anthony's truck doing here? I wondered
as the garage door lifted. I changed the locks but had
forgotten about reprogramming the garage door
opener. *I should have accepted Neal's offer to stay at
his place.* I haven't gotten used to sleeping in other
men's beds yet, although it's not for lack of trying. I was
a virgin when I began dating Anthony in high school
and he had been my only lover. Now at forty-six, I'm
making up for lost time.

I met Neal at my stylist's birthday party. Normally
I wouldn't mess around with an employee's relative.
But I'm learning not to have so many restrictions and
qualifications. I had always criticized Carolyn's choice
of men and told her to be more selective. But now I
understand. I've eliminated gay men, married men,
unemployed men, men under five feet six inches, men
under thirty-five (although I'm thinking about lowering
that to thirty), men who don't pay child support, those
that live with their mothers—unless she is ill, those that
live with a woman, men who drink too much or do
drugs, those with missing front teeth, men without a
car (I'm thinking about eliminating this one if they have
a job and a driver's license), and men with long
fingernails (too much like Anthony). If I eliminate my
employee's relatives, that would cover half of Memphis.
So Neal made the cut.

My first lover, after Anthony moved out was Rick, a
police officer in Dwight County. He's a widow and one
of the few eligible men in town that isn't in a wheelchair
or on a breathing machine. Growing up, I always felt
like the ugly stepsister so I was surprised and flattered
when he asked me out.

"I've always had a crush on you," he said. "And if Anthony is dumb enough to let you go, I'm not complaining."

Mama was appalled. "Beverly Ann, you are still a married woman," she said.

"But we're separated and getting divorced."

"Then wait until it's final."

"That could take months."

"What's your hurry? Why are you rushing toward hell?"

"Mama, please. Don't be so dramatic."

"I know you're grown, but some things just don't look right."

"I'm way past worrying about how things look," I said.

Mama fretted, but didn't have to worry long. Our one and only time together was so disappointing I almost called Anthony. I'm not sex-crazed, but if I'm headed toward hell, I want it to be worth the trip.

Surprisingly, my longest companion since separating from Anthony has been Mark. Because of him, I eliminated another restriction from my list; white men. I met Mark at a truck stop in West Memphis, Arkansas. I had forgotten that my windshield wipers were worn, until a downpour blinded me as I was driving to Eden. I crept slowly over the bridge and stopped at the first exit to buy new ones. Mark noticed me struggling to put them on my car, and put them on for me. He was a truck driver and part time instructor at a truck driving school. I decided to order lunch and wait for the storm to pass, and Mark invited himself to my table. Four hours later the storm was long gone, but we were still at the table nursing glasses of sweet tea. My stylists teased me for weeks when he came to pick me up for dinner.

"He's cute, for a white guy," Sharon had said. "Almost as cute as that guy in *Best Man Holiday*."

"I would never talk to a white man," Fatima said. "You know as soon as you get into an argument, he's going to call you a nigger, and then it will be on."

This was funny, considering that she didn't blink when her so-called boyfriend called her a bitch.

"Is it true what they say about white men?" Sharon asked.

I just smiled and said, "you know what the song says – it ain't what you got, it's how you use it." Our fling lasted three months until he was promoted, which meant he had to transfer to their headquarters in Atlanta.

"That's not far at all," he said when he told me the news. But I knew it would be the end for us and it was just as well. Things were fine when we were alone, but I was always self-conscious when we went out. I know I shouldn't care about things like that, but I couldn't really relax.

"Is everything okay in Eden?" Anthony asked as I walked in the door.

"Everything is fine," I said as I placed my purse on the counter.

"I know you don't like to drive at night, so for you to come in at this time, something must have happened."

"I'm not coming in from Eden. Although that really is none of your business."

"Oh," Anthony said quietly.

"What are you doing here anyway?"

"I stopped by last night to drop off my part of the mortgage payment and noticed all the outside lights were off. My extension ladder is at the rental house so I couldn't change the floodlight. I waited for you to get in since I know you don't like to come in when everything outside is dark, especially since Money is gone. I fell asleep on the couch. I didn't realize it was this late. So, did you and the girls go down to Tunica?"

"Too bad you weren't this concerned about my safety when you were living here."

"Beverly, can't we just have a conversation without you getting an attitude? So how did you do?"

"How did I do what?"

"At the casino."

"Who said I went to the casino?"

"Oh, I just assumed..."

"Don't assume anything, and quit trying to figure out where I've been. I don't question you."

"I can take a hint," Anthony said as he grabbed his keys. "But you need to watch the company you keep. Unless she's just a trick, I never let a woman drive home alone this late. Dude should have at least followed you to the house."

I rolled my eyes and walked upstairs. "Leave the money on the counter. You can see yourself out."

I took a shower and went to bed, but couldn't go to sleep. Once again, I had let Anthony get to me. Neal did ask me to stay, but I don't like him enough to actually sleep with him. Maybe that means I shouldn't be doing anything with him. *Neal could have at least texted me to make sure I got home.*

I picked up the remote control and found a healthy living show on CNN. *I'll either learn something or be bored to sleep.* The show actually piqued my interest and I made a note to ask Cecelia if I should be taking fish oil. Then there was a breaking news interruption. The anchor announced details of a suicide bomber in Afghanistan. I rarely watch the news. As long as I don't hear about the wars and killings, I can function without worrying about Tony every minute.

Tony is over twenty-one, but he's still my baby, my only baby. We tried to have more children, but after three miscarriages, my doctor advised me to have a hysterectomy. Tony was good looking like his father and maybe just a little spoiled. After attending two colleges and spending time working with Daddy in Eden, Tony enlisted in the military. I was devastated, but everyone else said let him go, it would help him grow up. "The terrorists can't be any worse than these gangbangers around Memphis," Anthony said. "The Lord will keep him," Mama said. Before I could even get used to the idea of him being away from home, he was deployed to Afghanistan. The military was one thing. War was another. I wish I had Mama's faith. If God is going to keep him, why did he allow war in the first place?

I changed to the business channel and that news wasn't any more encouraging. All the talk about the Fed, bulls, bears and Dow Jones – whoever he is – meant nothing to me. All I know is that Anthony moved, but the bills stayed. He still gives me money, but not like before. I have a mortgage, car payment, and salon utilities. Everything is going up, except sales. More women are doing natural styles and one barber left, so income is way down. Whenever we went through a slump, Anthony would get a roofing job or something to come up with the extra money. Now it's all on me.

I turned off the television and did what I always did when I felt bad. I went to the kitchen. I settled on a menu of cheese grits, eggs, hash from leftover steak, and biscuits for my pity party. As I cracked the second egg, I noticed a text. Mark was on his way to Tulsa, but the roads were bad so he was rerouting his trip and would stop in Memphis. Did I want to go to breakfast? He'd be here in two hours. I responded that I would cook and he could come by. I turned off the stove, put the hundred dollar bills Anthony left in my housecoat pocket and went to take a bath. Pity party over.

"The blues is when you drop your bread on the floor - and it lands jelly side down."

Leroy "Lefty" Bates

Chapter 4
JELLY SIDE DOWN

Cecelia slipped into the family waiting room and opened the bag of Cheetos that was serving as her lunch. She agreed to work three extra hours so her coworker could get off early to get to the beauty shop in time to be ready for her date to the R. Kelly concert with her new man. Millicent didn't lack suitors and always had a full social calendar. Cecelia didn't mind filling in. She would make a few extra dollars and Millicent always had a funny story the next day. That was before she knew that another nurse would call in sick and the emergency room would fill with flu patients, causing her to skip lunch. Millicent had half-heartedly said she would stay, but Cecelia told her not to worry about it. At least one of them was having fun. She couldn't remember the last time she had been to a concert. She and Michael loved reggae and went to festivals in Miami and Jamaica every year in the early years of their marriage. But once the children came, they stayed home and were content to do so. By the time they tried to recapture the sizzle, it was too late. Cecelia had laughed like Sarah laughed at God, when Millicent promised to return the favor by working late for her when she had a date.

Since her divorce, she had been on a handful of dates, but nothing close to a relationship. She had been amazed at how casually the men she went out with treated sex. She was not interested in hooking up. Men acted like sex came first, then you decided if you really liked each other. She had been accused of being a lesbian, still hung up on her husband, or having a relationship with the man in the drawer; none of which were true. Carolyn had suggested she try online dating. Cecelia wasn't interested. "That seems like shopping. Any man that I get with is going to have to find me." So far, no one had found her and she wasn't convinced anyone was looking.

"That's pretty sneaky – making a promise you know you won't have to keep. Millicent, by the time I have a date, we'll both be retired."

"That's because you need to do something more than work and go home. We're going out next weekend and I won't take 'no' for an answer." Cecelia had said okay, but already knew she wasn't going. Her grandbaby's birthday party was the following Saturday. She and Michael had spent Christmas at Sheree's apartment so Simone could stay home and play with her toys. They were actually civil to each other and shared a private joke about their daughter's cooking. They didn't want to discourage her, but it was apparent that cooking was not her strong suit. Cecelia was surprised at how easily they had settled into the role of grandparents and how much she had enjoyed his company. He had even hinted at spending New Year's Eve with her, but she was already scheduled to work. Sheree overheard them and teased her parents about going on a date.

"Mind your own business, young lady," Cecelia told her.

"Your mother and I will always have a bond," Michael said.

"Okay, whatever you say," Sheree had said with a smirk. Cecelia knew she and Michael would never get back together. But that didn't mean they had to be enemies. She had an early morning hair appointment on Saturday and was getting off early on Friday, so she would be fully rested without bags under her eyes. She wanted to look her best – for her granddaughter.

She was about to go back to the nurse's station when her brother's number came up on her phone. An ice storm had come through Dwight County and the cell tower wasn't working. Beverly had been to Eden and assured Cecelia that everyone was okay, but she still wanted to talk to her father and brother herself. She used to avoid his phone calls before he went to prison, and had a brief flashback of those times. He usually needed money, a ride, or a place to stay. Although Cecelia had been broke so long, she could hardly remember when she even had money to loan anyone.

"Finally," Cecelia said as she answered the phone. "How are you guys?"

"We're fine. Lots of people still don't have power, but Daddy has a generator, so other than no cable, some missing shingles, and a few trees down, we're doing okay."

"I hope Daddy isn't around there trying to fix things himself. Let me speak to him."

"He's not here right now. They went fishing."

"Fishing? It's not that warm down there. That man is determined to land himself in the hospital."

"He just wanted to get out of the house. Miss Emma promised they wouldn't stay long."

"Miss Emma?"

"There's no power at her house, so she's been staying here."

"Talk about taking advantage of a situation. She talked Daddy into buying new appliances, including a dishwasher. Mama never had a dishwasher. She's trying to take over," Cecelia said. "I guess next she'll be getting her mail over there. Why can't Daddy see what she's doing?"

"Daddy is a grown man and this is his house."

"It's also Mama's house and I don't think she would appreciate another woman sleeping in it. Dating a younger woman is bad enough, now Daddy is shacking up. He must be losing his mind."

"If it makes you feel any better, she's sleeping in your old room. But you've got to accept this."

"No, I don't. And it's not just me. Beverly and Carolyn both think Daddy getting serious is a terrible idea, but they won't speak up."

"Mama and Daddy kept their vows for over fifty years – until death do us part. So now they've parted. Daddy is still here and deserves to be happy. Don't be so selfish. Think about what Daddy wants."

"I'm thinking about what Emma wants, Daddy's money." Through a combination of thriftiness and hard work, C.W. Washington had pulled himself up by his bootstraps. He was part of a dying breed – a black farmer. In the early nineteen hundreds, African Americans owned fifteen million acres, but that number had dwindled to less than three million by the dawn of the twenty first century. Many families lost their land to unpaid taxes or heirs' property. But Daddy beat the odds. He started with forty acres and kept adding to it. He is now the largest black landowner in the county. He drives a truck that's twenty years old and rarely borrowed money. In recent years, he added to his holdings with a settlement from the Black Farmer's lawsuit, and then his wife's insurance money. Drilling in the area had driven up land prices. Not bad for a sharecropper's son.

"You don't give him enough credit. He's not a horny teenager going after the first woman that winks at him. Do you know how many good sisters of Eden and surrounding parts were after him – including some of Mama's so-called friends? We ate good for weeks. Somebody was bringing a homemade something or other over here every day. Daddy was fresh meat in shark infested waters."

"So was Emma's sweet potato pie the best?"

"I think Daddy likes her because she's a lot like him. He and Mama were opposites in many ways and that worked. Opposites attract, but it takes time to work through those opposites. I don't think Daddy is trying to spend time working things out or rediscovering the passion that he and Mama had. He just wants someone to hang out with. He and Emma enjoy the same things. They play cards every Tuesday at the community center. You know Mama didn't like to play cards. They watch *Sanford and Son* reruns and laugh like they've never seen the episodes before. Every Sunday morning they go fishing and he cleans them and she cooks them."

"That's because she doesn't go to church like Mama did."

"That doesn't make her a bad person. You don't go to church either."

"That's because I have to work."

"Don't give me that excuse. As long as you've been working, you could change your schedule sometime if you wanted to," Carl reminded her.

"Well, how often do you go to church?"

"I never claimed to be Jesus Jr. and I'm not criticizing anybody else about it. How did we get on this subject? I didn't call to argue with you."

"Then what did you call for?"

"Can't a brother call to talk to his sister?"

"It's possible, but I know you. What's up?" Cecelia asked.

"The storm made national news so I thought maybe you were worried about us."

"Umm. Well, obviously Daddy is doing fine. Was that it?" Cecelia said.

"There is one other thing. I want to reinstate my plumber's license and I need to come up there to take a test. Can I stay with you for a few days? All the hotels require a credit card to make a reservation, and I can't afford one anyway."

"Now you are talking crazy. You know you don't need to get a hotel. Is it all right for you to travel?"

"My parole officer said she would approve a one week trip."

"So when are you planning to come?"

"I'm not sure. I may wait until June. I'll be off paper by then. And I wanted to make sure it was okay with you first."

"Of course it's okay. You should know that."

"I know I burned a lot of bridges and wore out my welcome more than once, but—"

"Carl, what's past is past. Everybody makes mistakes."

"I appreciate that. I just hate that my mistakes affected the whole family. My brothers tried to talk to me. Carolyn quit speaking to me for years and wouldn't even answer my letters. You were so mean, I wished you wouldn't speak to me."

"It's called tough love. You were using and conning everybody and I wasn't buying your bullshit."

"I see that now, and it breaks my heart to think of what Mama and Daddy went through. I wasted a lot of time and money."

"You can't spend the rest of your life beating yourself up about it."

"I keep telling myself that. I'm lucky I had a family that would stick with me until I finally came to my senses."

"Now I need to use some of that tough love on Daddy to get him to come to his senses."

"Cece, his situation is totally different."

"Bullshit is bullshit. She may have sucked you in with sweet potato pies and fried fish, but that doesn't move me. And it certainly isn't worth giving away all that Mama helped build. Plus, since she works at the school, I'm sure she knows that Daddy gets a retirement check from driving the school bus all those years. Daddy is still grieving and not in the best of health and I refuse to let someone take advantage of him. I'm glad you called. I was planning to come down there next month, but it sounds like I need to get there sooner. This madness has gone on long enough. I thought you guys would handle this, but Carolyn is too busy being a newlywed and Beverly is too busy trying to date every man in Memphis. I see I need to come myself. Plus, I heard U.S. Energy is signing people up for mineral leases and Daddy wouldn't even talk to them."

"How did you find out about that?"

"I have my sources. He's listening to Raymond and not reason. What could be better than getting a check for doing nothing? I need to talk some sense into him."

"Cecelia, don't come down here starting trouble."

"I'm not starting anything. But I definitely plan to end it. You'll all thank me one day," Cecelia said as she stood and pushed her chair under the table. "I'm going to put in for emergency vacation days first thing in the morning." Now where she would find some emergency money was another thing.

"I would hardly call this an emergency," Carl said.

"Daddy losing his mind is an emergency. I'll be there as soon as I can get away. And tell that gold-digger to get out of my room."

CAROLYN

"Good evening, Miss Rock Star," Carl said as he opened the car door and stepped aside for me. "You look mighty jazzy with those dark sunglasses on."

"I guess this is how celebrities feel. Let's see, am I Beyoncé or Oprah?"

"What about Miss Daisy? Can I go make water?"

"Funny. The drops make my eyes extra sensitive to sunlight. I go to the doctor next Friday, and hopefully I'll be done with the drops and can start back driving. I don't mind being chauffeured to and from work, but I don't like being stuck at the house."

Spring signaled the arrival of bountiful azaleas, fragrant honeysuckle, and delicate dogwood blooms. Unfortunately, allergies, migraines and a sinus infection came along too. I thought I had a cold I couldn't get rid of, but when my eyes started burning and turning and staying red, I finally made a doctor's appointment. Then my head hurt so bad I couldn't even hold it up. I struggled through the night, then Derrick insisted that I not wait for my appointment and took me to the clinic the next morning.

"I never had a problem with allergies when I was a kid, and we stayed outside from sunup to sundown," I told the doctor when given the diagnosis.

"Didn't you say you only recently moved to Eden? Your immunities have changed."

"I can live with smog and pollution, but I'm allergic to fresh grass and flowers," I said as I shook my head.

"I'm seeing more and more people with allergies, especially since they started drilling around here. Although, some researchers believe because we live in a cleaner world, our tolerance is lower. Also, you've been wearing your contacts too much. All of that has aggravated your condition. I'm going to prescribe some drops for your eyes, but you won't be able to drive for ten days." Carl agreed to drive me to work during my driving moratorium.

"Carl, wait, go back," I said as we approached the gate.

"What did you forget this time?"

"I just got a text from Portia. Her car won't start. Do you mind looking at her car?"

"I don't have any jumper cables or tools with me. I don't know how much I can do."

"She just needs a ride home. Her car can stay here overnight. She lives near Forrest City and sometimes we ride together."

"No problem, just know I charge by the hour," Carl said.

"Turn left, she's in the back lot," I said as he swiped my badge and drove through the gate.

"Too bad I don't have the truck," Carl said. "Then I would have had my cables."

"But then we'd all be squished in the front seat. There she is," I said and let the window down and waved. "You don't mind, do you?"

Carl looked at the petite, honey-colored lady and smiled. "I don't mind at all."

CARL

"That was a good practice," Raymond said as he unlocked his office.

"The boys will need it, playing Forrest City this week. I watched the film you gave me. They're tough," Carl said.

"I'll look at your notes tonight. Thanks for watching the film. I'll look at it, but it's always good to get another perspective."

"No problem. It's not like I have other pressing commitments," Carl said.

"I know it hasn't been easy for you. But I want you to know how proud I am of you. A lot of guys would have given up or returned to their old habits. You've been a big help to me and a good example for the boys."

"I've been so frustrated, I can't even describe it. All I do is watch all the morning news shows, spend a couple hours at the library on the computer, then come home and watch more TV. So working out with the team has been good for me. But no matter how frustrated I get, I would never consider going back. I must have gone temporarily insane to get on that stuff in the first place. I can't undo what happened, but I don't have to repeat it."

This week had been another in Carl's frustrating search for work. Mr. Jones had promised him he could work at the car wash, but not until the week before Easter. During the winter, only the automatic services were available. In the spring, he added vacuuming and hand waxes. The pay was abysmal, but it would be better than nothing, barely. And, he paid in cash, so his check wouldn't be garnished. That would hold him a few months until his parole was over. Then he was leaving. He hadn't told anyone, but he had found a job, just not in Dwight County. North Dakota was booming, and he had gotten three call backs for jobs he had applied for. They knew about his record and were willing to pay his relocation expenses. His father and siblings all had their own lives, and he needed to go get one. They were begging for plumbers up there, and he could be an apprentice for a few months, then take the test to get his license. He would have had to start all over to renew his license in Illinois. He even thought about starting his own company once he got there. He hated the idea of being so far away from his boys, but he wasn't doing them any good in this situation. "It's hot in here. Can you plug in your fan?"

"I know I sound like Mama, but if we sit under this fan, then go outside, we'll both have pneumonia," Raymond said.

"Can you believe we used to practice then go play ball for hours? I'm worn out," Carl said as he took his phone out of his gym bag. "I missed a call from Daddy."

"Call him back and make sure everything is okay," Raymond said. "He never calls anyone."

"He left me a message. Mr. Franklin called about a job with his contracting company. He wants to set up an interview."

"That's great. They're one of the few local companies that's hiring. If he called, you must have a good shot at a job, although I'm going to be selfish and say I hope your hours don't conflict with practice."

"Mr. Washington—"

"Tevin, didn't you see my door closed? You know you're supposed to knock—"

"But there's a fight in the bathroom! And Mario is bleeding."

Raymond and Carl rushed and followed Tevin to the boy's bathroom. When they entered the restroom, there was a crowd of boys yelling, cursing, and pushing.

"What's going on here?" Raymond asked making his way to the center of the crowd, where he spotted a boy on the floor in a pool of blood. "Damn," he shouted, "Who has a cell phone? Call 911. Everyone get back, right now," he said, as he pushed the boy in the chest that was kicking the boy on the floor. As the boy stumbled backward, an older boy grabbed Raymond from behind. Raymond flung around and punched him in the stomach. Carl had been trying to break up three other boys when he spotted the older boy reaching in his pocket. Carl rushed toward him, knocked the gun out of his hand and backhanded him so hard, he fell on his butt. He got up and charged head first toward Carl, just as the sheriff walked in.

"All of you line up against the wall," he said as he talked on his radio. "I need an ambulance right away."

The rest of the day was a blur filled with paramedics, an emergency room wait that lasted hours, and mountains of paperwork. Raymond had to complete incident reports for the police, expulsion papers for the boys, an incident form for the union that was tracking all instances of violence against teachers in their effort to demand better security in the schools, and other forms for the school board to protect them from lawsuits. His hand was bandaged, so Carl filled in the papers and Raymond signed them. Geneva came and double-checked everything the doctors and nurses did and made them re-do things to her satisfaction. After three hours, Raymond was free to go, but they stayed until they knew Mario was going to be all right.

His mother and grandmother were understandably upset and vacillated between tears and rage. They found out the boy with the gun wasn't even a student at the high school. There was some kind of rivalry going on that no one could satisfactorily explain. It was a good thing the boy was locked up because Mario's brothers were ready to get him. Raymond and Carl tried to talk them down, explaining that revenge wasn't going to get them anything but time in jail. C.W. and Emma came and sat with them. Finally, they got the word that Mario had pulled through surgery and was responding well. His mother and grandmother thanked Raymond and Carl, while the boy's brothers were still bent on payback.

"Did you ever find out what the fight was about?" C.W. asked as they walked to the parking lot.

"I don't think they even know themselves," Raymond said as he winced in pain. "Just some wannabe gang members."

"We never had gangs and drugs here. It's getting as bad as the big cities," Emma said.

"It's them rappers and all that mess on TV," C.W. said.

"I'm just glad it wasn't any worse. The principal told me they found another gun, a bag of weed, and some pills on the floor," Raymond said.

"You want to ride home with us?" C.W. asked. "We're going to Walmart, but we can take you home first."

"I can drive," Carl said as he searched for his keys. "I'm going to the house and watch some ball. I think the Lakers are playing tonight. Wait – I completely forgot about your message from Mr. Franklin. I was supposed to call him."

"If you tell him what happened, he'll understand. Just call him in the morning," C.W. said.

Who would think I would do four years in Cummins without a fight and come home to fight some kids? Carl thought as he pulled out of the parking lot. He thought about his boys and as soon as he pulled in the driveway, he pulled out his phone and called them. To his surprise, they were both in a talkative mood. Terrell bragged about his report card and Carlton warned him about the failing grade he had in History and his 'F' in conduct in Homeroom. "I turned in a paper late and then I was out a few days with a bad cold and missed a test. The teacher let me make it up, but I didn't understand what she had covered, so I did bad on it. I don't know why we have to learn that stuff anyway. Who cares about what happened in England thousands of years ago?"

"I know it seems irrelevant, but it's how the system is set up," Carl said, as he lit a cigarette. "You're a smart kid, you can catch up. I'll call and quiz you every night this report card period. Now tell me about the conduct grade."

"That was bogus too. The teacher said I kept breaking the uniform rules – just because I didn't have a belt. Isn't that crazy?"

"Son, don't you have a belt?"

"Yeah, I just forgot it a few days and if I had gone back to get it, I would have been tardy, and I'm at the limit for tardies. Any more and I'll be suspended."

"Then put it in your backpack when you take it off. That way you'll always have it. The teacher doesn't want to have to remind you every day. She has other things to do."

"I should have known you would take their side. I don't see why they have to tell us what to wear. Here's Terrell. You can talk back to him."

"Wait, don't go," Carl said. "I'm on your side. But if you don't get an education, you could end up locked up, and they'll tell you what to wear, when to eat, when to go to bed---"

"Not wearing a belt doesn't mean I'm going to end up in jail. Just because you messed up, doesn't mean I will."

"It's not even about the belt. It's about following rules. The smartest guys in the world are locked up because they had problems following rules. They've got this system waiting for you. They're shipping jobs overseas and the only thing they're building in the United States is jails for black boys. Don't fall into the trap. If I have to come over there and live in a shelter so I can see you off to school every morning, I'm going to make sure it doesn't happen to you."

"Dang. It's not that serious. I'll wear the belt. Mama just got home and wants us to help her with the groceries. Talk to you later."

The mention of groceries set off Carl's hunger pangs. He ate a banana and yogurt in the morning before practice and hadn't had anything else all day. He went in the house and headed straight for the kitchen. As he searched the refrigerator, he received a text from Portia. She had heard about what happened and called while he was at the hospital. He had told her he would call when he got home.

"Hey there," he said when she answered. "I just got home. I'm going to raid the refrigerator, then watch a ball game."

"If you wait twenty minutes, I can bring you something decent to eat," Portia said. "I know hospital food can be pretty bad."

"It's worse than that," Carl said. "I haven't eaten anything."

"I'm on my way," she said.

He didn't have any money for his sons, but maybe what he did offer was even more valuable. And Portia was turning out to be a little more than all right. He was almost sorry when her car got fixed and he no longer had an excuse to see her every day. He finally asked her to a movie and they'd been dating ever since. Her days were long since she commuted to Memphis, so they primarily saw each other on the weekends. It had only been about a month, but he felt like he'd known her all his life. *Maybe the call from Franklin Contracting is a sign that I need to stick around here.*

Carl heard footsteps on the porch and a knock at the door. "That was a quick twenty minutes," he yelled as he went to the door. But it wasn't Portia. Rick and another police officer were at the door. "Is everything okay?" Carl asked as he opened the door.

"Carl, I know your family, and hate to do this, but I have to arrest you," Rick said.

"What? What is this about?"

"The fight today – you're charged with assault. One of the parents is pressing charges."

"But I was breaking up the fight. You saw what was going on."

"And you're also charged with being a felon in possession of a firearm."

"I didn't have a gun."

"Your fingerprints were on the gun. I'm sorry, I have to take you in," Rick said.

"Don't I get to call somebody?"

"You can do that when you've been officially booked."

"This is bullshit."

Portia drove up as the officer opened the squad door for him. "What happened?" she asked.

"Call my sister. Call Carolyn."

BEVERLY

"You reap what you sow." That's what Mama used to say. Mark is in town and wanted to take me out. Any other time, it's me and the remote, but this time I had two suitors. I lied and told Mark I didn't feel well, so I could go out with Louis. He was a beauty supply sales rep and always flirted with me when he came to the salon. I figured he was a better prospect since he was local. We had plans for a movie then dinner. We went to the theater across town, because he said there was a restaurant over there he liked. But when we came out of the theater, his wife was parked next to his car—yes, I said wife. She called me everything but a child of God. I wanted to tell her it wasn't that serious, and she could keep her short, no-kissing, man. I left them arguing in the parking lot and went back inside the theater to call a cab. I had to wait an hour for the cab, then the driver got stuck in construction, and it took an hour to get home. That's two hours of my life wasted that I won't get back—make that four, because the movie was sorry, too. I should have gone out with Mark, avoided the drama, gotten a good meal, and saved cab fare.

I just never knew the dating pool was so shallow. I've heard my customers complain for years, but I didn't think it could be that bad. It's worse. I'm fine by myself, but if you ask me out, I assume that means you're available. Silly me. I didn't know I had to do a background check and lie detector test before every date. Sometimes I think I should just stay with Anthony. Better the devil you know than the devil you don't.

CAROLYN

"Hey, Sis, are you busy?" Carl asked.

"Eating dinner. What's up?"

"I won't hold you long. Just wanted to tell you, I had an interview with Mr. Franklin this afternoon and while we were talking, one of his customers had a pipe burst. So guess who rode over to Johnson City with him and fixed it? Yours truly. As the old folks say, 'I can show you better than I can tell you.' He hired me and we didn't even finish the interview."

"Carl, I'm so happy for you. That's great news."

"Just one problem, I start tomorrow, so I can't take you to work. I asked Perry to take you."

"Uhh, does he even have a license?" I asked. "That's ok. I can find a ride with someone else. Don't worry about me."

"Are you sure? I hate to leave you stranded. I already owe you for getting me out of the jam at the school," Carl said. "I'm too close to getting off paper to have something stupid hang me up."

"I have one more form to file then everything should be cleared up. I'll just add it to your bill. Call me tomorrow and tell me how it went."

"So who was that?" Derrick asked when I put the phone in my pocket. "Pretty rude to talk on the phone during dinner."

"That was Carl. He got a job and starts tomorrow, so I need to find a ride to work."

"Why don't you just take off a couple days?" Derrick asked.

"I can't drive, but I feel okay. Kym lives in Dwight County. I'll call and see if I can catch a ride."

Derrick left early and was gone by the time my ride came to pick me up. Derrick beat me home that evening and was waiting for me when I got dropped off.

"Hey, honey," I said as I stepped on the porch and waved good-bye to Kym.

"Why are you so late?" Derrick asked, as I stepped in the house. "It's almost eight o'clock."

"Kym had a late meeting, so I worked until he finished."

"He?"

"Yeah. You know Kym Walls."

"You mean Kymball Walls?"

"Right. I just always called him Kym."

"So you've been out half the night with another man?"

"I wouldn't call working late out with another man."

"Well, that's what I call it and you won't be riding with him anymore."

"You can't be serious," I said.

"I'm sure there's someone else you can ride with."

"I could probably find someone, but that's not the point."

"What is the point?"

"You're acting like my master instead of my husband. I'm a grown woman. "

"A grown *married* woman. I don't see what's so wrong about me not wanting my wife riding around with other men."

"Because it means you don't trust me. We spent a whole year living in separate cities. The only way that could work was if we trusted each other."

"I trust you, but I'm not stupid, and I don't see why we're even debating it. I'd better not see or hear about it."

I hadn't heard that word since the fourth grade. "Who do you think you're talking to? I'll do what I want," I said as I took off my shoes and headed toward the kitchen.

"Don't walk away from me," Derrick said as he grabbed my arm and snatched me back, ripping the seam of my blazer and causing the buttons on the sleeve to pop off.

"Derrick, stop. Let go."

"Well, don't dismiss me, like one of your employees. I'm still talking to you."

"Okay," I whispered as tears filled my eyes. "Please let go."

"Don't cry, baby," Derrick said as he loosened his grip and put his arms around me. "I love you and can't bear to think of you being with another man. If I didn't give a flip, you could do whatever. I just don't think it's appropriate for a married woman to spend hours alone with another man. Especially if there are other alternatives. Stay home tomorrow. I'll take off early."

"I can't believe you did that." I dated a guy a long time ago that put his hands on me one time and I never gave him the chance to do it again. "I'm scared Derrick."

"I am so sorry," Derrick said. "You don't need to be afraid of me. I just love you so much."

"I love you too. So why are we fighting like this? Maybe we should go to counseling."

"We don't need to go spend a bunch of money to tell some white folks all our business."

"We can find a black one and it's free and confidential through my job."

"I don't care if he's purple, we don't need that. Do you really think they don't track who uses those services? You don't want that on your record," Derrick said as he held my hand between his.

"I've never seen this side of you," I said.

"And you'll never see it again. If you want to go to counseling, fine. I'll do whatever you want. Just let me make it up to you. Take off tomorrow and we can spend the day together."

"But I hate to waste a sick day when I'm not sick."

"So spending time with me is wasting a day?"

"You know that's not what I meant," I said as I rubbed my arm.

"You're under a doctor's care. That's what the leave is for."

My head was throbbing, and all I wanted to do was lay down. To keep the peace, I agreed to stay home. In a backhanded way, Derrick had told me he loved me. Something he rarely did anymore unless we were horizontal. It's strange how things work out. If we hadn't argued, I wouldn't have taken off work. We spent the next day together, fishing, tending to the yard, and making love, not the rushed, tired, end of the day sex we'd been having. We agreed we were both working too hard and needed to spend more time together. I rode to work with Portia the rest of the week.

They say if a man puts his hands on you once, he'll do it again. But there are exceptions to every rule and Derrick promised he would never hurt me again.

CECELIA

Cecelia locked the door behind her, put her purse on the kitchen counter, and hung her Jason Wu coat on the back of the barstool before she picked up the ringing phone. Since her phone was off, she had given the hospital the condo number as a second contact. She saw her sister's name on the caller ID and answered.

"Girl, where have you been?" Carolyn asked.

"Well, hello to you, too."

"I'm not in the mood for pleasantries. I've been calling and texting you for two days. I got worried when I didn't hear from you so I called the hospital. They said you worked the early shift. Do you have a new man or something? Why are you ignoring my calls?"

"I'm not ignoring you. I dropped my phone and haven't had time to get a new one. What's up?"

"You know I'm trying to sell the condo. The realtor called. She wanted to show my condo to someone who is moving to town and needed to see it right away. She couldn't get in, and they bought another unit in the building, even though mine was priced lower."

"What can I say? I'm sorry."

"I'm getting very frustrated with this situation. Last time I had a potential buyer, you missed two appointments to meet the realtor."

"I told you I was called to emergency surgery. Patients don't arrange their emergencies around my schedule."

"Well, I know you didn't want me to, but I'm sending her a copy of the key. She needs to be able to get in on short notice. "

"Okay. Do what you need to do. I told you I'm sorry. How's Daddy?"

"He's fine. Miss Emma invited us to dinner tomorrow. I've run out of reasons to decline her invitation," Carolyn said.

"Why do you need an excuse? Just tell Daddy the truth. You're not in the mood to break bread with him and his mistress."

"I'm not as skilled at being rude as you are."

"You can call it rude. I call it being real. You don't see Daddy asking me nothing about that woman. He knows how I feel. I never liked her anyway. She gave me a 'B' in her class, when I know I did enough work to get an 'A'.

"Raymond says we're being selfish and should try for Daddy's sake."

"Raymond is a man and they stick together. He used to take Michael's side in everything too."

"You're my sister, but Michael was right most of the time."

"Et tu Brutus?"

"Michael was a good man. I bet you two could get back together if you half tried."

"Who says I want to get back together?"

"I was single a long time. I know it's slim pickings out there, especially the older we get. Just call him sometime."

"Why would I want to get back with a man that has taken my children and my money? If it wasn't for him, I'd still be in my house. He wasn't satisfied to just let me lose the house, he wants a chunk of my paycheck so I can't afford another one. I don't know what I would have done if you hadn't let me stay here."

"It's not his fault if Junior said he wanted to go live with his dad, and so by all rights you are supposed to pay child support."

"Carolyn, whose side are you on?"

"I'm just being real, like you said. You staying there worked out for both of us. My place isn't empty and you can save some money to get back on your feet. "

That was the plan, but things hadn't quite worked out that way. If anything, she was deeper in debt, and her plan to save money while staying in Carolyn's condo seemed doomed from the start. She had taken out Parent PLUS loans to help her daughter get through college. She was in an accident one evening on her way home from Lady Luck. She didn't have gap insurance and her insurance settlement didn't cover the repairs. She applied the insurance payment to a new car, and now she had a larger car payment. Then she dropped her computer and after spending hundreds of dollars to get it fixed, it still didn't work properly and she had to get a new one. Last year was the first year she had filed her taxes as a single person and her withholding was too low. Instead of the tax refunds that she was used to, she ended up owing almost three thousand dollars. She thought she could get an extension until October. But she didn't realize that the extension to file her taxes didn't mean an extension of time to pay, so penalties and interest were added. She knew Carolyn was disappointed that her condo hadn't sold yet, but it was a break for Cecelia. She didn't know where she would be if she had to add rent to all these bills.

"Well, I'm not exactly on my feet yet, but at least I'm not on the street. Thanks again for letting me stay here," Cecelia said. "I may give you a hard time, but I do appreciate it, and I'll do a better job of keeping in touch with your realtor."

"Girl, you are so dramatic. You wouldn't have been on the street. But you are welcome."

"All right, talk to you later."

Cecelia called the bank to be sure her paycheck had been deposited, then found her cell phone bill and called to get her phone turned back on. She had been given a reprieve so far, but she couldn't stay in Carolyn's condo forever. She needed to get some money together soon, and living paycheck to paycheck wasn't going to get it. This was not how she envisioned her forties. She was supposed to have money in the bank, take at least one expensive vacation a year, and be close to burning her mortgage. She hadn't expected to be rich, but she certainly expected more than this. True, she was healthy and weighed almost the same as when she graduated from college. She had a career that she loved, her children were healthy, and Simone was the cutest granddaughter alive. Seeing so much death and illness at work, she didn't take these things for granted. But starting over at this age was demoralizing. She felt she deserved more, and she was determined to get it.

"It's not going to come to me. *I'm going to have to go get it,*" Cecelia thought, and went through her boxes and found her test prep materials for the RN- two position. She also found a Lady Luck coupon with forty dollars in free play. *No need in letting this go to waste.* She grabbed her jacket, purse, and keys, as she set out for one last hurrah.

"If you don't like my ocean, don't fish in my sea
Stay out of my valley, let my mountain be ...
You'll never miss the sunshine till the rain begin to fall
You'll never miss your ham till another mule be in your
stall."

Ma Rainey

Chapter 5
DON'T FISH IN MY SEA

Mary J. just finished her mini-concert and Charlie Wilson is up next. I'm supposed to be cleaning out things Anthony left behind, but when I ran across his extensive CD collection, my cleaning session turned into a one-woman party. The CD player and tower had been collecting dust in the guest room. Before you could program Ipods or get satellite radio, we played CDs all day in the salon. I started with Prince then the soundtrack from *Cadillac Records*. We played that one so much, we bought at least three CDs. I tried to listen to Luther Vandross, but ended up reminiscing about Anthony and fighting back tears. I pulled Luther out, found Mary J. and my daddy's peach wine, and the party was back on.

All that's left downstairs is to pull the last of Anthony's stuff out of the closet. On this day last year, he moved out. Or should I say, I broke his phone into pieces with a hammer, then threw it out and told him if he knew what was good for him, he would follow that phone out the door. We were separated, but I thought we were giving each other space to work on our marriage. But he took it as permission to do what he had been doing all along anyway, and that day I had had enough. I've been asking him for months to come get the rest of his stuff. Every now and then, he'll stop by to get something he needs. Last week it was his boots. Aunt Belle says it's a tactic to keep one foot in the door. Maybe I wanted him to have one foot in the door. I've never been alone. I went from my father's house to being Mrs. Anthony Townsend. But it's been a year and I'm ready to close that door. *If he won't remove his foot, I'll do it for him*, I thought as I stuffed old jerseys in a bag.

I turned down the CD player when I heard the doorbell. "Sounds like I'm just in time for the party," Anthony said when I opened the door.

"Yes, you are just in time. Follow me to the bedroom."

"This is a surprise, but music always did put you in the mood."

"Anthony, please," I said shaking my head. "I need you to take these bags outside for me. The garbage man comes in the morning."

"Wait a minute," Anthony said as he looked in one of the bags. "You're throwing away my bowling shirt?"

"It's too small. You left it. I figured you didn't want it."

"Well, you figured wrong. I wore this shirt the first time I won a trophy. We were in that league for years. Remember when our team went to the tournament in Milwaukee? We just missed third place."

"I remember catching you coming out of Melinda Walker's room."

"I told you I was just returning her gloves—"

"Anthony, quit. I didn't believe you then, and ten years has not made the story any more plausible. If you want the shirt, put it in the box on the dresser."

"You got somebody moving in here? Why the urgent need for space?"

"It's not an urgent need for space. I just see no need for you to keep stuff here. It has been a year. You've moved out. It's time your stuff moved with you."

"Sounds like you've been talking to your sisters," Anthony said as he sifted through the CDs.

"If you must know, I'm bringing the treadmill out of the garage and turning this room into an exercise room. I don't need my sisters to point out the obvious. I can think for myself."

"Okay, okay. I didn't mean anything by it. I see you've already played Luther. Remember when we went to his concert in Nashville?"

"Yes. It was advertised as ladies only, but you insisted on going."

"No way was I going to have my woman listen to all that romantic music and me not be around. As I recall, that turned out to be a smart move on my part. We ended up getting a motel room in Nashville and not returning home until the next day."

"As I recall, there was heavy rain and tornado warnings when the concert was over and we decided it wouldn't be safe to get on the highway," I said.

"Umhuh. Keep telling yourself that if it makes you feel virtuous. Wow, here's one I haven't heard in years," Anthony said as he put the Luther Vandross disc in the player. "It still doesn't seem like he should be gone."

"He could really sing," I said as I poured myself another glass of wine. "These days it's all about the look and sampling. They don't make music like that anymore."

"You know our parents said the same thing about our music."

"I guess that happens with every generation. But I don't feel like the older generation. Where did the time go?" I said.

"We spent it raising a fantastic son and building a home and a successful business."

"I never would have thought it would end like this," I said.

"It doesn't have to. I was stupid," Anthony said as he put my glass on the dresser and took my hand and spun me around. My feet fell in step like a soldier called to formation. "You know I've never loved anyone but you."

"I've never loved anyone but you, but—"

"No but, a period," Anthony said. "What else matters? People make mistakes, but we don't have to make it worse by throwing away our whole life together."

"Anthony, how many times have we had some version of this conversation? At some point your actions have to match your words."

"Let's not get into all of that. If we've learned nothing else this past year, it's that life is short. Let's just think about right now. We're here, in our home. Regardless of all the other stuff going on, you're the love of my life. I believe we were made for each other and nothing will change that." As if he planned this very moment, *Here and Now* filled the air. Anthony pushed the stuff from the bed to the floor, then pulled me next to him on the bed. I leaned my head on his chest in the spot that seemed made just for me.

I raised the jar to check the expiration date on the bottom. The coffee had been in the cabinet almost a year. It was the brand Anthony liked and I hadn't bought any since he left, but I hadn't thrown it out either. The biscuits were the last item on my menu of softly scrambled eggs with cheese, grits, bacon and Mama's pear preserves.

"It smells great in here," Anthony said as he walked in the kitchen. "I can't remember when I've had such a full breakfast."

"I can't believe I used to eat like this every day, and this was just the first meal. No wonder I was big as a house," I said.

"Your weight never bothered me, but I must say, you've lost it in all the right places. Last night was fantastic. In fact, let's put these plates in the microwave on a keep warm setting and go back and get this day started right," Anthony said as he pulled me to him and kissed my neck. I followed him through the living room, stepping over boxes and bags. The food would keep.

My eyes opened as my stomach growled. I sat up in bed and searched for the origin of the buzzing noise. Anthony's phone was on the nightstand and it kept vibrating. He was in the shower and I knew I should have ignored it. Aunt Belle always said if you look for trouble, you'll find it. But old habits die hard. I picked up his phone and noticed he had gotten three texts from K. He thought he was being slick by just putting initials after I busted him years ago about numbers in his phone. Like I couldn't figure out that full names were guys and initials were women. K thanked him for agreeing to go car shopping with her today. She said she understood about him having to break their date and go to Eden to check on his folks, to be safe on the highway and she had something waiting for him when he got back in town, with a smiley face.

I threw the phone on the bed and went to the kitchen. I was spreading preserves over my fourth biscuit when Anthony came in. "I have some errands to run, but I'll call you later," he said.

I nodded my head, but remained silent. Anthony hastily put two slices of bacon in a biscuit, kissed me on the cheek and left. I scraped the rest of the breakfast into the garbage. I still smelled like Anthony, but decided there was something I needed to clean before I cleaned my body. I spent the rest of the morning cleaning out Anthony's stuff. Instead of carefully sifting through boxes and drawers and putting things in a keep or toss pile, I dumped everything in garbage bags. For years, I've been the long suffering wife and made excuses like, "boys will be boys, if every wife left every husband that played around no one would be married, a black boy needs his father, at least he brings his money home." But I'm through making excuses. I have been long-suffering, understanding, forgiving and tolerant (some called it stupid), but I will not be a booty call.

When the downstairs closet and his side of the bedroom closet was clean, I dragged the bags to the landing then kicked them downstairs and dragged them to the garage. I heard the garbage truck turning the corner, tightened my housecoat belt, then dragged the bags to the curb. I am officially out of the Anthony Townsend business. This time I really mean it.

CAROLYN

God don't like ugly. I heard Mama's words as I tried to wipe the cranberry juice stain out of my new cream colored comforter. Derrick had brought me breakfast in bed and I knocked the juice over when I got up to turn on the ceiling fan. I guess ruining the comforter is the price for the lie I told my husband.

This morning I claimed killer cramps as an excuse to stay home. My cramps were no worse than usual, but I did feel bad. Getting cramps meant I had gotten my period and am not pregnant, again. I fought back tears when I felt the sharp pain in my lower side and got the pimple on my chin, both signs that my monthly was coming.

"We're hosting the Usher Board anniversary this afternoon," Derrick said this morning as he entered the room with a tray of sausage, eggs, yogurt, toast, cranberry juice, and the Dwight County Times. "Hopefully you'll feel well enough to come to the program."

I had no intention of attending the program but just smiled. I felt like a kid lying to my parents to get out of going to church. Mama always said to be careful what you ask for. That was definitely true in this case. I had prayed for a God-fearing, church going man, but didn't mean go to church every time the doors opened. Derrick attended Sunday School, was president of the usher board, and a trustee. I was proud to accompany him to church, even though we rarely sat together. Since he was an usher, he was usually at the door. When he wasn't on his usher post, he sat on the front row with the deacons and trustees. The Sunday School classes were separated by gender, so we didn't attend classes together. Then after church, he usually had

107

some meeting or other church business. So we were in the same space, but still not together.

While we dated, whenever I came home, it was understood that I was going to church with my mother. Derrick invited me to his church, but I declined until my mother told me, "go mark your territory." I went a few Sundays, then returned to Friendship, my mother's church. One of the last things she and I did together was go to church. The smell of cinnamon, a special treat she reserved for Sunday morning coffee, still triggered memories and tears.

I haven't been back to Friendship since her funeral. Once I moved to Eden, I went to church with Derrick, although I haven't officially joined. I consider myself a Christian, but I'm not used to going to church every Sunday, and don't think I'll be condemned to hell if I don't. When I lived in Chicago, I attended Bedside Baptist. French toast, vanilla roast coffee and T.D. Jakes had been my usual Sunday morning routine. Going to church with a husband seemed like a dream of a perfect life that I would never have. I got the church-going husband, although maybe my request should have been more specific, but I'm not complaining.

The past few weeks, Derrick has been more like the sweet man I married. Flowers, breakfast in bed, and date nights remind me why I fell in love with him. I moved to Derrick's side of the bed to let the comforter dry and grabbed the newspaper. The Dwight County Times was less than twenty pages, but the weekly paper kept us up to date on area happenings. Instead of the usual news about who shot john and what politician was under investigation, there were stories that touched me personally. I noted that a planning group was meeting at the library this week, and Raymond was listed as the contact person. Raymond had mentioned that a group was forming to oppose fracking in Dwight County. The bottom half of the front page was devoted to the Eden High School basketball team, with a picture of Raymond and his team. The team was now one win away from going to the district tournament. I grabbed my tablet, went to the online version of the paper and sent Beverly a link to the article.

I was about to turn off the television and concentrate on the newspaper, but something the minister said caught my ear. His title was, *Let It Go.* He was speaking on forgiveness and he quoted Colossians chapter three, verse thirteen: *Bear with each other, forgive one another if any of you has a grievance toward someone. Forgive as the Lord forgave you.* He went on to quote several other scriptures. He said not to deny the hurt or injustice, but if you hold on to it, you're the one suffering. It's easy to love someone when they are good to you, but a characteristic of unconditional love is sticking with someone when they aren't so loveable. Not that you turn into a doormat. Sincerity and repentance are key ingredients, both traits Derrick has displayed. I guess it's time to let it go and move on.

I thought about how blessed I am. But I also know God hasn't run out of blessings and there are things I still want for my life. A baby is at the top of the list. Funny how life changes. A year ago, having a child wasn't even on my radar.

I had gone in for my regular checkup before I moved. "I see you'll be forty-two in a few weeks," Dr. Turner had said.

"Don't remind me," I said.

"What's wrong with forty-two? If you continue to take care of yourself and watch your weight you'll still be a knockout. But you do need to start getting regular mammograms. I will schedule one for you. And one more thing, you may not look your age, but your body knows how old your eggs are. I know you're a newlywed, but if you plan to have children, you better get busy."

"Children? I gave that notion up long ago." When I turned thirty, I considered using a sperm donor or just getting pregnant and raising a child on my own. A few years later, a coworker and I dated. We were so in love, I transferred to another department so our relationship would not be a problem. We moved in together and planned to have children, so I threw my birth control pills away. I knew we were doing it backwards, since he hadn't put a ring on it. After six months of trying to get pregnant, I went to the doctor and learned that my tubes were blocked due to endometriosis. This was a shock because I hadn't had any symptoms or abnormal pain. I was prescribed medication and even tried acupuncture. Then I had a laparoscopy and it seemed to do the trick. I got pregnant and was prepared to announce a long maternity leave, sit home and rock babies, but I had a miscarriage. Then I found out he was seeing his ex-wife. Luckily, in our effort to keep up appearances, I had kept my apartment. I moved out of his place, and hadn't been with anyone I remotely considered father material since. A child just wasn't in the cards for me. The picture on church fans with a caramel colored mother, father, and two children was so out of reach that I had stopped praying for it. I had found a husband who loved me, and Derrick said he was happy with just the two of us. I figured asking for a child was just being greedy. I accepted my fate as aunt and godmother and was content, or so I thought.

"I know you've had some miscarriages, but you are not infertile. You may just need a little help. In vitro fertilization is much more common now than even ten years ago," Dr. Turner said.

I listened to Dr. Turner's explanation of the mechanics, risks, and costs associated with the procedure. After my conversation with Dr. Turner, I began reading and searching the internet for information on infertility. My periods were regular, so ovulation was not a problem. Dr. Turner referred me to a specialist in Memphis. I scheduled an appointment and had a pelvic exam, blood test and ultrasound. Those tests revealed no issues and I went on fertility pills. This is my second period since being on the pills, so it looks like the next step will be in vitro fertilization. That will be expensive and insurance doesn't cover it. We aren't rolling in money, but I can figure out a way to pay for it. We've saved money for a down payment, so we can dip into that fund. Everything is clear now, and I feel like the sermon was specifically for me. I said a special prayer for God to bless my marriage with a child, then made a note to schedule an appointment first thing in the morning. I don't have time to sit around licking my wounds. Forgive and move on.

CARL

Carl walked out of the office a happy man. He was officially off paper. He had paid his debt to society through almost twenty two hundred days of incarceration and parole. He hadn't gone to his sister's wedding because it was a last minute deal and he couldn't get permission to travel that quickly. Potential employers had told him they wanted to hire him, but couldn't hire anyone on probation or parole. He initially reported once a month and now had gotten to every eight weeks, but it was still a nagging reminder that he wasn't quite free. Some guys stayed inside and did all their time so they wouldn't have to be on parole. Carl just wanted to get out. If he had to jump through one more hoop, so be it. He was now finished jumping. No more drug tests or filling out the same stupid form each month. He had felt like a slave with a traveling pass having to check in and get permission to do anything. Now he could go to the moon if he wanted and it was nobody's business.

The fight at the high school had been another unexpected hoop. He was just trying to help and ended up the one being taken into custody. Luckily there were several witnesses to corroborate his story. He wasn't charged, but did end up prohibited from helping Raymond with the team. They claimed felons were a bad influence on the young men, and Raymond was reprimanded for not following school board policy. Ironic, since he was probably the best one to talk to the boys about why they needed an education and didn't want to go to prison. But keeping his own sons in line was job enough for him. He didn't have as much time to volunteer anyway. He had gone to see his sons for the past three weekends and he was working.

He had already gotten his first paycheck from Franklin Contracting. C.W. said he and the owner knew each other and Mr. Franklin happened to mention his vacancy when they saw each other at the bank. Carl applied to appease his father. He didn't expect to be hired, but he was. Carl enjoyed working for Mr. Franklin and having contact with the owner. He liked not having to punch a time clock. He was hired as a painter, but once they discovered he was a plumber by trade, they took advantage of his skills. They would ask him something, knowing he knew the answer and would volunteer to do it. They couldn't hire him as a plumber since he didn't have a license, but he hadn't complained. He was just glad to have a job. He could see his boys without begging someone to take him or loan him money, and he and Portia were settling into a comfortable routine.

Looks like things are finally starting to go my way, he thought.

CECELIA

Cecelia finished her teeth whitening treatment, then laid out her undergarments, including Spanx to hold in and smooth out her rolls and folds. She weighed almost the same as when she graduated from college. As a teen, she was jealous of her sisters' curves and boobs. Now, she realized it was a blessing since she did not struggle with weight like they did, although, the pounds had shifted. Even though she was now a grandmother and her hot date was only with Chuck E. Cheese, she didn't want to look like a grandmother.

Cecelia searched through ten boxes before finally finding her navy Jimmy Choo shoes. She worked six days a week, and rarely wore heels, but that hadn't stopped her from amassing an extensive shoe collection. She had even more boxes in storage. The shoes would look perfect with the jeans and ruffled powder blue blouse she planned to wear to the party. The jeans were almost two years old, but she had only worn them once. They were a little tight now, so she decided to skip breakfast and only eat a salad at the party so her stomach wouldn't poke out. The blouse was last year's color, but she could pair it with pewter accessories and it would still look classy.

Phyllis R. Dixon

She had come a long way since her shopaholic days, when every event required a new outfit. Not having a credit card helped. Filing for bankruptcy had been a humbling experience, but didn't curb her shopping. The bankruptcy erased their maxed out credit card debt. Then to her delight and Michael's chagrin, they received even more credit card offers. The banks were eager to sign her up since she had a clean slate. Before she knew it, the new cards were at the limit. Michael said it was the last straw, but he didn't complain when she bought him new golf clubs, or got the furnace fixed. After she paid her divorce attorney, and helped with her daughter's tuition, she was broke again. But now, she didn't have shopping as an escape. Credit card offers weren't filling her mailbox and paying bills by herself was a struggle. So shopping was a thing of the past. She even cut back on her casino trips. Designer names and nightly take out dinners didn't look as appealing when she had to pay cash. Cecelia got a secured card with a small line for emergencies and was learning to survive without plastic. It was definitely inconvenient though. She needed to get down to Eden to see what was going on, but she didn't have the money for a plane ticket and didn't have enough time to drive or take the train. Now she realized spur of the moment trips had to be planned and she didn't have to buy something new with each paycheck, or for each event, especially since she spent most of her time in hospital scrubs. When she moved from the house, she was embarrassed by the number of items that still had price tags on them. But it wasn't every day that her only grandchild turned two, so Cecelia fell off the wagon and splurged. She bought her two outfits from Neiman Marcus and a collector Black Barbie doll.

Simone was an unexpected gift. She was so smart and her laugh was an instant mood lifter. She was a carbon copy of Sheree, who had been a gorgeous baby. She had the longest eyelashes, a full head of curly hair and milky smooth almond colored skin. Of course she was biased, but even people they didn't know would stop them and comment on how cute Sheree was. She was growing up so fast. Seemed like her daughter was a toddler just a few years ago. Now Cecelia could see she had been so busy trying to make a living that she hadn't taken time to enjoy the living she was making.

Cecelia was proud of the way her daughter had matured. She was working and going to school, and hadn't inherited her mother's shopping gene. She took good care of Simone. The university had a reduced price day care program for student parents, and Simone was the teacher's pet. She already knew her colors and could count to ten. Cecelia and her ex-husband didn't agree on much during the last years of their marriage, but they both agreed that Simone was a blessing. A blessing they almost missed.

When Cecelia found out her college-bound, debutante, teenage daughter was pregnant, to say she wasn't pleased would be an understatement. Cecelia had planned Sheree's life, and a baby at seventeen was not part of the plan. She had given Sheree ballet, piano, and gymnastics lessons. Her children had gone to the best schools in Chicago, despite their father's objections. Why were they paying taxes to be in a good school district? Good according to public school definition was still way below the best private school, and Cecelia wanted the best for her children. She justified that the high tuition would pay off in the long run, as they would score well on tests and get scholarships, lowering college costs.

Cecelia got the news about Sheree being pregnant while they were at a family reunion in Eden. Within two minutes of finding out, Cecelia already knew which doctor to send her to for an abortion. She even said it was good it happened in July because Sheree would be recuperated by the time the fall semester started. Sheree refused, saying she and the boy were getting married. Cecelia ranted about her daughter's immaturity, naiveté, and lack of resources. Having a baby was out of the question. Cecelia could still hear the slap and feel the sting of her mother's words when she announced her plans for Sheree's baby. It was the first time in thirty years that Lois had laid a hand on her daughter. Cecelia had just wanted the best for her daughter and knew she needed an education. Of course now Cecelia was ashamed that she even had those thoughts, and hoped that her mother was putting in a good word for her with the man upstairs.

Simone turned out to be the best thing for all of them. She helped her daughter grow up, and once Simone was born, Cecelia and Michael could be in the same room without arguing. She hated Michael for filing for divorce and she hated him even more for filing for custody of their son. She understood all of that *let a man raise a man* stuff, but only unfit mothers lost their children. Michael could have spent as much time with Junior as he wanted. She had planned to switch to days so she would be at home in the evenings. They spent mediation and their first court hearing arguing about it. Then the judge asked Mike who he wanted to live with.

"Young man, you're old enough to make a decision for yourself," the judge declared.

Her stomach still churned whenever she recalled her son's words. "My father."

She worked even more hours and immersed herself in work to mask her hurt. But she and Michael were civil now and had even been partners when they played cards on Christmas. She realized it was probably for the best. Junior was doing well in his new school. He went out of his way to reassure his mother that he loved her and even said he was thinking about becoming a nurse. When she visited, the three of them played Scrabble and a couple times Cecelia had even spent the night – sleeping on the couch. Junior and his sister hinted that their parents should get back together. Cecelia knew the odds of that happening were even lower than her hitting the progressive, royal flush, Ace high. But just because the odds were low, didn't mean it was impossible, or that she didn't want to look her best.

Cecelia arrived a few minutes early and recognized the midnight blue Mercedes in the parking lot and parked next to it. It was three years old, but still looked new. The car that Michael didn't want to buy. Michael had wanted to get their old van fixed. Once she finally convinced him to get a new car, she had to talk him into getting a Mercedes. For just a hundred dollars more for a few more months, they could get the top of the line. Michael kept the car as part of the divorce settlement. Cecelia hated to give up the new car, but couldn't afford rent, child support, and a car note so she traded in the van for an older car and focused on straightening out her finances. Her budget worked on paper, but Sheree's tuition, Simone's day care, and back taxes weren't in the plan. As she double-checked her hair in the rearview mirror, a lady walked to the Mercedes and opened the trunk. She took out a large box wrapped in Minnie Mouse paper and walked back inside.

The decibel level smacked Cecelia's ears as soon as she entered the restaurant. She could hear her mother's voice chastising them for making such a big deal for a two year old's birthday. But Simone loved 'shuckshe' as she called it, and Cecelia was more than happy to spoil her. She spotted Michael from behind as soon as she entered. The clear spot in the top of his head had expanded from the quarter it had been last year to almost two inches. He was keeping his hair cut lower and doing a good job of hiding the spot. But she had seen that head for twenty years and knew where the hair used to be. He still looked good though. He had even lost a few pounds.

"Well, hello, Grandpa," Cecelia said as she got to their table.

"Hey, Granny," he said, as he stood and pulled out a chair for her.

"Cecelia, I'd like you to meet Kelly," Michael said as he introduced her to the Minnie Mouse box lady. She was cute enough, not the type she would have guessed Michael would be attracted to though. Cecelia wasn't jealous, but she was perturbed that the key to the Mercedes she had struggled to make payments on was inside the Minnie Mouse box lady's purse. This was supposed to be a family event. Simone didn't need a parade of girlfriends confusing her. Cecelia was going to let him know the next time she talked to him.

"I can't believe he brought his girlfriend to a family gathering. How tacky," Cecelia said when she and her daughter went to the ladies room. "If he didn't have good sense, she should have had enough class to decline his invitation."

"Mother, it's okay."

"No, it's not, and I'm going to let him know."

"Really. It's okay. Simone likes her."

"She's been around Simone?"

"Yes, I've met her before too."

"Why didn't you tell me?"

"What did you want me to say? I didn't want to upset you. I know you and Daddy haven't been divorced that long."

"This isn't about me and your father. I just don't like the idea of her being around my granddaughter. People are crazy these days."

"Mother, you don't even know her."

"And neither does your father. At least not well enough to be subjecting Simone to her."

"You can tell yourself that if you want to. I think you're just a little bit jealous. I understand. You guys were together a long time. It's natural to be jealous and feel some resentment."

"Just because you're taking psychology, don't think you can analyze me. I went to college too. This has nothing to do with anybody being jealous."

"If you say so. Although the maiden doth protest too much methinks."

"I studied Shakespeare too. I'm only looking out for your daughter, since her mother and grandfather have no problem exposing her to strangers."

"Okay, Mother, whatever you say."

Cecelia dried her hands and loosened the top button on her jeans, then headed to the counter to order a pizza.

CAROLYN

"I think my heart has finally stopped pounding," I said as I reached across the table for a second slice of pizza. "I don't know if I was more worried about the game or Daddy getting arrested."

"That ref knew he was cheating, and y'all know I can't stand nobody messing with my children," C.W. said. "I'm getting mad now just thinking about it."

"No need in getting mad. We won, but I still can't believe we played two overtimes," Raymond said. "I'm so proud of the boys."

"I thought Carolyn was going to burst my eardrum," Beverly said. "I'm going to send you my ear doctor bill," she said playfully shaking her finger in my face.

I had been to the NBA finals, NFL playoff games, and Wimbledon to watch Serena, but none of it was as exciting as watching my brother coach our alma mater to a win in the second overtime to secure a spot in the state tournament. Every seat in the gym was filled, although, by the end of the game, everyone was standing. Three players fouled out and Raymond got a technical in the last overtime for walking on the court to protest a call. The game came down to free throws and the Eden player made both to tie the game with eleven seconds left. Eden's player stole the ball when the other team tried to inbound after the free throw, ran the length of the court, and made the winning shot from just outside the key as the game clock turned to zero.

We lingered in the school parking lot after the game, savoring the win and good feelings. I saw several of my old classmates and couldn't remember having a better time. No one wanted the evening to end, and when Raymond suggested we go out for pizza, everyone quickly agreed, even though it was a school night. Everyone except Derrick.

"We'll have to pass. Carolyn and I have early starts tomorrow," he said.

"Oh come on, let's go. An event like this doesn't happen often. It's worth going just to see Daddy eat pizza," I said in what was left of my voice.

"Well, I'm going home. You do what you want," Derrick said, as he pulled his keys out of his pocket.

"You can ride with me," Beverly said. "I'll drop you off at home."

We had almost as much fun at the pizza parlor as at the game. Raymond ordered a vegetarian pizza that no one touched other than him.

"He just ordered that so he wouldn't have to share," Beverly teased.

Carl and Raymond recited a play-by-play flashback of one of their games, each remembering who made the clutch shots differently. One of my classmates who was at the game, joined us. His son was on the team. We reminisced about boring teachers, school dances, and who had crushes on who. We were having so much fun, we hadn't noticed that the restaurant had emptied and the workers were sweeping around us.

"Looks like we're closing the place," Beverly said.

"Before they kick us out, I'd like to make a toast," Carl said, and raised his cup. "To my brother, no matter what happens at the state tournament, congratulations on a great season. He could be somewhere making real money, but he chose to come back to Eden. And to my sister-in-law, you two make a great team. I want to be just like you, big brother, when I grow up, except with more money. Here's to you."

Next, Raymond stood and raised his cup. "Thanks to my family, especially to Carl. I don't care what the school board says, you're the assistant coach and we couldn't have done it without you."

"I'd like to make a toast too," C.W. said as he stood and raised his sweet tea. "I'm proud of all of you and happy to have you living nearby. I don't know what I would have done without you this past year. But I want to thank someone else for being by my side, and that's Emma. Stand up, Honey," he said, and pulled her chair out. "You know we been keeping company and we're going to make it official. I asked her to be my wife and she said yes. So here's to my future bride. She's going to retire at the end of the school year and we're getting married July third."

I grabbed my glass to disguise my discomfort at hearing him call another woman, 'honey'. When he announced a wedding date, I choked on a piece of ice. Raymond slapped me on the back.

"Are you ok, Miss?" the manager asked rushing to my side.

"Yes, just went down the wrong pipe," I mumbled. Beverly kicked me under the table so hard my shin was throbbing.

"Congratulations, Daddy," Carl said.

"Welcome to the family," Beverly said as she hugged our future stepmother.

"You folks have been great, but we have to leave by eleven. The alarm is automatically set and I don't have the code to override it," the manager said.

"I didn't realize it was that late," I said, rubbing my leg.

"Time flies when you're having fun," Emma said as she picked up her purse.

"Or when you're in shock," Beverly whispered.

C.W. honked and waved as he pulled his truck out of the parking lot.

"Can you believe that?" Beverly asked as they drove off. "Daddy has lost his mind."

"What happened to all that welcome to the family jazz?" I asked.

"I was just being polite. What else could I say?"

"I'm happy for him," Raymond said.

"You're kidding, right?" Beverly asked.

"What?" Carl asked. "I think it's good too. He needs somebody."

"A girlfriend is one thing. Getting married is something else," Beverly said.

"Daddy didn't waste any time," I said.

"We've got to talk to him," Beverly said.

"I don't think anything we say will make a difference. Seems like he's made up his mind," I said. "If they picked a date, does that mean they're planning a real wedding?"

"I can't believe we're even having this conversation. Mama would never have forgotten about him so quickly," Beverly said. "This whole thing is ridiculous."

"Now who sounds ridiculous?" Raymond said. "Mother is gone. Daddy is here. I would think you'd be glad he won't be alone."

"I believe she just wants his money," Beverly said, as she pulled her keys out of her purse. "It's not a coincidence that she's decided to retire."

"It happens all the time," I replied.

"You two have been letting Cecelia poison your thinking. You know she doesn't trust anyone. I'm going to leave you guys to stew about this. I've got to get up early," Raymond said.

"So does Carolyn," Carl said. "Derrick didn't want her to stay anyway. She's going to be put on punishment. Do you need us to write you a note?"

"Ha-ha," I said. "You're just trying to change the topic from Daddy's announcement."

"Actually, the original topic was celebrating Raymond's coaching victory. Good job, Coach," Carl said as he got in his car.

Raymond honked as he and his wife drove off.

"Should we call Cecelia?" I asked as I fastened my seat belt.

"I'll call her on my way to Memphis. Hearing her fuss will make the drive pass faster," Beverly said.

"It's kind of late for you to be driving. Why don't you stay in town?"

"I'm going back. I'll be okay."

"I may take a mental health day tomorrow. I am worn out. I must be getting old. I can remember when I didn't leave the house until eleven," I said.

"Old? Speak for yourself," Beverly said.

I *was* speaking for myself. I enjoyed the evening, but tonight was the exception. I missed the theatre, Cheesecake Factory, and watching the Bulls. I had only been in Eden two months and had settled into a routine of going to work, eating dinner, and going to bed. I've already gained seven pounds. We need to accelerate our house hunt so we can get closer to Memphis. Maybe then we'll get out more and Derrick won't feel obligated to spend almost every evening with his grandmother. I noticed the dining room curtain move as we turned into the driveway, and the porch light came on.

"That's sweet," Beverly said. "Anthony was so busy doing his own dirt, he never paid attention to when I came or went."

I limped out of the car and waved to Beverly as I opened the front door.

"Where you been?" Derrick asked as I stepped in the house.

"At Mazzio's," I said and limped to the couch.

"They close at ten o'clock. It's after midnight."

"We stayed while they cleaned up. Then we hung out a little while in the parking lot.

"You expect me to believe that? It's cold out there."

"We had an unexpected surprise that made us oblivious to the time and the weather. Besides, why are you interrogating me?"

"Because nothing is going on in Eden at this time of night. Maybe you were hooking up with Antoine. I saw you two at the game."

"Antoine Parker? You've got to be kidding."

"You seemed mighty glad to see him."

"Derrick, I haven't seen him in twenty years."

"You hadn't seen me in twenty years either. All I know is you defied me when I said we were coming home."

"Defied you? I wanted to celebrate with my family. You should have come too."

"You keep forgetting, I'm your family now."

"It's not an either or. And I don't have to jump when you say boo."

"Well don't let me catch you or hear about you doing something or being somewhere you're not supposed to be."

"Are you threatening me?"

"Call it what you want. You've been warned."

"You're acting crazy. First Daddy, now you. This must be the twilight zone," I said as I stood. "I'm going to bed. Maybe I'll wake up and find this was all a dream," I said wincing and walking toward the bedroom.

"What happened to your foot?"

"It's my leg, not my foot, and that's what you should have asked me about."

"What happened?"

"I twisted it jumping out of Antoine Parker's window when his wife came home."

"Lucky for you I know he's not married. But don't take me lightly. I'm not playing."

That's what worried me.

"Trouble, trouble, I've had it all my days.
It seems that trouble's goint to follow me to my grave."
Alberta Hunter

Chapter 6
DOWN HEARTED BLUES

Carl had worked eight consecutive days and was looking forward to his day off. He and C.W. were going to Little Rock to watch his son play in his first game. Another boy on the baseball team had to withdraw from school when his father's job transferred him and the coach asked Carlton to join the team. Right now he was a backup catcher, and last in batting order. But Carl knew that would just be temporary. His son was as passionate about baseball as he had been about basketball. It had even motivated him to improve his grades. Carlton asked his dad if there was any way he could send him to a hitting camp this summer. All the other boys were going. Carl agreed without hesitation. His ex-wife hadn't been too crazy about the idea, especially when she found out how much it cost.

"You must be back on the pipe to talk about spending that kind of money on some baseball mess," she said. "If you have extra money to throw around, I can use it for dental bills and school clothes."

"Kids take clothes, shoes, and food for granted. This is something extra I can do for him that he will appreciate."

"I'd rather see you pay that kind of money for a tutor or something that will help him in school," Pat said. "Besides, I already told him 'no.'"

"I didn't know he asked you. I don't like him playing us against each other," Carl said. "I'll talk to him about that. But it's not like it was when I was coming up. Kids these days have trainers and there is no off season. His teammates have been playing organized ball for years. This will help Carlton catch up. And if baseball keeps him motivated, then his schoolwork will be better. He has never asked me for anything. Let me do this." Their double-team worked and Carl paid the registration fee.

He had also paid on a birthstone bracelet for Portia's birthday. The jeweler in Forrest City let him do a layaway. He had offered him an account, but Carl didn't want any debt. He noticed Portia admiring Carolyn's bracelet and decided it would make a perfect birthday gift. They hadn't talked about it, but they had become a couple. Carl almost felt like he had a regular life. He was working, spending time – and money – on his children, and had a lady to share his off time with. He was still living in his parent's house and driving his mother's old car, but at least he had a reason to get out of bed, and a little spending money in his pocket.

The thought of money reminded him that his paycheck was late – again. He was hired as a painter, but did plumbing too, and since Mr. Franklin had been out, Carl also supervised the jobs.

Mr. Franklin had emergency surgery five weeks ago and the company was unraveling. Customers were complaining because jobs had gotten out of order. They were running out of supplies because the materials order hadn't been placed and most importantly, their paychecks were late. His son was filling in as best he could, but he had a full time job of his own.

"I'm sorry to trouble you," Carl said as he entered the office. "I hope Mr. Franklin is doing better."

"Hello, Carl. He's progressing slowly. I'll tell him you asked about him."

"Well, I won't trouble you long. I just came in to pick up my check. You told me when I called that I could come pick it up today."

"Oh, Carl. I totally forgot to call you. Since Dad's been sick, it's been hectic around here. Mr. Washington gave me the money, but I'm not sure which account to run it through."

"What do you mean?" Carl asked.

"Mr. Washington and my dad had an arrangement and—"

"You mean my father gives your father the money to pay me?"

"That's my understanding of the deal. I thought you knew."

"No, I didn't."

"Well, I know you need your money. I'll just write you a check out of my account. And my dad and I can settle up later."

Carl went to the bank and cashed the check, put the money in an envelope and put it on his father's dresser. He couldn't get mad at his father for trying to help. Carl knew he faced an uphill challenge with a record, but he was determined to be the exception to the rule. But now he felt maybe Perry was right. He had been unrealistic and was ready to accept reality – like when he realized he was not going to the NBA, or when he realized he was in jail for more than a few days. He had tried to beat the odds, but they were stacked too high. He went to the library to use the computer and pulled up the information about the job in North Dakota. Hopefully that window was still open.

He heard his phone and saw Portia's number. He didn't answer.

BEVERLY

Dating is hard work. With Anthony, I didn't spend much time figuring out what to wear. I didn't touch up my roots or get my nails done as often. I didn't care if I ate beans or not and I never worried about my weight. Maybe that's why I hung on to Anthony so long. It's easier to stick with the familiar. We never had to decide where to eat, we already had our favorite restaurants. We never had to decide what to do. We either went to Eden, the casino, or bowling. That's called being comfortable — or you could call it a rut.

Well, these last few weeks, I've gotten out of my rut. I've been in Memphis almost twenty years, but it's as though I'm seeing it for the first time. I finally stopped making excuses and went out with Mark again. Who knew Memphis had a ballroom dancing club? It always looked like so much fun on TV, but it never crossed my mind that I could actually do it. And how could I have lived here all this time and not known about The Pancake Shop and their butter pecan pancakes? I've never liked exercising, but we've been doing things that don't seem like exercise. We've walked through Shelby Farms, the largest public park outside of Central Park in New York City, rented bikes, and paddleboats. I've driven through the park on the way to the eastern suburbs, but never taken the time to actually visit. I grew up on land and got enough of nature by doing chores. But going to the park is like getting to enjoy nature without the work or responsibility. Mark couldn't believe I had never been to Graceland, the largest tourist attraction in town. I explained that Elvis wasn't quite as revered in the black community, but I do have a new appreciation for 'The King'. We toured the National Civil Rights Museum. The last time I had been was as a chaperone on a field trip with Tony's class. It's easy to forget the struggles and atrocities black people endured. I thought I would feel funny going there with a white person and was reluctant to go when Mark suggested it. But it was educational for both of us. We went to the Stax Museum and I was surprised how well versed Mark was in soul music. We even went to the BBQ contest, something else I've always wanted to do.

Our relationship has been out of order. We had sex a couple times before he moved. But after my epiphany with Anthony, I've cut off all friends with benefits. Aunt Belle was right. I've never been wined and dined so much in my life. But after about four dates, when guys realize I'm serious, they move on. Mark has been the only one to hang in there. Maybe he has a steady woman in Atlanta. If he does, he does. Without the sex, I'm not as invested and can just enjoy the relationship for what it is.

This morning we went to The Pancake Shop. Mark has to work late tonight, so we decided to get together early. If I'm not careful, I'm going to gain back all the weight I lost last year. I know I need to get on the treadmill, and that was my plan when he dropped me off at home, but my pillow was calling my name.

As soon as I laid across the bed, I heard my phone and saw a text from Sharon. She said I should come by the shop as soon as possible. *What could it be now?* I started to call, but knew Sharon wouldn't send such a cryptic message unless there was a reason. When I walked in, Sharon handed me an envelope. I opened it and felt my blood pressure rise. It was two sentences from Grant saying he was resigning immediately with an address and phone number to give his clients that called.

I was stunned. In the four weeks Grant had been at the shop, he had quickly become a hit. He came with an established book of business and was great with natural hairstyles, bringing an all new clientele to the salon. He paid his booth rent a month ahead and kept his station immaculate.

I have two stylists, Sharon and Fatima, who have been with me for years. Sharon always has man issues and Fatima always has issues with her children, but they're both good workers, trustworthy, and pay their booth rent on time – usually. In some ways they are closer to me than my own sisters. I have an older lady that works limited hours. She's the best at press and curl, and patient with children, and those people are hard to come by. That fourth station seems to be jinxed. No stylist has worked there longer than eighteen months. After I caught the last heifer in the storage room with Anthony, I decided to just let the chair sit idle. I half-jokingly said the next stylist would be a man – then I wouldn't have to worry about Anthony. But that wasn't why I hired Grant. He had excellent references and I was lucky to get him. He had run his own shop, but the landlord lost the building to foreclosure and the new owner remodeled the shopping center and doubled the rent. Grant had invested all of his money into leasehold improvements in his salon and couldn't pick up and move somewhere else. He put his equipment in storage and said he would just work for a while until he decided what to do. I knew he probably wouldn't stay long. Once a person has their own shop, it's hard to go work for someone else, but I would have thought he, at least, would have the consideration to tell me in person.

I went to the back office and called him. "Grant, I cannot believe you would leave on such short notice and without having the decency to tell me to my face. Here I am making changes to the website to include you and all the time you're planning behind my back to move. If you don't have any more regard for me than that, then I'm glad you're gone. You're a fantastic stylist, but I value honesty and loyalty so it's just as well that you leave."

"Are you finished?"

"I suppose so."

"Well, first of all, I did not go behind your back and plan a move. You, of all people, should know that changing locations is not good for business. Clients like stability. I have built my reputation on reliability and integrity. But I was no longer able to work in such a hostile environment. Your husband and I have exchanged words more than once and I finally told him what I thought and he fired me."

"What?" I said. "I had no idea any of this was going on. He had no right to do that."

"Well, I told him I thought I was working for you. He informed me that he is half owner of the shop and has just as much say-so as you do, and that my services were no longer needed."

"Did he say why?"

"Beverly, in the dictionary under homophobic, there will be a picture of your husband."

"I've tried to talk to him about that, but this is business—my business. If Anthony is the issue, I'll take care of him. I want you to come back. I apologize and promise this won't happen again."

Anthony's number wasn't on my call log and I had to search my contacts for his number. I haven't spoken to him since he spent the night a few weeks ago. He called a couple times, but I didn't return his messages.

"Hey, baby," he answered. "I'm glad you called. I've been meaning to call you, but my schedule—"

"Save it for one of your tricks. This is not a social call. You had no right to fire Grant."

"What are you talking about?"

"Grant, the new guy at the shop."

"You mean that funny boy with the braids?"

"I don't know if he's funny or not. I didn't hire him for his comedic skills," I said.

"You know what I'm talking about," Anthony said.

"I don't know anything about his personal business and I don't care. He pays on time. He's a great stylist, and he's a nice guy."

"Well, I can't have no funny boys around the shop. I know you ladies seem to love them, but men won't feel comfortable around him. And I know they won't bring their sons in for haircuts. They don't want that type of influence around. They convert kids."

"Anthony, you sound ridiculous. He's been there a month and I haven't noticed any drop off in business. In fact, business is up."

"Well, I still don't want him around. I can't stand faggots."

"Don't say that. That's like calling someone a nigger. They have civil rights, too."

"I don't give a damn about their civil rights. You cannot compare being a slave, suffering discrimination and lynching, to faggots getting their feelings hurt. I cannot believe you are defending him. Maybe I need to keep my eye on you, too. First, you go off and get a white boyfriend. I guess next you're going to tell me you have a girlfriend."

"Not that it's any of your business, but Mark is not my boyfriend. And no, I don't have a girlfriend, but I don't have anything against gay people. I don't understand it, but I'm not judging. As long as they aren't hurting anyone, that's their life."

"Well, that sissy can just live his life somewhere else."

"There you go again, calling him names. What if Tony told us he was gay?"

"That would never happen."

"But what if it did?"

"It won't, so there's no need talking about it."

"We don't always know everything about our children. On Oprah there were guys and girls who announced they were gay and their families never suspected a thing."

"Well, there's your first mistake. Oprah is not gospel. Maybe you should read the actual gospel. For someone who grew up in church, I would think you would be the last person to tolerate that mess. Now I'm through talking about it."

"Good. I'm tired of hearing it. Grant is coming back." Technically, Anthony was correct. Even though we're separated, we have an arrangement for the salon. Since he has a full time job, he rarely takes customers anymore. But he keeps the supplies stocked and fixes anything that breaks. Business is down now, but when we were both in the salon, things were booming. Our teamwork helped provide the three thousand square foot house, high end vehicles, cruises, and platinum American Express cards. When the older lady next door died, Anthony talked her children into selling us the house. He remodeled it and we moved my salon in that space. Working close to home meant less time in transit, and it was easier to manage the salon. Sometimes I wished we had worked as hard on our marriage as we did on the business, but today is not one of those times.

"Just because we aren't living together doesn't mean I don't have a say. In case you forgot, I'm more than an employee. I own half of that place, and I have as much say about who works there as you do. This isn't about him anyway. You're just mad that I left that morning."

"I cannot believe you. No, Anthony. This is not about you leaving that morning. Actually, you did me a favor. As Aunt Belle says, when one says 'scat cat' another one says, 'here kitty'."

"So that white boy is saying 'here kitty kitty'? Remember, you are still my wife."

"In name only. You think you can just do what you want and still claim rights over me and my salon?"

"Our salon."

"Whatever. Just don't come around here making trouble," I said and hung up the phone.

I searched through my contacts and found Sandra's number. Sandra is from Eden and when I got my license she was one of my first customers. I did her hair at a reduced price while she was in law school and Sandra did the paperwork when we opened the salon. She helped get charges dropped when Tony got in trouble a few years ago and represented me after the shooting incident. Now I have another job for her.

"Sandra, can I come to your office in the morning?" I said as soon as she answered. "I want to file for divorce."

"Beverly, are you sure?"

"I'm positive."

"I knew you and Anthony were separated, but I didn't know things were this bad. I may be prying, but you are more than a beautician to me. Have you guys gone to counseling?"

"If we go to counseling, after five minutes, the counselor will ask, what took me so long."

"Then think about mediation. It's cheaper and quicker."

"Will you still represent me?"

"Usually there aren't any lawyers; that's why it costs less. But I can advise you if you're sure this is what you want."

"I'm positive. When is your first opening?"

"My calendar tomorrow is pretty full. Is seven too early? I can get with you before my first meeting."

"Seven is perfect. I'll be there."

How ironic that my final straw with Anthony was not over a woman, but a man.

CAROLYN

One thing about moving home, everyone thinks I'm their personal lawyer and accountant. Raymond keeps bugging me about working with his protest group. I had to get my brother out of jail. Aunt Belle wants to sue every business that doesn't meet her demands. One of my cousins called and wants me to help him and his siblings straighten out the deed to their parent's land. And, Derrick wants me to help the church apply for a loan. Now I know how Beverly feels when we all show up for free hair dos. But Daddy doesn't fall into that category. I've always done his taxes and it's the least I can do for him. It's an annual reminder of how much my parents accomplished.

Phyllis R. Dixon

During a time of overt segregation, and elusive
bank loans, Mama and Daddy survived and thrived. As
a child, I was embarrassed by my homemade dresses,
rotary phone, and sack lunches. I couldn't understand
why we only had one TV. The kids uptown seemed to
have more, while we seemed to be still living in the dark
ages. Later, I learned that the tractors, tillers, and
combines I had considered little removed from a mule
and whip, were expensive pieces of equipment, and a
better investment than televisions and clothes. Instead
of worrying about how to keep the land, he has to worry
about estate planning, wills and trusts. Besides his
taxes aren't complex, although it did take me longer
than I had planned. I promised Derrick I would be
home before noon, but the time went by faster than I
realized.

"Daddy, I'll print a copy for you when I get home,"
I said as I turned off my laptop and checked my watch
again.

"You're sure I don't need to sign some papers? I
really don't like sending my taxes over the computer
like that," C.W. said. "How do I know that no one else is
going to get my information? I've seen warnings about
identity robbery on the news."

"Nothing is one hundred percent foolproof, but
filing online is more secure than shuffling and mailing
all those papers. Daddy, I wouldn't let you do anything
unsafe," I said as I grabbed my computer bag and
purse. "I've got to get home. Derrick and I have an
appointment to look at houses this afternoon, but I
know you've been up since before day, so you're
probably ready for lunch. Want me to fix you a
sandwich or something?"

"That's okay," C.W. said as he opened the freezer. "I've got some plates up here that Emma fixed. I'll just stick one of them in the microwave."

"All right then, I'll see you later." As I opened the door, my brothers stepped on the porch. "So what have you two been up to?" I asked as I searched for my keys.

"I'm getting the boys ready for a track meet. Carl and I jog around the lake and whoever wants to show up does."

"The way I've been eating, I should join you guys. Call me next time."

"I guess that's the only way we'll get to see you," Carl said. "We haven't seen you much since the tournament. Looks like married life is keeping you busy."

"Before you dash back to your honeymoon nest, don't forget the CARE meeting," Raymond said.

"What?"

"Remember, I told you about the Coalition Against Resource Exploitation?"

"Oh, yeah. Derrick said that's just a bunch of outside agitators trying to stir up trouble."

"Wow, the Carolyn I knew would make up her own mind. Does he tell you what clothes to wear too?"

"Don't even go there, Raymond. I'm sure it's a worthy cause, but I don't have time for politics."

"Clean air and water is something everyone can agree on. We are getting legal counsel from some national organizations, but it would be good to have local help too."

"It's still tax season. I may have to work late."

"Surely you can leave on time one day. This is important."

"I know it's important and to do it justice, will require a lot of time, something I don't have. I feel like I spend half my day on Interstate 40. Derrick and I have been looking at houses and we're getting his ready to sell. Plus, Derrick seems to think those leases will bring a lot of money to the landowners around here. Let me think about it."

"What's to think about? No disrespect to my brother-in-law, but those big companies fund all of the state commission members' campaigns. So of course, Derrick is going to say what his bosses say. This is the reason we stayed in slavery so long – those in the big house didn't want to sacrifice their comfort. Not realizing what enslaves one enslaves us all. You need to decide whose side you're on."

"I know I've been gone a while, but where did all this fracking business come from? I know we were kids, but I don't remember any talk about drilling oil when we were coming up," Carl said.

"It's not oil, it's gas. The gas has always been there, but it was too expensive to detect and retrieve. Prices have gone up because gas is more energy efficient than oil and doesn't pollute the air. Technology has improved and now the companies can locate the reserves and extract gas at a profit," Raymond said.

"So how can they do that without buying your land?" Carl asked.

"It's called mineral rights," I said. "Mineral rights entitle the owner to the minerals below the surface. They have the right to extract the minerals from the earth or mineral owners can lease their minerals to a third party like U.S. Energy to extract. If a third party extracts minerals, the mineral rights owner will receive payment in the form of royalties. Mineral property is considered a real property much like surface property and it can be retained, transferred and leased in whole or in part. In most states, it's legal to own or lease the mineral rights but not the surface property. The deed will disclose who owns the mineral rights."

"See, you already know enough to be of help to us. How you can turn your back on this with a clear conscience is a mystery to me," Raymond said. "Harriet Tubman said she could have freed more slaves if she could have convinced them that they were slaves. Your refusal to help is just as bad as—"

"Don't preach to me. Just because—"

"I'm going inside," Carl said. "I've seen this fight before."

"No one's fighting," Raymond said as he held up a peace sign. "But this is our family legacy. Daddy could have made a lot of money if he had sold to Consolidated Farms a couple years ago. But he didn't. If they start all this fracking, the value will decline plus there will be toxins to worry about. Maybe you don't understand since you don't have children."

"What's that supposed to mean?" I asked.

"I'm just saying. Your line stops with you, but we need to think about future generations of this family."

"I seriously doubt that Malcolm or Rayven want to be farmers."

"Even if no one farms the land, we can't sell it if the water is contaminated," Raymond said.

"This is such a mess. I should have listened to your mama. She wanted to sell this place and move uptown. I told her she could do what she wanted after I was gone," C.W., said as he sat in the porch rocking chair with his steaming plate. "I never imagined I would be here without her."

"I know, Daddy," I said and kissed him on the cheek. "I miss her too."

"Then we should honor her memory by making sure her legacy is intact."

"Raymond, give it a rest," I said as I picked up my computer bag.

"While we're resting, the white man is poisoning our land. Do you want me to talk to Derrick?"

"I don't need you to talk to Derrick. I can think for myself."

"It doesn't look that way to me. You are still a Washington."

"I said I would think about it."

"Well, don't take too long. They're already drilling on the Martin's place. You know that's only five miles away. We're running out of time."

CARL

"*Sanford and Son* is over forty years old and the show is still funny," Carl said as he turned up the volume. "These shows they come out with now aren't worth watching."

"I enjoy *Sanford and Son* as much as the next person, but I'd rather not watch a new show or an old show," Portia said as she took the remote control and turned off the TV. "Let's do something this weekend."

"Something like what?"

"You haven't been to see your boys in a while. How about going to Little Rock tomorrow? You can drop me off at the mall, go visit them, then come pick me up and we can go down to the Rivermarket for drinks or dinner."

"I don't like to see them when I don't have money."

"I'm sure they just like spending time with you. There are lots of free things you can do. They could care less how much money you have."

"But I care. I missed my last two child support payments and I refuse to show up at their front door empty handed."

"Then let's go to a movie. The new Denzel Washington movie has finally made it to Forrest City."

"What part of 'I don't have any money' don't you understand?"

"My treat," Portia said.

"You paid the last two times. You can't keep paying for everything."

"I don't care how much money you have or don't have. I wouldn't offer if I were going to resent doing it. And if you're that concerned about money, you can start by quitting smoking. Cigarettes aren't cheap."

"Even guys on death row get cigarettes," Carl said as he stood.

"That's because they're going to die anyway. Why don't you go back to the job your father lined up? Their business may have picked up by now."

"They didn't lay me off. I found out my father was paying them. He may as well have just been giving me the money." Carl had caulked all of his father's windows, cleaned the chimney, weeded his mother's flower beds and helped the guys mend his father's fences. These tasks kept him busy while he looked for a job. But prospects looked bleak.

"He was only trying to help. You're letting your pride get in the way of your relationship with your boys and letting people help you."

"Sometimes I feel like that's all I have left."

"The Bible says, pride goeth before a fall."

"The Bible also says, if a man doesn't work, he shouldn't eat."

"Well you definitely need to eat. We've got to keep your strength up. I've got some work for you to do," Portia said as she tried to grab Carl's hand.

"I'm not in the mood," Carl said.

"So much for my pride," Portia said. "How about going to the lake? That's free."

"I see the thrill is gone. You used to say you didn't care what we did, you just wanted to be with me."

"I do want to be with you, but that doesn't mean we have to sit around the house all the time. All we do is eat, fool around, and watch TV."

"Maybe you need to find someone with a more exciting itinerary. Sounds like you're getting bored with me."

"I just don't like you feeling sorry for yourself all the time. It's depressing."

"I'm already depressed. No need in both of us being depressed," Carl said as he pulled his keys out of his pocket. "Maybe we've taken this thing as far as it will go."

"What does that mean?" Portia asked.

"I think you know what it means. Take care of yourself," Carl said as he walked out the door.

CAROLYN

Who knew one of the best restaurants in the state was in Forrest City, Arkansas? Before it became known as the place where T.I. went to prison, Forrest City was known for Maggie's Kitchen. The décor wasn't fancy but the food was scrumptious. They were even featured on an episode of *Diners and Dives* on the Food Network. Ordinarily, I would have left a little food on my plate, but the food was too good to try to be cute. I swirled the last morsel of blackened catfish in the teriyaki sauce and cleaned my plate.

"Looks, like you enjoyed it," Derrick remarked. "How about dessert?"

"I'm already afraid the button on my skirt is going to pop. I know you don't want to be embarrassed."

"Now, Carolyn, you can't have a birthday without cake," Derrick said as a chorus of waiters emerged with a hunk of red velvet cake with lighted candles, singing Happy Birthday.

Unable to resist, I took a small bite. "This is so good," I said as I fed a mouthful to Derrick. "But I can't eat another bite. Let's box up the rest to go."

Cecelia gave me a surprise party when I turned thirty, and some friends and I took a cruise when I turned thirty-nine. But I couldn't remember a happier birthday. Even though it's my birthday, I have a gift for Derrick. I've barely been able to contain my excitement about the news I got today.

I took off work today, but still left this morning at my regular time. I told Derrick I was going to Beverly's shop, and I did, but only for a wash and wrap. I didn't get a retouch or have my nails done. I arrived at the clinic by ten o'clock. Memphis Fertility Associates has one of the highest success rates in the country and was highly recommended by my doctor in Chicago.

I listened to the doctor's explanation of the mechanics, risks, and costs of in vitro fertilization, but I was already familiar with the process. I had researched online and read numerous testimonials from successful parents. Dr. Turner transferred my records, but the clinic retested me. I had a pelvic exam, blood test, and ultrasound for fibroids two weeks earlier. Derrick doesn't know any of this yet. I wanted to have all the test results back and surprise him. I got my FSH test results this morning and couldn't have asked for a better birthday present. The specialists said all my tests were normal and encouraged me to bring my husband in so we can finalize the details.

After dinner, we drove to Lake Council. We parked right next to the water's edge and could see twinkling lights glowing from the houses on the other side of the lake. This was one of our favorite places in Dwight County. Derrick cracked the windows and the movement of the water created a melody so relaxing we didn't even turn on the radio. It was early spring so the night air was a little nippy, but that meant there were no mosquitos yet. The reflection of the full moon on the water was hypnotic. We sat quietly for a few moments with my head nestled on Derrick's shoulder.

"Thank you for dinner. You are always doing things for me. I want to do something for you," I said and kissed him on the cheek.

"Oh boy," Derrick said licking his lips. "Do we need to get a room?"

"Why, Mr. Roberts, I'm a good Christian woman," I teased.

"You got that right. You are very good," Derrick said softly as he kissed my neck.

"Derrick, listen to me," I said, scooting away from him. "I need to talk to you about something."

"Okay, talk," he said holding my hand and guiding it to the hardness between his legs.

"Derrick, this is serious," I said and jerked my hand away.

"All right, I'm listening," Derrick said.

"I want us to have a baby."

"A baby? You can't be serious."

"I'm very serious."

"We just got married. And, we're not exactly kids."

"We've been married over a year and Halle Berry had a baby at forty-six."

"She probably had her own doctor like Michael Jackson did. Isn't pregnancy at your age a high risk?"

"I've been to a specialist and she said there's no reason..."

"When? Why didn't you tell me?"

"I wanted to be sure first. I didn't want to get your hopes up."

"My hopes for what? I love our family—you and me. We should be planning for retirement, not kindergarten. We're finally together and I'm satisfied with our life. I thought you were too."

"It isn't that I'm not satisfied. But wouldn't a baby just make everything complete?"

"You told me you didn't want children."

"I think I told myself that to lessen the sting of not having any. Finding someone to love me seemed like such an impossible task, so I gave up. But then you appeared and now there are new possibilities. They have all kinds of new procedures now."

"You want some kind of operation? Is that safe?"

"No, it's not an operation. I'm talking about in vitro fertilization."

"Now, I know you're kidding. You want us to have a test tube baby?"

"They don't call it that anymore. It's not like that at all. Did you know that one-third of the procedures results in a healthy baby?"

"Well, just because man can do it doesn't mean it should be done. You want me to go in some doctor's office, jack off, then let them mix up my sperm and your eggs like they're making a cake, let it hatch, then stick it back inside of you? It might not even be my sperm or your eggs. Who knows what they'll concoct?"

"Derrick, it's not like that at all. Come to the doctor's office with me and let her explain it. She says I'm a good candidate."

"She means guinea pig. This stuff is crazy and I know why you're saying this. Your birthday is a reminder that you're getting older. Let's be happy about it and be satisfied with what we have. You can't bring back your youth."

"I'm not trying to bring back my youth," I said. "But we have a very short window. I don't want us to look back in five years and regret not trying."

"Well, I promise you. I won't regret it. If we do, we can always adopt. Besides, it's not of God."

"How can you say that? Thousands of children are conceived by in vitro fertilization. Are you saying all those children are not God's creation?"

"I just know what the Bible says and—"

"Don't preach to me. I know what it says. I don't see you turning away from doctors and medicine when *you* feel bad. You couldn't get to the hospital fast enough when you had those kidney stones removed."

"Baby, this is different. You're talking about creating a life."

"Well, I thought God was in control. If he created the doctors who created the technology, who created the procedure to create the life, isn't that his handiwork?"

"Are you having a midlife crisis or something? People our age are grandparents. We're not twenty-five anymore."

"I've always wanted a family. I thought you would be happy about this."

"You really should have talked to me about this before you ran off to see all these doctors. I could have saved you the hassle."

"It came up because I took my old behind to the doctor to get a checkup. There are certain tests you should have when you turn forty. She asked me about our childbearing plans."

"You should have told her we don't have any plans. I am not interested."

"So that's it? That's the end of the discussion?"

"Yep." Derrick turned the key and started the car. I turned and looked out the window at the water as he slowly backed over the bumpy cobblestones. It never crossed my mind that Derrick would be opposed. I thought he made all those negative comments to spare my feelings, and that he would be excited about being a father. He's so good with the children at church. He just needs more time to get used to the idea. This won't be easy, but I know he'll come around.

"Listen, people to what I'm telling you
Don't let your left hand know what your right hand do."
Lil Johnson

Chapter 7
NEVER LET YOUR RIGHT HAND KNOWWHAT YOUR LEFT HAND DO

Carl smiled when he read his ex-wife's text message. She thanked him for the money he sent and said she was able to get caught up on her bills. He had paid several months back child support and sent Pat extra money for the boys. It felt good to be able to take care of them. Rather than sit around and whine about his situation, he finally decided to do something about it. His wake up call came when he didn't get a call at all. He hadn't spoken to his boys for weeks and when he did call, their mother's phone was out of service. He drove to Little Rock and discovered her transmission had gone out. The first week her car wasn't working she and the boys took the bus. They had to leave home ninety minutes early for her to get them to school and she to her job on time. The routine in the evening was even worse. The last three weeks she rented a car, but this meant she couldn't save money to get the car fixed and was actually spending more money. By them getting home so late, she didn't have time to cook in the evenings, so they were spending money on takeout.

Her phone had been cut off and she was a month behind in her rent.

"Why didn't you call me?" Carl asked.

"I guess I'm so used to handling things myself it never occurred to me. Besides, I know you're not working."

She hadn't said the words in anger, but her statement was worse than being cursed out. What good was he if he couldn't help his boys when they needed something? So he had done what he said he wouldn't do. He called Perry. Within two weeks, he had money to send his boys and one thousand dollars in his pocket - thanks to a skill he learned while locked up.

He had lived in Chicago and Little Rock and his crack addiction followed him from one place to the other. He smoked crack for ten years and couldn't seem to shake the hold it had on him. Eighty-five percent of the U.S. prison population has a history of substance abuse, and once inside many just exchange one drug of choice for another. The prison wall is not a barrier and people would be surprised at the availability of drugs inside. Drugs get in via relatives, staff, even the mail, since legal documents are exempt from search in mailrooms. Inmates die of overdoses and the drug counseling programs are a joke. People sign up for counseling just to look good at the board. The first six months of Carl's time, he stayed almost as high as he had on the outside. But when he failed his first urinalysis and was then assigned to the laundry – where he was surrounded by never ending piles of clothes, towels, sheets, and funky underwear with no air conditioning - he decided to quit getting high for good. He signed up for everything he could to pass the time, and one of the classes he signed up for was computer classes.

The computer classes helped him stay sane. Some of the guys acted like they were just away for a while and the prison environment was as normal as anything else. Carl never felt that way. Access to the internet gave him a window into the outside world. He had never been much into computers, so he didn't realize how restricted their access was. He was just glad for the access he did have. He started with computer privileges of one hour a week. By the time of his release he was spending hours in the library. He completed their introductory computer classes then taught himself coding and basic programming. He even thought he could pursue a computer related job when he got out. Unfortunately, there weren't many of those jobs in and around Eden. He thought about moving in with one of his sisters where those jobs were more plentiful, but he would need more training. He wasn't eligible for training programs since he had a felony on his record, and he couldn't afford to pay for the program.

He ran into Perry one day when he was picking up a pack of cigarettes at the gas station. He usually dismissed Perry's 'job' offers, but that day he listened. When Perry told him all he had to do was deliver a package, and it wasn't drugs, Carl couldn't believe how easy the money was. He knew it wasn't legal, but couldn't see another way. He had tried longer than most. He thought maybe others just hadn't tried hard enough to get in the game. Carl tried to work his way off the bench but he couldn't even get in the stadium. Then when ex-felons end up back in prison, folks act like it's a validation of their weakness. Carl never thought of himself as a criminal. He was just a victim of the system. True, it was a situation he created, but he saw no way out. Perry was the only one offering a way out, so he took it.

Most offenders know the statistics and that the chances are high that they will eventually be caught. They also think they are smarter than others and start out with a plan to get enough money to go legit. That was Carl's plan. He had done a few runs for Perry and made a little money. Carl hadn't asked what was in the package and hadn't looked. But Perry had let him in on a plan to make even bigger money. Turns out the bag was full of credit cards. Perry had a source that had a connection that had a hook-up with a computer hacking ring in Russia. Every month or so, his hook-up bought thousands of stolen credit card numbers, made cards, and distributed them. Carl and Perry were in the distribution chain. Perry said they could make more money if they made the cards themselves. The equipment wasn't expensive and anyone could buy it. Carl said he didn't want this to be a long term deal. He'd do the computer work, but only for a month or so. He just wanted to do a few more runs, until he got enough money to pay down his back child support and saved enough to move to North Dakota. Then he'd be gone.

CECELIA

Cecelia's stomach growled so loud she looked around to see if anyone else heard it. *Today's not going to be a salad day,* she thought as she walked past the salad bar and headed to the grilled food line. She rarely ate in the cafeteria. She usually ended up working through her lunch break and grabbing a snack from the vending machine on her floor. She also kept nuts and raisins in her desk. But today she was hungry. She arrived at work last night at eleven and was working a double. They admitted two cardiac patients and she missed her six o'clock break. So it was about ten-thirty but her stomach didn't know if she wanted breakfast or lunch.

She checked her account balance on her phone to make sure she had enough to pay for a meal. Today was payday, but she didn't want to chance using her debit card until she was certain her paycheck had been deposited. She had given Sheree two hundred dollars on Friday to pay for her car insurance. Sheree said she would pay her back, but Cecelia knew not to count on that. She didn't mind helping her daughter. It just seemed that she needed help whenever Cecelia could least afford it. But Cecelia had a full tank of gas and a full pantry, so she knew she would be okay until payday. There was a time she would have just gotten a cash advance on one of her credit cards and headed to the casino. She got complimentary meals and rooms whenever she wanted. But she now realized those meals and rooms weren't really free. Besides, all that buffet food ran up her cholesterol.

She wasn't worried about her cholesterol today. Cecelia splurged and ordered an omelet with extra cheese, pancakes, coffee, and an apple for later. She was surprised to see a line at the cash register. The cash only line was moving, but of course, she didn't have any cash. The computers were down and the cashiers had to manually input credit and debit transactions. "My food will be cold at this rate," she said to no one in particular.

"Computers run everything these days," a baritone voice behind her said.

"What did we do before we had computers?" Cecelia said, as she glanced at her watch. "The one day I decide to come to the cafeteria, they have issues. Like the blues song, if it wasn't for bad luck, I wouldn't have no luck at all."

"Well, I'm going to say this is my lucky day. If the computers were working, I wouldn't have had the opportunity to talk to such a lovely lady."

Cecelia turned all the way around to get a good look at the man who had just complimented her.

"Gabriel Andrews," he said as he extended his hand. "I haven't been sick much, but I certainly didn't have a nurse as lovely as you."

"Thank you, but my patients usually are in such distress they could care less what I look like. They just want me to do my job and do it well," Cecelia snapped.

"I didn't mean to offend you. I forget that women are touchy about compliments over here."

"What do you mean by 'over here'?" Cecelia asked, noticing his accent for the first time. She also noticed that he was clean shaven with a low hair-cut, medium build, about six feet two inches, with Hershey chocolate skin and perfect white teeth.

"I'm not from the states. I forget that people here are more sensitive, and even innocent comments can be construed as sexual harassment. I promise I meant no disrespect. I apologize."

"I apologize as well. I didn't mean to be touchy," Cecelia said. "I guess that's the hunger talking."

Seven minutes later they finally made it to the front of the line. Cecelia paid for her food, then found a table. Gabriel grabbed his tray and followed her. "Mind if I sit with you?" he asked, and sat before she could answer.

In the next fifteen minutes, Cecelia found out he was a Johnson Fellow in a doctoral program co-sponsored by the hospital university. He was born in Petionville, a suburb of Port Au Prince, Haiti, spent his teens in London, and now lived in Miami, where his parents, both college professors had retired. Just as she was putting sweetener in her coffee, an announcement came over the speaker.

"Code blue, 3016 Stat. Code blue, 3016 stat."

"That means I have to get back to work," Cecelia said, as she quickly finished her coffee and put the apple in her purse.

"But you just sat down. Your hour can't be over yet."

"Tell that to whoever they just wheeled out of the ambulance."

"I've enjoyed talking to you. Can we go to a real lunch sometime – not in the cafeteria? Unless there's a man in the picture?"

"No man in the picture. I feel like I'm married to this hospital," Cecelia said as she grabbed her purse.

"We need to do something about that. So can I call you?"

"I really need to go," Cecelia said.

"Here, put your number in my phone," he said as he handed her his cell phone. "Now when you see this 305 area code, that will be me. When's your next off day?"

Cecelia had to think. She had gotten into the habit of working on her off days, even if it was just to do paperwork. "Thursday."

"Okay. It's a date. I'll call you before then and we'll set something up for Thursday."

Cecelia nodded, took another gulp of coffee and left. Anyone looking at her would never guess she was on her way to someone's emergency by the smile on her face. But she had just done something almost as elusive as getting a royal flush. She had been asked on a date.

Cecelia was supposed to be showing Gabriel the city but felt like a tourist herself. Between the hospital and her family, she rarely ventured outside of her routine. But she had seen more of Chicago in the last three weeks than she had in the twenty years she had lived there. They were both working nights and spent their days touring the city. They had been to Buddy Guy's Legends, the Chess Records Museum, Navy Pier, and the Field Museum. Like some people close a club, they closed the International Museum of Surgical Science, a place Cecelia had heard about, but never visited. She had taken him to several pizza places and had even broken her "no meat" rule and indulged in Chicago style hotdogs. Riding the 'el', was also on Gabriel's 'to do' list. Cecelia rode it at the beginning of her marriage when they just had one car, and it wasn't an experience she coveted, but she joined him in his adventure.

Cecelia was the longtime resident, but Gabriel was teaching her a few things too. They went to the DuSable Museum of African American History, a place Cecelia had been on field trips with her kids' schools. But she hadn't realized that DuSable, regarded as the first non-native resident of Chicago was of Haitian descent. There was a sizeable Haitian community on Chicago's north side that Cecelia had been oblivious to and Gabriel had introduced her to some awesome Haitian restaurants over there. She took him to Lady Luck but he quit playing after he lost twenty dollars. He described the players as irrational fools and couldn't understand how people could throw their money away. She tried to explain to him that people didn't always lose. "They wouldn't build them if they weren't making millions," he said. He didn't complain, but Cecelia felt uncomfortable with him watching her play, so they left after two hours. She had actually won one hundred dollars, but Gabriel wasn't convinced.

Their best date was the tour of the old Sears Tower, not because of the view, but because Gabriel bought postcards in the gift shop and quickly wrote a note to his parents and mailed them. He told them he was enjoying Chicago, work was going great, that he had met a special girl, and couldn't wait for them to meet her. That told her he was feeling what she was feeling. Maybe she had finally hit the jackpot.

CAROLYN

The garlic and onion aroma overwhelmed the car and I cracked my window even though it was raining. Derrick's been gone all week on field visits throughout the state. My initial plan had been to cook his favorite dish; smothered steak and rice, and have it ready when he walked in the door. Cooking is one byproduct of marriage that I hadn't fully considered. I had a chef's kitchen in Chicago, but my oven was primarily storage for the Martha Stewart cookware I rarely used. Being the youngest girl, I guess I didn't spend as much time in the kitchen with Mama as my sisters. When I did venture near the stove, my culinary skills leaned more toward pasta or grilled fish, especially since I've lost weight. Derrick expected meals with a meat, preferably coated in flour or meal and fried, with at least two vegetables every day. I now have a new appreciation for both of my sisters. Taking care of houses, husbands, children, and a job requires superwoman skills. Of course, I don't have the children part— at least not yet.

Primarily because it's tax season, Derrick doesn't give me a hard time about cooking. If I don't cook, he'll go to Mother Roberts' house. She seems to cook a Sunday dinner every day as though she expects me not to cook. True, I don't relish cooking and planning meals every day, but I don't appreciate my mother-in-law assuming I'm not taking care of my husband. I made it my mission to learn to fix Derrick's favorite meals. Beverly confided the secret to good smothered steak was low heat and lots of bell peppers, (my first two attempts were on the bland side and a little chewy). Sweet potatoes, baked in the oven, just as Derrick liked (microwave would have been fine with me), and some pickled beets would complete the meal.

I left work early with plans to chill some of Daddy's plum wine, spruce up the house, and have all this waiting when Derrick got home. But I got stuck behind an accident on the Mississippi River bridge. Then, Rick stopped me just as I crossed the county line. Luckily, he's always had a crush on Beverly, so he only gave me a warning and told me to tell her to call him sometime. Now, it's almost six o'clock. Enter Plan B - pizza with salads from Wendy's. It's not fancy, but I'll spruce it up with my mother's dishes instead of paper plates and light Bird of Paradise candles from our honeymoon.

Maybe the few days apart have done us some good. Derrick sent me several romantic texts and even agreed to go house hunting in the morning. I have a Victoria's Secret nightie that still has price tags that I plan to surprise Derrick with. I'll be the dessert. I parked in the garage and could hear voices in the kitchen. The aroma of greens met me as I unlocked the door.

"Hey, babe," Derrick said as he rose to greet me. "Mamalil cooked for us. Isn't that great?"

Our pizza date for two ended up being a soul food dinner for three. Ordinarily I would have relished a dinner of greens, homemade fried chicken, pinto beans and cucumber salad with cornbread. Derrick's grandmother cooks almost as good as Mama – although I would never have let my mother know that. But I wasn't in the mood for company. And by the time Derrick took his grandmother home, took out her garbage, looked at her dryer to see why it was cutting off early and stopped her toilet from running, he was so tired he fell asleep as soon as his head hit the pillow. However, my Victoria Secret purchase didn't go to waste. We made up for the night before with an early morning loving session. We had a morning appointment with the realtor and grabbed granola bars on our way out the door to keep from being late. Five hours, and ten houses later, we were finally back home.

"I feel like I've put in a full day's work," Derrick said as we walked in the door.

"So which house did you like the best?" I asked.

"They were all good enough," Derrick said as he grabbed the pizza box and a bottle of water from the refrigerator.

"I liked everything about the house in Wellington except the color. Who paints their house royal blue? Then again, the house in the new development in Pine Hill was stunning. I know we said we didn't want the headache of building, but we can have a large lot and an updated kitchen. Supervising a remodeling job in some of the older houses will probably be just as much work as building a house. You still haven't said which one you liked."

"They're all so big," Derrick said. "I'm not trying to spend my weekends doing yardwork."

"I'll help you. I always wanted a flower garden like my mother."

"You don't even fool with the few flower beds we have here. We don't need a house that big."

"I guess we don't need it, but we can afford it, so why not? For now, we can each have an office and we can use the other extra bedroom for a guest room. Who knows, we may have some little people in those bedrooms one day."

"Carolyn, don't start. And, don't take this the wrong way, but I'm very uncomfortable with the prices. Our mortgage payment is going to be over fifteen hundred dollars."

"I was paying that much for a smaller place in Chicago."

"You may be used to those big numbers, but I'm not. This house is paid for."

Derrick's two bedroom, one bathroom bungalow was built right after World War II for returning veterans. I feel like I'm living in the yesteryear exhibit at the Smithsonian with popcorn ceilings, window air conditioner units, and florescent lights. A hand-held hose connected to the tub faucet serves as the shower and worst of all, there is no dishwasher. My mother said these houses were considered ultra-modern when they were new because they were the first houses in town built on a slab, rather than a crawlspace, and they had an attached garage. The one car garage is now pretty much storage, although some neighbors have insulated them and converted it to living space. If it weren't for the late-model cars in the driveways, the street looks the same as it did back then, with one key difference. The neighborhood is now almost all black with just a few older white residents left.

Derrick offered to enclose the garage, add a bathroom, and get new appliances to update the house. I don't want to hurt his feelings, but that would be like putting lipstick on a pig. Most of my boxes remained in the garage. I don't intend to unpack until we move to our real house.

"We can afford it. We actually prequalified for twice that amount."

"Just because we qualified, doesn't mean we should do it," Derrick said.

"It's not just to get a big house. I still feel like this is your house. I want us to have *our* house," I said as I pulled paper plates from the cabinet.

"Yeah, our house and our big mortgage. Why get in all that debt? We can use the money we were going to use for a down payment to remodel the kitchen and add another bathroom. Then, it will feel like your house and we'll save money. If we're going to spend that kind of money, I'd rather get a house on Lake Council. I'd have easy access to my boat and still be close to Mamalil."

"We'll be able to spend more time together if we move. I'll be closer to work and can cut my commute time."

"Well, I have another solution. Why don't you find a job closer to Eden? Your brother and his wife found jobs."

"Raymond is in a teacher certification program. They pulled strings for him because they wanted him to coach. And nurses can always find work. Sick people are everywhere. Geneva got a position at the new dialysis center."

"You're selling yourself short. There aren't a lot of lawyers around town. I'm sure you could find something."

"But I've been with the IRS almost twenty years. I'd lose my retirement."

"If we stay where we are, we don't need as much money for retirement. If you find another job, you'll probably make less money, but we'll need less and we can spend more time together. Makes perfect sense to me. And if you're not so tired, maybe we can make a baby the regular way."

"What did you say?" I asked as I put the pizza in the microwave.

"I believe you heard me. Shall we get started?"

BEVERLY

April fourth is always a day of reflection in Memphis. It is the day Martin Luther King Jr. was assassinated. Historical programming is on TV all day. There are prayer breakfasts, heavy-weight politicians come to town, and we close the salon. Some of it is depressing, but it also makes you realize that we have made progress. It's easy to think current problems are insurmountable, until you remember how bad things used to be. But today is a day of reflection for me, not because of Dr. King, but because of Mark.

He's been to Memphis twice this month and we talk almost every day. His texts make me smile and I enjoy his company. Right now we're just friends, although he hasn't hidden the fact that he'd like it to be more. I've been the one putting on the brakes. He thinks it's because I'm still hung up on Anthony. But that's really not it. If I'm honest with myself, it's because he's white.

Black men have no problem dating any race as long as the woman has a vagina and two legs (the legs aren't even mandatory). I've always thought of myself as a caring person and race doesn't matter. I was the one Paul came to when he was concerned about bringing his wife to the family reunion. I told him this is the twenty-first century and a black and white couple isn't news anymore – even in Dwight County. But on a day like today, when race permeates the media and conversations, I wonder what Mark's family was like back in the day. Were they part of the lynch mob, or to go further back, slave owners? And what if they were? That doesn't have anything to do with Mark – or does it? We've spent hours on the phone and together, but race is the one thing we haven't discussed. Every time I think there's no way for us to be a couple, he gives me another reason to keep him around.

We talked three hours last night. The first call lasted an hour and within ten minutes he called me back. "Are you sure you're all right?" he asked when I answered the phone. "Before you brush me off and say you're fine – you don't sound fine, and unless you say you don't want to talk to me, I'm going to bug you until you tell me what's wrong."

"I guess I'm just in a funk. I went to Eden to spend the weekend with my father and felt like a visitor. His lady friend has taken over the house. She's taken the plastic off the couches and rearranged my mother's kitchen."

"I would think that would be a good thing. Unless your father is a chef, he probably needs someone to cook for him. Don't you like her?"

"She's okay, and I try to be nice. But that's the problem. I don't want to be nice and polite when I go down home. It doesn't feel like my parents' house when she's around."

"Just focus on your father. If she makes him happy, that's what matters. At least you don't have to worry if he's lonely or eating properly. So that's what has you in a gloomy mood?"

"I was going to spend the night since the salon is closed today, but I felt out of place sitting with them while they watched TV, so I came back to Memphis. You know Daddy sat next to her on the couch? I don't ever remember him sitting on the couch. He was always in his recliner. Then, this morning, my son called. He was supposed to get leave this summer, but they've cancelled it and now he doesn't know when he'll be home. I'm so worried about him."

"You've got to have faith, and knowing you, you'd worry no matter where he was. Worrying won't help him and would probably make him feel bad if he knew."

"I just wish I had kept him from enlisting."

"You should be proud that you raised a responsible young man. That was a very mature thing to do. These days' kids think their parents are supposed to take care of them until they're thirty. My mother felt the same way when I went in the Army. I left Tupelo and came to Memphis to get a job, but couldn't find anything paying a decent wage. The factories weren't hiring like they used to. From the end of the war until the sixties, my uncles and cousins moved up here, got good jobs at places like American Can, Kellogg, and Goodyear. But by the time I got out of high school, those jobs were gone and if you didn't have a degree or know someone at the post office, the best you could do was to find a minimum wage job. That wasn't enough money to pay for my own place and help my mother too, so I joined the Army. That was the best thing I could have done. I served my twenty years, retired, got my own truck, then met you.

"I guess you've always been industrious," I said.

"I don't know how industrious my motives were. I just wanted my own place so I would have a place to take girls."

"Now the truth comes out. And I thought you wanted to serve your country," I said, smiling at the thought of Mark as a player.

"I hear a smile. That's better," Mark said.

We talked another hour, and by the time we hung up, I was in a much better mood.

He sent me a text at five this morning. It was a quote from Dr. King. *"Faith is taking the first step, even when you don't see the whole staircase."* How sensitive of him to know what day it is since this isn't generally a red letter day for people outside of Memphis. And, he sent it just four hours after we hung up. It's nice to know someone woke up with you on their mind. I know people are basically the same and Mark is definitely saying and doing all the right things. *So why am I tripping?*

CARL

Since leaving Franklin Contracting, Carl had pretty much given up on trying to find a job. Every now and then, he answered an ad or posted a resume online. He did that to keep up appearances. His real plan was to build up his savings. His arrangement with Perry was working fine so far. He now had a five-figure savings account, and sent money to his sons. He was grateful for this opportunity and vowed he would not be greedy. As soon as he made enough money to catch up on his bills and move, he would be gone. He was meeting Perry in Memphis for a pick up at a post office box. Perry was going on to Atlanta and Carl would make a delivery in St. Louis then turn around and come right back to Eden.

Carl went to the kitchen and made a cup of coffee to take with him.

"So where are you headed this early son?" C.W. asked as he entered the kitchen.

"I'm going to put in a few applications in Memphis," Carl said. "I was hoping the rain would subside."

"All this rain isn't good for the watermelons," C.W. said. It had rained ten consecutive days as a weather system stalled over the mid-South. "But I guess we shouldn't complain. Cece said they got snow."

"That is one thing I do not miss," Carl said. "A little snow is all right, but we would get buckets of snow in Chicago. At least down here when it does snow, everything stops. Up there you have to make your way through it. Although, I guess it really doesn't matter much now since it's not like I have a job to go to."

"When it does dry out, we're going to have a short window to get the sorghum. I'll need your help."

"No problem, Dad. I doubt if anything comes up between now and then."

"You mean anything like a real job? You've been looking in Memphis and Little Rock, and trying to work with whoever will hire you, and you're ignoring a job right under your nose."

"What's that?"

"This farm."

"I helped out during planting time and I fixed the fences and the irrigation pipes, but I need a real job."

"Don't you see those men coming here every day? This is a real job. And I'm not talking about just driving a tractor or combine or fixing stuff. This place needs a manager. You were dropping fries working your way up to assistant manager and trying to earn your own store, when you have your own business right here. I grossed almost two hundred fifty thousand dollars last year. I just assumed Charles would take over. Then when he died, I thought maybe Tony would take over since he showed some interest in the place. But he left too, so I thought maybe I should just sell out. But this land has been in our family almost one hundred years. I know I always said having this land meant you always had a home. But it also means you always have a means of support. You can make your own living."

"I guess I never thought about it like that."

"And I blame myself for that. I wanted all of you to have more opportunities than I did. I wanted you to get an education and be able to go anywhere you wanted. But just because you have an education and choices doesn't mean you have to reject what you already have. You need an education to be a farmer these days. Farming isn't like it used to be, just putting some seeds in the ground and hoping for rain. Derrick showed me new trends in seeds and planting techniques. He told me I could improve my yields and fuel costs if I got a computer, but I'm just not ready for all that. But I see how smart you are on computers. It would be easy for you to catch on. I'm not a religious man, but maybe the reason none of them other jobs panned out is because this is what you're supposed to be doing. Just think about it."

"I will, Dad," Carl said as he grabbed his jacket. "But I got to go now." The phone rang and C.W. waved as his son opened the screen door. Carl rushed to the car and glanced at his watch as he put it in reverse. He sent Perry a text to let him know he was on his way and happened to look in his rear view mirror and saw his father on the porch waving his arms.

"What is it?" Carl asked as he backed up and rolled down the window.

"There's been an accident. We need to get to Memphis right away."

"O way down yonder by myself
And I couldn't hear nobody pray."

Negro Spiritual

Chapter 8
AND I COULDN'T HEAR NOBODY PRAY

It's only eight o'clock and it feels like I've already put in a day's work. I was too tired last night to finish Aunt Belle's wash, so I got up at sunrise to wash and fold her last two loads. How can one person have so much laundry? When I got to her house, she said she was hungry and I was taking too long, so she had tried to fix coffee and oatmeal. The walker got caught on the kitchen table leg, and she dropped the milk. I mopped, cooked then did dishes. She's always been independent and I know being housebound is working her nerves. But she's working mine. I know I shouldn't complain. Her injuries from the accident could have been much worse.

Her Sassy Seniors Social Club was on its monthly bus trip to the casino, in Mississippi when an eighteen-wheeler hit the bus. She broke her leg in two places and spent two weeks in the hospital in Memphis. They released her with instructions to strictly adhere to her exercise regimen if she wanted her leg to fully heal. That meant I went to her house three times a week to help her do her physical therapy exercises. Carl was home all day and could have gone, but she said she didn't want a man handling her leg. I could tell she was disappointed that I didn't sit and eat with her, but Derrick and I have an appointment this morning. So when I finished my shift with Aunt Belle, I came home and cooked another breakfast. I should be worn out, but I'm too excited. Between our jobs, the weather and family obligations, Derrick and I haven't done much house hunting. Our calendars today are clear and I'm glad we're finally getting back on our schedule. It was beginning to feel like we'd never move.

"This is the last stack, I promise," I said as I placed a stack of papers next to Derrick's coffee cup. "I've already emailed a list to the realtor and we're meeting her at the house in Forrest City. But if there are some you absolutely don't like, no need in wasting time looking at them."

"Carolyn, let's do this later. I told Mamalil I'd take her grocery shopping this morning. She says the food is fresher the earlier you go. Knowing her, she's already waiting on her porch," Derrick said as he put on his jacket.

"But I told you we have an appointment with the realtor this morning."

"I thought we decided to stay put and you were going to look for a job closer to home."

"We discussed it, but it was contingent on me finding a job, and I haven't seen anything worth even applying for. I'll keep my eyes open, but we should continue house hunting. There are some good deals out there."

"I already told you these prices are too high," Derrick said as he thumbed through the stack.

"I guess I'm still in the Chicago mindset. I can't believe we can get such a great house for these prices."

"I don't want any avoidable debt. By the time I get through fixing everything on your list to get this house ready to sell, we might as well stay here. What do we need with four and five bedrooms?" Derrick asked.

"You filled this house up by yourself. Although you could toss a lot of the stuff around here. Your drawers are filled with old bills and statements and the closets are full. You must have every article of clothing you've ever owned. Now with both us of we're bursting at the seams."

"I prefer to think of it as cozy."

"I haven't even unpacked all of my boxes. And what happens when we have children?"

"Carolyn, I'm worried you're becoming obsessed with this baby thing."

"Is that what you call us having a family – this baby thing? Why are you so against us having children?" I said as I ran water to wash the breakfast dishes.

"I'm not against us having children, but it doesn't consume my every waking hour. You know the odds are against it and that's just fine with me."

"What if I get pregnant? You know we're not using anything and the doctor said I'm healthy."

"The doctor also said there's a low probability, and it would be high risk if it did happen. Why can't you just be happy as we are?" Derrick asked.

"I *am* happy," I said as I put my arms around his neck, pecked him on the lips, and rubbed the back of his neck. "I just want to be prepared. For now, we can use the extra bedrooms for an office and an exercise room, and still have a guest room."

"You wouldn't be trying to seduce me now, would you?" Derrick said, as he pulled me to him. "I'm beginning to think you only want me for my sperm," he said, then kissed my neck.

"In the words of James Brown, a woman's got to use what she's got to get just what she wants. Whoa. Did you feel that?" I said and grabbed his arm.

"What?"

"The house just shook. Did a plane fly too low or something?" I asked and went to look out the window. "It is cloudy, do you think it was thunder?"

"I'd like to think my good kissing and hugging shook you up. But it's probably only a tremor," Derrick said.

"Tremor, as in earthquake?"

"Just a little one."

"Are you serious? Earthquakes? In Arkansas?"

"I'm very serious. It's not as unusual as you might think. We live on the New Madrid Fault. The largest earthquake in America occurred on this fault. Of course, the area was sparsely populated back then, but there's always the potential for it to become active."

"There aren't any tall buildings around here. But still, that can't be good," I said, as I noticed the ceiling fan still swaying. "Well, I'm going to text the realtor and tell her to take the two story houses off the list. I don't want to wake up with my upstairs bedroom downstairs."

"Plus we need a one-story house in case Mamalil has to come live with us." Derrick said.

"You're right," I said, glad I was facing the dishpan and he couldn't see me roll my eyes. "It does look like rain is coming, though. Can't you take Mother Roberts later?"

"All right. She has a doctor's appointment on Monday anyway. I'll call her and tell her we'll go when we leave her appointment," Derrick said as he took off his jacket. "Your daddy told me the secret to a successful marriage is happy wife, happy life. Pick the houses and we'll go look at them. All I ask is that it be move-in ready and within thirty minutes of Eden. I don't want to be too far from Mamalil."

"Deal," I said. Thirty minutes is still too close as far as I'm concerned. Mother Roberts is polite but distant. My sisters-in-law said Mama was the best. She treated them like daughters, didn't judge, and would call out her sons when they were wrong. Maybe it was different when you only had one child. Mother Roberts' life revolves around Derrick, and she never misses a chance to let me know I'm not measuring up. She doesn't like me working in Memphis. She hinted that I don't cook enough when she commented on Derrick's weight. When she saw that I had filled the garage with racks of clothes, she commented on how wasteful that was. When she was staying here last year, she kept telling me the place needed a woman's touch and she was surprised I hadn't already changed anything or planted some flowers. I have no intention of decorating since I don't plan to be here long. The only changes I've made are new bedroom comforters and slipcovers for the couch, since she let her dog lay all over it. I was thrilled when she and Poochie went home. Of course, I'm glad she's feeling better. But it also means we aren't tied to Eden. When Mother Roberts was in the nursing home, Derrick wanted to be available at a moment's notice. She's back in her house and has Life Alert, an alarm system, and security cameras, but she won't turn them on. She says she can't remember the password or that she doesn't want people spying on her, or they run up her electric bill. So Derrick is still at her beck and call. I love his devotion, but it feels like our marriage is on hold. Now that his grandmother is better and I've transferred to the Memphis office, things are finally getting on track. All I need is a little help from the fertility gods and things will be perfect, *and* a dishwasher.

I finished the dishes and put Derrick's plate in the microwave. "Let's hurry. I don't want to be late this time," I said as I entered the bedroom with two glasses of orange juice.

Derrick waved his hand at me to lower my voice as he listened on the phone. "Okay, I'm on my way," he said then put his phone in his pocket.

"Mamalil fell. Her neighbor said Poochie has been howling all morning. She went to knock on the door and could see her on the kitchen floor. I'm going over there now. "

"Should I call 911?" I asked.

"I've already called them, but they come from St. Francis County. I'll be there before they arrive."

"Wait, I'm coming with you," I said as I put the glasses on the table.

"I was never comfortable with her living alone," he said. "But she didn't think you wanted her to stay with us. I told her that wasn't the case, but she insisted she would be okay. If something happens to her, I'll never forgive myself."

Or me, I thought.

CARL

Carl loaded his toolbox and the weed-eater in his trunk, then called Aunt Belle and told her he was on his way. He had cut her yard the day before, and was putting the finishing touches on it today. Carl felt a tremendous debt to her. If she hadn't been in a bus accident, he would have been on time for his meeting with Perry. Which meant, he would also have met a policeman with a warrant. It seems their pick-ups and deliveries had not gone unnoticed and Perry was arrested in a sting that spanned five states. Perry was out on bail, and didn't seem the least bit phased by the ordeal. Carl would have been crushed. He couldn't bear to disappoint his father again. Carl wasn't a religious man, but took Aunt Belle's leg as the sacrifice made for him to stay out of trouble.

He would have been at her house earlier, but his father needed his help on the farm. One of the workers was sick and another one's wife was having a baby. C.W. said it was supposed to rain all weekend and he really needed to get the rest of the soybeans in. Emma's car wouldn't start, so he was going to take a look at it, then they were going to breakfast. Carl had been in the field since seven. By eleven, he was starving, and decided to go to town to get a catfish lunch and would drop one off at Aunt Belle's too. Carl was sweaty with mud on his boots, but didn't bother to change. He had just gotten in the car when he spotted a vehicle turning into the driveway. He didn't recognize the van or the driver, but he could see two white men in the front seat. Uninvited white men at your house was rarely good news. Usually, they were coming to tell you someone had died or been arrested, or to arrest someone. His father had told him stories about how white men came to his aunt's house and took his cousin for a ride and no one ever saw him again. Carl opened the center console and spotted the hammer just in case. As an ex-felon, he could not have firearms. He could be sent back to jail just for riding with a gun. When he was in Chicago, he never left home without at least two guns. He never had to use one, and the one he had when he did the robbery that got him locked up wasn't loaded. The primary purpose he had used them for was to pawn them for money to get high. When he moved back to the farm, guns were just a natural part of living in the country. You used them for four-legged trouble. Usually, just firing a gun in the air was enough to scare off any ill-intentioned animal. Two-legged trouble was a different story. Carl had been shocked to learn the tranquil Eden of his youth was just a memory, like a Norman Rockwell painting. A hammer was no match for a bullet, but at least he wouldn't be totally defenseless if some wannabe gangster walked up on him.

He knew a visit from the parole office was a possibility, since he hadn't gotten his final release papers, but he hadn't violated any rules, hadn't missed any meetings, and had passed all his pee tests. Sometimes he dreamed men came to take him away. He and his mother were crying like when Kizzy was torn from her parents in *Roots*. They escorted him on each side back into prison. Just as they pushed him into the cell he would wake up. No waking up today – this was reality. Maybe Perry had struck a plea deal and given up Carl's name. Maybe they had him on some surveillance camera with a package, he thought as sweat beads formed on his forehead. Maybe they were just lost, he thought as he took deep breaths to calm down. He took his key out of the ignition and hopped outside his vehicle.

"Can I help you?" Carl asked.

"I'm looking for Charles Washington Senior," the younger man said.

"He's not here. Can I help you?" Carl said as he checked to make sure the door was locked.

"Do you live here?" the older man asked.

"Charles Washington is my father. What do you want with him?"

"We have some paperwork for him. We've been trying to make an appointment but don't have a current phone number, and our letters haven't been answered. We'll have a crew out here next week, so we wanted to get back with him to let him know."

"A crew for what?"

"They'll just be doing some surveying. It will be a few months before they start drilling."

"What are you talking about?"

"Mr. Washington signed a mineral lease with U.S. Energy."

"Hey, maybe we aren't supposed to be talking to him," the older man said.

"Are you sure you have the right house? My father would never sell this land."

"It's not a sale. We're leasing the mineral rights. I'm sure you've seen the equipment along the highway."

"Yes, I've seen it. And like I said, my father said he would never do that. He loves this land and he doesn't need the money."

"Well, I hope I haven't disclosed something I wasn't supposed to. Although it wasn't going to be a secret much longer when our trucks start showing up. Just give this package to your father. It explains everything. Here's my card if he has any questions."

Carl took the envelope in the house and tried to call his father. Carolyn got him a cell phone and paid the bill, but he rarely answered it. He seemed to think it was for him to call people and not so they could call him. Next, he texted Carolyn and Raymond and told them to call him right away.

"What's wrong? Nothing's happened to Daddy has it?" Carolyn asked as soon as he answered the phone.

"No. Some men from U.S. Energy just left here. They say Daddy signed a lease giving them mineral rights and they plan to start drilling in a few months."

"That's crazy, Daddy would never do that," Carolyn said.

"I'm holding the envelope in my hand right now. It's addressed to Daddy so I didn't open it."

"Where is he?"

"He didn't come home last night. He's probably at Emma's."

"He stayed out all night? Are you sure? Have you talked to him?"

"Not today."

"I can't believe Daddy is hanging out at his age. Mama would never have carried on like that."

"He's grown and he didn't ask my permission. Anyway, back to the subject – what do you want me to do with this letter?"

"Hold on to it until I get there this evening. We'll ask him about it, if he can pry himself away from his girlfriend. In the meantime, I'll check for any filings in Daddy's name. I'm sure there is a mistake. Daddy would never do this. Although I never thought he'd remarry either. He's like a totally different person since he met Emma. Beverly and Cecelia both think she's after his money. Maybe they're right."

"Daddy's love life isn't the issue right now," Carl said. "I'll go to Miss Emma's and tell him what's happening."

"I can't believe they use these tactics to intimidate people into signing contracts. Luckily, Daddy has us to look out for him, but many of the older people have no one to help them. I'm going to check with Raymond on his next CARE meeting. Maybe I need to learn more about this," Carolyn said.

Phyllis R. Dixon

CECELIA

Cecelia decided she could no longer ignore her bladder and pressed the cash out button, and pulled her player's card out of the machine. The wild joker had come out of hiding, allowing her to work her way back from a loss of three hundred dollars. Her machine had finally turned in her favor and she was eight hundred dollars ahead. She knew she could ride that even higher, but she really had to use the bathroom. She was getting nauseated since she hadn't eaten in almost twenty-four hours, and her eyes were burning from wearing her contacts too long. Despite these issues, she felt better than when she arrived. She had enough money to pay her cell phone bill, with extra to tide her over until payday.

She missed Gabriel and told herself she would stop in just as a way to pass the time. She didn't know it was possible to miss someone so much who had just entered her life. She and Gabriel had been inseparable for the last six weeks. As inseparable as possible, given her sixty-hour workweeks and his research and class schedule. It had been nice to have someone she could talk to about microbes and infectious agents. And it was nice to be with someone who didn't think it odd when she cooked a full meal at three o'clock in the morning.

She and Gabriel were at Perfect Pizza when his sister called. He let it go to voicemail the first two times. But when it rang a third time, he asked if she minded if he answered. Their father had been in a serious car accident and was in surgery as they spoke. They went to his studio and she searched for the first flight to Miami while he packed. She took him to the

180

airport and instead of coming home, she went to the casino. She hadn't been in almost a month. Her plan was just to stay an hour or so, but she was still here, with less than fifteen minutes before her shift started.

The attendants and waitresses had been her human alarm clocks and usually reminded her when it got to be a certain time. She'd tip them and didn't have to worry about staying too long. Since she hadn't been in a while all her regulars had switched to different areas and shifts. She couldn't believe the time.

She rushed back to the ladies room and pulled her cell phone out of her purse. She had missed two calls from her daughter, a call from Millicent, and two text messages. One was a sweet text from Gabriel and the other was from Carolyn. The condo had sold and the buyer wanted to take possession next week. This was a curve ball she hadn't expected, but before she called her sister, she knew she needed to call the hospital. She figured Millicent had another hot date and wanted Cecelia to work late for her again, so she would just talk to her once she got to the hospital. In her best, scratchy, soft voice Cecelia called the nurse manager and explained that she had taken Nyquil and overslept, but she still didn't feel well. Her daughter was in the kitchen fixing homemade soup and hopefully she could come in later.

"Miss Brown, your daughter just left here. She was bringing your granddaughter to the clinic for a checkup and stopped in to surprise you. Please report to human resources tomorrow at eight am."

CAROLYN

Everyone in Dwight County must be here, I thought as I gingerly walked along the roadside. Curbs and sidewalks are a luxury that Friendship Missionary Baptist Church doesn't offer. The parking lot was full and I thought about parking on the field that doubled as overflow parking on Family and Friends Day, Mother's Day, Easter and revival, but it had rained all day and I didn't want to get stuck. I balanced my purse on my head since I left my umbrella in my desk at work and rushed to the church. I didn't expect there to be this many cars. I knew Raymond was passionate about the encroaching gas drilling and figured he was probably exaggerating the dangers. Apparently, others shared his concern.

The church was packed and the meeting had already started, but my eyes met Derrick's as soon as I entered the sanctuary. I caught the tail end of his remarks as he assured the audience his office was available to help them and recited his phone number, email address, and his department's website. He turned and sat behind the pulpit next to Raymond. I smiled as I thought of how pleased Mama would be to see her son and son-in-law in the pulpit. They both urged me to come so I left work early, but got hung up in construction and was still late. I knew Derrick was having extra pressures at work lately, so I decided to surprise him by bringing some Gus' Chicken from Memphis for dinner.

I know the fresh vegetables and home cooked meals I'm eating now are better for my health and wallet, but I do miss the food in Chicago. Despite having a designer kitchen in my condo, I rarely cooked. If I wanted Italian I ordered from Vinnie's. If I wanted ribs, I went to Jones and Company. If I wanted a good salad, I stopped at The Greek Station. What passed for fine dining in Eden was a Waffle House, Mazzio's Pizza, and Cook's Diner.

Derrick usually got home before I did and was a better cook, so he cooked dinner most of the time. The dinner menu on my nights to cook usually consisted of doctoring up a McDonald's salad or adding a Wendy's baked potato to grilled chicken breast or a steak. Daddy had been amazed to find out Derrick did most of the cooking, since he never even toasted bread when Mama was alive. Derrick's not perfect, but he's perfect for me. Everyone says marriage takes work, and we're working through our issues. I love being a wife. That's why I want to give him a child. I want us to be a family, not just a couple, and a child will bring us closer together.

"You would make such a great father," I had told him when we walked past a couple at Walmart with twins.

"Let's not plow that row again. You know how I feel about that subject. Can't we just be happy with what we have?"

I said yes, but hadn't given up, and had more treats other than Gus' Chicken planned. I smiled as I thought of the night I had planned when I was startled out of my reverie. Everyone was clapping and looking toward the back. I joined them, and turned around too, wondering why we were clapping.

"Stand up Chub--I mean Carolyn. Let everyone see you," Raymond said. "My sister is a lawyer, and has agreed to be our legal advisor. They want to pacify us with legalese and new regulations. They are extracting natural gas from shale layers underground with high pressure water, sand, and a cocktail of toxic chemicals that they won't disclose to anyone. We already have higher respiratory illnesses and earthquakes. Earthquakes in Arkansas! What more evidence do we need? We don't want fracking regulated, we want it banned."

The crowd cheered and began chanting, 'no fracking way, no fracking way.' Raymond raised his hand and continued. "The other side has money and lawyers and money and accountants and money and so-called scientists and money and politicians. But we put those politicians in office and we can kick them out. Everyone feels compelled to vote in the presidential elections, but the local election has a more direct effect on our everyday lives. What could be more basic than clean water? We have a voter registration table in the back and we want everyone to vote. Everyone can play a part, if it's taking someone to the polls or folks like my sister lending their expertise. We don't have money, but we have right on our side."

Raymond had moved back to Eden first and couldn't sing enough praises about the slower, cheaper, warmer, cleaner, safer pace of living. But according to Raymond, the cleaner aspect was in jeopardy. He was quoting statistics and calling for action. I have a new appreciation for my brother as he spoke to the crowd with the right combination of preacher, motivational speaker, and teacher. Even though we spend most of our time together arguing, I do admire his conviction. Once his mind is made up, he goes all the way. But this time he had gone too far.

I felt like a Miss America contestant as I wore a pasted smile, but inside I was seething. This is tax season, my busiest time at work. I told Raymond I would think about it. Actually I told him no, but said I would think about it when he tried to play the guilt card.

"I know we can't pay you—"

"Raymond this isn't about the money at all. Environmental law is not my specialty. That's a very exclusive branch of the law. "

"You're right, it is a very expensive branch of the law," Raymond said. "We could never afford an environmental lawyer, but I bet you're underestimating yourself. You're relentless when you set your mind to something."

"That's just it. I haven't set my mind to this."

"I don't see why not. You live here too. You'll be drinking the same contaminated water we will. I could have stayed in Chicago if I wanted to absorb pollution. Maybe you don't think generations ahead since you don't have children, but it's different—"

"What does having children have to do with anything? For all you know, I could be pregnant right now."

"Carolyn, you're missing the point. I'm just saying this is more important than us. Daddy worked hard for that land. We can't let them contaminate it like it's no big deal."

"I'm not saying it's no big deal. But this may be a battle too big for you to fight."

"Well, I can't give up without trying. Maybe this is why the Lord led me here."

"Wow. Too bad Mama didn't live to see this day – you quoting scripture. I thought you said the Bible was a tool used by the white man to control people."

"Just because I don't believe in the organized church doesn't mean I don't believe in God. And maybe Mama would have lived to see this day if they hadn't started contaminating our air. Some people have reactions to the dust that is generated from those trucks and drilling. I know what the doctors said, but I believe drilling contributed to her illness. This is so clear to me. How can I get you to see the connection?"

"I get it. But this is more than me donating my time to charity. It could be a conflict of interest with my

Phyllis R. Dixon

job and I'd have to report my activities to our Ethics Official for clearance."

"See, that's the problem. People get their degrees and their good jobs and they don't want to help anybody else. Everybody can't afford bottled water and water filters, and they shouldn't have to. Daddy would have been better off selling his land for the peanuts that Consolidated Farms offered him a few years back. Once drilling starts, we won't be able to give it away. This is our legacy. How can you not care?"

"I didn't say I didn't care. I'm a newlywed and I work sixty miles from home. I want to spend time with my husband."

"Don't you think Martin Luther King and Malcolm X wanted to spend time with their families? Would you have your job if others hadn't made a sacrifice? Didn't you feel that earthquake last month? You know there aren't supposed to be earthquakes around here. Those companies don't care about the people here. They just come in, rape and pollute the land and move on. We must stand up for what's right."

"I admire your commitment, but I'm just not in the mood to save the world."

"Don't admire me. Join me. At least say you'll think about it. You won't have to attend any meetings. I'll bring you paperwork every now and then and ask for your advice."

"All right. I'll think about it." Those were the last words we spoke on the topic. *I should have known to stick to my guns,* I thought as I sat back down. A lady from Reed County spoke next. She talked about the promises U.S. Energy made and the ruin they left behind. "The paper mill closed and people thought U.S. Energy was a godsend. Gas lease payments and royalty checks replaced mill paychecks and financed new cars,

186

paid tuition, and remodeled homes. After three years, they abruptly terminated the contracts. There was some obscure clause in the contracts that allowed them to do that with just ten days' notice. People had car loans and mortgages they couldn't pay. They not only left financial havoc behind, they left a toxic trail of bad water and elevated instances of respiratory illnesses. We brought a class action lawsuit and they settled. Every landowner got fifteen thousand dollars. We now know the cost was much more than fifteen thousand dollars. We would all gladly return the money if we could reverse our decision. I urge you to do all in your power to keep them from coming in."

The crowd gave her a standing ovation. Rev. Handley quickly seized the moment by making an impassioned plea for donations. I disappeared out the side door and dashed home. At home, I opened a can of corn, washed and pierced some sweet potatoes and put them in the microwave, and put the chicken in the oven – not a bad dinner for a Monday. I was setting the table when I heard Derrick drive up.

"Hey, baby," I said as I met him at the door.

"Thanks a lot," he said as he walked past me and threw his keys on the counter.

"What's wrong?"

"I can't believe you're asking me that."

"I didn't wait for you after the meeting because I wanted to have dinner ready for you. I brought you—"

"I could care less about dinner and it would have been better if you hadn't come to the meeting. But I guess that was the only way I would discover you were working on the lawsuit."

"Oh, is that it? I haven't told Raymond I would definitely do it."

"Well, you could have fooled me and about two hundred other people that were there."

"I told Raymond I would think about it, but you know how he hears what he wants to hear."

"Yes, I know that and you do, too. So you should have been clear in your response."

"I turned him down, but he made some good points, so I told him I would think about it. This is tax season and I have enough work already. Besides, I want to spend as much time as I can with my husband," I said and placed my hands around Derrick's waist. "Raymond was so excited, I didn't want to burst his bubble."

"I hear concern about your job and your brother's feelings, what about my job and my feelings?" he said as he stepped away from me. "You know my department is named in the lawsuit, and I'm the one who handled the permits. They've been picketing our regional office in Little Rock."

"No, I didn't know that."

"You would if you had discussed this with me."

"I'll just tell him, no. I'm sure he'll understand, and even if he doesn't—"

"Carolyn, this is about more than the lawsuit. I get the strong black woman thing and I don't expect you to ask my permission on everything. But I'm tired of being treated like a roommate. You wanted a husband, but I'm not sure you wanted to be a wife. Mamalil's sink is stopped up. I'm going to change clothes and go take a look at it."

I stood in the kitchen, stunned by Derrick's words. I was furious with Raymond and got my phone to call him and tell him. I had forgotten to turn the ringer back on after the meeting and had missed two phone calls and a text from my realtor in Chicago. My condo didn't pass inspection and I would have to lower my price or make repairs to sell it. *Great,* I thought. Next, I called Raymond. It went to voicemail, and I waited while a snippet of *Man In the Mirror,* played before I left a message.

Mama always said a couple's arguments were rarely about whatever they said it was about. This was about more than the lawsuit. I wish I could talk to Mama. I know Derrick and I love each other. So why are things so hard?

Derrick came in the kitchen and grabbed a bottle of water out of the refrigerator. With his Cardinals baseball cap and perfectly fitting jeans, I remembered how cute he was. "I think your dinner is burning," he said as he walked out the door.

I hadn't noticed the sharp smell. I threw the phone down and quickly turned off the oven and opened the oven door. I forgot to grab a potholder and burned my hand as I reached inside. The chicken was charred and the rush of smoke set off the smoke detector. *What else could go wrong?* I shook my hand and fought back tears.

"If you don't think you've got the blues, just keep living..."
Buddy Guy

Chapter 9
KEEP LIVING

"I appreciate you handling my car for me today," Carolyn said as Carl pulled out of the Burger Barn drive-thru.

"No problem. It's not like I have much else to do," Carl said. "Besides, I like driving. I do my best thinking and planning when miles of highway stretch out in front of me." Carolyn's check engine light was on and there wasn't a BMW dealership in Dwight County. Carl was going to drop her off at work then take her car to the dealership in Memphis. He had gotten up earlier than usual and shaved for the first time in two weeks. Perry's arrest had shocked some sense into him and he hadn't done any more 'work' for Perry. The service department had promised to give him a loaner and his plan was to spend all day answering want ads and completing job applications. Carolyn said since he now had some recent work experience, maybe he'd have better luck finding a job. Carl wasn't optimistic, but said he'd try.

By the time he picked his sister up that evening, he felt like he had been chasing his tail. Some of the places that supposedly had openings, said those were put in the paper by their corporate office and they didn't know anything about it. Some told him they only took applications online and some said they had already filled the position. When he went to the dealership he was told they had to order a part, and Carolyn's car wouldn't be ready until Friday. C.W. had a doctor's appointment in Memphis on Wednesday so Carl volunteered to bring Carolyn to work again, take their father to the doctor, then visit Beverly.

His 'to do' list expanded when Miss Emma's hairdresser and Aunt Belle's neighbor asked him to pick up some items at the Costco in Memphis. They offered to pay him. News travels fast and he had two new passengers on Thursday. Friday, he took Aunt Belle to a doctor in Memphis. Her leg was healing very slowly and Cecelia wanted her to see a specialist. He also took two of his mother's church members to the casino. They were spending the night, which was good since Carolyn's car was ready as promised on Friday, and there wouldn't have been enough room in her car. He returned the loaner, picked up Aunt Belle, then Carolyn, then headed back to Eden.

"I miss working there, but my pants definitely fit better. It's amazing how much weight you can pick up in a short time," Carl said as he pulled away from the Burger Barn drive-thru window. "I probably absentmindedly ate three bags of fries every day, then at night took home the food we had left."

"They gave me the wrong order," Carolyn said. "I ordered a pecan cranberry salad, not Caesar, and they gave me barbeque wings instead of hot wings. And there's an order of fries in here. I didn't order these."

"You want me to go back?"

"No, they were already slow. It would probably take them twice as long to actually get my order right."

"I didn't see any familiar faces," Carl said. "Looks like they've had a lot of turnovers. When I started working there, that store had the lowest customer service rating in this district. In three months, I helped turn it around."

"You were always good with people. That's why I know you'll find something else."

"I wonder. If I can't work at Burger Barn, I don't know where I can work. And people wonder why ex-cons return to crime. How are we supposed to support ourselves?"

"I must admit, I never thought about the issue until it affected you. But there are thousands of men in your same situation, and something has to be done to help you guys."

"People don't care."

"That owner should care. He's probably getting lots of complaints and has lost business if this is how they serve customers," Carolyn said as she pulled two fries out of the bag. "No need in letting these go to waste."

"So you're taking a break from the rabbit food?"

"I've eaten more fast food in the last five months than I have in three years and it's starting to show. By the time I get home, the last thing I feel like doing is cooking. In Chicago, I'd just eat a piece of fruit and skip dinner. But Derrick wants a full meal and a piece of fruit isn't going to do the trick."

"He knows you work long hours."

"He's not demanding about me cooking, but inevitably when he brings in a bag of something fried or pizza, I join him for a bite and end up eating a whole portion. Or else he'll go to his grandmother's for a full course meal and bring home leftovers."

"She probably doesn't mind. I'm sure she's glad for his company."

"I know, but this isn't exactly how I envisioned marriage."

"You two seem like a good couple. There'll be some bumps in the road, but just stick with it. It's hard to find someone who really cares about you."

"Listen to my little brother, trying to give me advice. While we're talking about relationships, someone's been asking about you lately," Carolyn said. "You two break up?"

"Portia was getting a little too serious. It was time to move on."

"What about all that advice you were just giving me? You men – you'd rather jump from woman to woman than be with someone who really cares about you. I don't understand it."

Not that Carl was doing much jumping. He had thought about calling Portia a few times, but decided against it. He wasn't planning to stay here long anyway. He had saved enough money from "working" with Perry and planned to leave after Father's Day. No need in getting tied down.

"Well, it's actually been nice hanging with you this week. We've spent more time together this week than we have in years. Are you coming inside?" Carl asked as he pulled in front of his porch.

"No, I need to get home. I'm going to bake some potatoes in the microwave to go with this salad and wings."

"Carolyn, you know I don't want to get in your business, but are you okay? Riding with you this week, you haven't seemed like your usual self. You haven't been quizzing me about Portia, well at least not until a few minutes ago. You haven't asked about my job search and you haven't been telling me how to drive. I admit it's been peaceful, so I'm not complaining – just want to make sure you're alright. Are you mellowing with marriage?"

193

"I'm okay. Just a little tired."

"Take a few days off. They'll get along without you. Spend a few days at home."

"Between me and you, I think home is the source of my stress. Do you like living here?"

"It's an adjustment."

"That's an understatement. I knew it would be a culture shock, but I thought the warmer weather, proximity to Daddy, slower pace and of course Derrick made up for the move."

"And it hasn't?"

"There have been a few wrinkles I hadn't counted on, like living in a shoebox with someone with enough clutter to have two episodes of *Hoarders* – and our move date keeps getting pushed back. I love Aunt Belle, but sometimes I feel like I'm the one with the broken leg. She won't stick to her diet, won't do her therapy, and when I ask her about it, she gets an attitude with me. Then there's Derrick's grandmother. Being caretaker to a woman who can't stand me is giving me an ulcer."

"I'm sure you're overreacting. Miss Roberts is just a lonely lady and all she has is her grandson. She'll relax once she realizes you aren't trying to keep them apart. Hang in there. Derrick seems to be a good guy," Carl said as he handed Carolyn her keys. "Looks like Carl's shuttle service is shutting down."

"You know, there seems to be a demand for this service. Just based on the few people we talked to, you had someone calling you every day. Maybe you could turn this into a business."

"And what would I drive? My car isn't up to putting a lot of miles on it, and your car is nice but it's small and I doubt you want me to drive it every day. I have some money saved, but don't want to spend it on a new car."

"Well, how about this, run an ad in the paper, name your start date, and ask people to pay the first trip in advance. If you get enough responses, you'll know you're on to something. If not, you just give everybody their money back. You can use my credit card to rent a van, pay me up front from your deposits, and keep the rest."

"I did have people asking if they could ride with me next week."

"See, there you go."

"Big sister, you may be on to something."

CECELIA

Cecelia checked her rearview mirror for a third time before exiting her car. She could have made an appointment in the hospital and gone on her lunch hour, before, or after work, but she had chosen an office in the western suburb of Lombard to avoid running into anyone she knew. She wasn't ashamed, but didn't want everyone all up in her business. As a medical professional, she knew there shouldn't be a stigma associated with going to therapy, but that was easy to say when it wasn't you. She had been raised that therapy was for white folks. Black folks had enough Jesus and common sense not to need to pay someone to listen to their troubles. In truth, they probably just didn't have the money, but she could hear her mother telling her all she needed was to get closer to the Lord. True, she couldn't remember the last time she had been to church. She blamed it on her hospital hours, but that really wasn't it. She believed in a higher power, but didn't see the need for organized religion to get to that power. Outside of her mother, the church folk she had run into had more problems than the non-church folk.

It would be different if this had been her idea; it wasn't. Counseling was a condition of her disciplinary action. She had never been a union advocate, and was known to grumble when she thought about the dues taken out of her paycheck. She always thought those people were just whiners. Now she was a believer. She had done something stupid and could have lost her job. Once she completed these mandatory sessions, her record would be cleared after twelve months.

Her union rep informed her of rights she didn't even know she had and said her offense was miniscule compared to some other indiscretions. She reached the third floor and the office was right across from the elevator. The name on the door, Woodland and Associates, could have been a law firm or accounting practice. The name didn't tell you there were crazy people inside. But Cecelia knew she was lucky. She knew she could have been fired, suspended without pay or demoted, so she vowed to survive this penance and move on.

The perky receptionist ushered her from the waiting room to a room that looked more like a hotel lobby than a doctor's office. The doctor was waiting when she entered and directed her to sit in one of the two recliners.

"Hello, Ms. Brown, it's a pleasure to meet you."

"Don't take this personally, if I can't say the same. Where is the couch? I thought all psychiatrist offices had couches."

"That's only on television. Have a seat. So I see you're a nurse."

"Yes, I am. Look, if you've read my file, you'll know that it wasn't exactly my idea to come here."

"I didn't see a guard accompany you and I don't see handcuffs. So it looks like you walked in of your own free will."

"It was either that or lose my job."

"Some people do make that choice."

"I may have done something stupid, but I do have good sense. I'm not going to risk my job," Cecelia said.

"But you did risk your job."

"I just lost track of time."

"Is that the first time this has happened?"

"You know it's not."

"You're right. I can see you've been reprimanded three times in the last year. So you don't think not coming to work was risking your job?"

"Look, I know I screwed up. I hadn't been to the casino in weeks and just wanted to have a little fun."

She had wished for a hot machine and got one. But she missed her daughter's phone calls and was caught in a lie when she was late for work – again. Cecelia's summons to human resources had been humiliating. She felt like a misbehaving schoolgirl sent to the principal's office. Because of concerns with substance abuse, her supervisor told her she would have to refer her for drug testing. Cecelia thought it was better to admit to gambling than to have drug allegations in her file. So here she was. Hopefully she could skip from step one to step twelve and get this over with. She had learned her lesson.

BEVERLY

Murphy's Law is definitely in effect today, I thought as I put the speeding ticket the officer had just

Phyllis R. Dixon

given me in my purse. My shampoo girl didn't call and didn't show. I had gone against my instinct by hiring her in the first place. As I washed a client's hair, I forgot my phone was in my vest pocket and it fell in the shampoo bowl. The bowl cracked the screen and the soapy water ruined the display. I hadn't thought about it being the first of the month. It seemed as if all of Memphis was at the AT&T store paying their bill or getting a new phone. When I was finally waited on, I had a trainee and that took forever. Then on my way to my doctor's appointment, I got this speeding ticket. Any other time I would have cancelled the appointment, but I had already missed two and I was hoping to get something to regulate my symptoms from the change. I didn't want to ruin my weekend with Mark by sweating like a football player.

All of this and I still haven't packed. Mark and I are going to the Blues and Jazz Festival in Greenville, Mississippi this weekend. I'll admit I'm a little nervous. It's not like we haven't been together before, but this time will be different. It will kind of be like making our relationship status official.

"What are you looking for?" Mark asked me last week out of nowhere.

"What do you mean?" I asked.

"In a man, what are you looking for?"

"I'm not looking for anything or anyone," I said.

"Well, you won't be unattached forever. If you could create the perfect guy, what qualities would he have?"

"I guess I value honesty above all. He doesn't need a lot of money, but he needs to make enough to take care of himself. I want someone who treats me like I'm special and I want to laugh a lot."

"I believe you just described me," Mark said. Then he pulled me to him and kissed me. A real kiss.

"What's wrong?" he asked.

"Nothing, I just wasn't expecting that," I said.

"We have a great time together. You're beautiful, smart, and sexy. Any man would be crazy not to want to be with you. Look, I know it takes time to unwind from a marriage. I'm not pressuring you. But I want to be first in line to scoop you up when you're ready to be scooped."

We hadn't spoken about it since. But when he asked me to go with him to the festival, we both knew what that meant. I'm still a little nervous about it. I knew he wouldn't be satisfied with passionate kisses and patting my behind forever. But how long to wait? I can hear Mama saying, I should wait until marriage. But I'm not even divorced yet and certainly not interested in getting married soon – maybe not ever. So am I supposed to be celibate the rest of my life?

Maybe I've had my bad luck for the day, I thought as I pulled into a parking space next to the door. All of this rushing just to check in and wait. When they finally called my name, it was just for lab work. Then I went back to the waiting room to wait some more. Half of the women were pregnant, and most had a man with them. How precious to be at that stage of life. My baby is in some foreign land protecting people who could care less about him or his country.

I was startled to hear my name and embarrassed to realize I had dozed off. This was my first time seeing Dr. Madison. I had been in the waiting room almost an hour, so I already had a negative opinion. My doctor retired and referred her patients to this office. I was surprised how young she was. I know this is a necessary service, but what kind of person wants to be a gynecologist, I wondered. Mama told us stories about our great-grandmother, who was a midwife, and who delivered all of us except Carl and Paul. Maybe the joy of helping bring life into the world was worth the rest of it. We spent most of my visit discussing menopause treatments, bone density, and weight control. Quite a change from the days when birth control and family planning were the primary topics. Just as we were wrapping up, a nurse knocked on the door, then handed the doctor a folder. Additional fodder for my negative opinion. *How rude of her to read her reports while she's supposed to be taking care of me,* I thought.

"Mrs. Townsend, we have your lab results and there is a slight abnormality." Apparently, Murphy wasn't through with me yet.

"It could have been worse." The doctor's words kept ringing in my ear. I knew I had been feeling funny but thought I was experiencing yet another effect of the wacky world of menopause. Mama set me down and talked about the birds and the bees, warned me about boys and gave me a box of Kotex. They even talked about 'the monthly' in high school gym class. But no one prepared me for the change. When I heard others talk about it, I didn't see what the big deal was. I had several customers who couldn't sit under the dryer for longer than a few minutes – saying they were too hot. That seemed like a slight inconvenience to me. No more cramps, bloating, or bleeding accidents – sweating a little bit didn't seem like a bad trade-off. But no one had told me that instead of cute little sweat beads, I would feel like I was on fire inside. My gown and sheets were drenched some mornings and other times I had to get my winter comforter because I would be so cold. My back aches, my privates' itch, and moles emerge daily. Where's the mother-daughter talk for the change? I miss Mama every day, but even more at times like this. I'm the big sister, so I can't ask Carolyn or Cecelia. But I've heard enough conversations in the salon to know I could get some type of treatment from the doctor. So after sucking enough ice chips to freeze my liver and taking cornstarch baths to soothe the itching, I made a doctor's appointment. It confirmed what I already knew. I am indeed in menopause; the blood test proved it. But the test proved something else, too.

"You're kidding, right?" I had said.

"No, I'm serious and this could have been serious. You should have come in as soon as you started having symptoms."

"What symptoms?"

"Itching, burning... What did you think you had?"

"I didn't think I had anything. I thought it was part of menopause. I don't know what to say. I didn't even know you could get an STD at this age."

"Now you sound like one of my teen patients, saying they didn't think they could get pregnant the first time."

"I am so embarrassed. I feel like crawling under this table."

"Just be glad it's nothing worse. At least this is something that will go away. Black women have a disproportionate incidence of new HIV infections and data suggests one in thirty black women is or will be HIV positive. I know this is a sensitive situation, but you must talk to your husband."

"We're separated."

"Well, talk to whoever your partner is, and you must use protection."

"I know. I have clients with unplanned pregnancies and I tell them the same thing."

"Well, you need to follow your own advice." She then explained the regimen of antibiotics I would need to take and sent me to the lab for a shot. I felt like all of the staff was whispering about me. They're probably used to this sort of thing, but I couldn't help it. So much for my weekend with Mark. Instead of listening to blues this weekend, I'm living it.

CAROLYN

I grabbed the pages from the printer when I heard the car in the driveway. Raymond had called to tell me he was on his way a few minutes ago. I got a late start because I waited for Derrick to leave before I finalized the letters. CARE has gotten five-hundred signatures on a petition and Raymond asked me to draft a cover letter to go with it to submit to the state Water Commission, State Environmental Board, and Department of Energy.

The last thing I expected to do was get involved in Eden politics. Raymond was always crusading for some cause when he was in Chicago. Those were usually established organizations and the extent of my involvement was a donation. This time CARE needed my expertise more than my money.

I still haven't told Derrick I'm working with Raymond on the fracking protest. He said it was my decision, but I know what he says and what he means don't always match. Why can't he understand that my involvement with CARE has nothing to do with him? I know I need to tell him, but we've been getting along so well lately. I hate to break the spell.

"Hey, open up," Raymond shouted through the screen door.

"I'll be finished in a few minutes," I said as I opened the door. "I planned to have the document ready when you got here but I got sidetracked. Aunt Belle always seems to need me when I'm in the middle of something."

"That's okay. We never get to visit you. It gives us a good excuse to stop by," Raymond said as he and Carl headed toward the kitchen.

"I love you guys, but the odor is really strong. I'm going to have to spray when you leave," I said as I fanned with my hand.

"We just left the track," Raymond said, as he opened the refrigerator. "What you got to eat?"

"I don't need to look in the refrigerator. I see what I want, right here on the counter. Let me get a piece of cake," Carl said.

"You're baking now?" Raymond asked.

"Mother Roberts baked it."

"Good. Then we know it's safe to eat," Raymond said.

"Ha-ha," I said as I pulled out two paper plates.

"So you guys are getting together and didn't invite me? Beverly said as she walked in the kitchen. "I went to the house and no one was there."

"We just stopped by on our way home from working out," Carl said.

"Carolyn worked on the CARE legal papers for us. The next meeting is Thursday. I want all of you to come. The bigger the audience, the better," Raymond said. "And don't forget the primary on Tuesday. The county commission members are on the ballot."

"I haven't changed my driver's license yet, so I doubt if I can vote," I said.

Phyllis R. Dixon

"And I'm not registered," Carl said.

"Here I am lecturing the town and my own family members aren't registered."

"I've had a few important things on my mind," I said. "So forgive me if your organization is not front and center on my list. I do have a job you know. And for some reason, Aunt Belle acts like she only knows my phone number. Beverly, I wish you would let me know when you're coming to town. I can really use some help with her."

"Well, it's not like I have a nine to five job, and can tell you when I'll be off," Beverly said. "Even Mondays end up being hectic. This is just a quick trip to check in with Daddy."

"I thought you can do what you want when you're the boss. I don't think it's fair that you guys leave everything to me."

"Everything like what?" Carl asked. "I'm the one taking her up and down the road to her doctor visits."

"That's maybe once a week. How about paying her bills, washing her clothes, making sure she eats, hiring help for her since she seems to fire everyone the Aging Agency sends over there."

"Can we get back to the subject?" Raymond said.

"Sorry to interrupt Raymond's World, but this is important," I said.

"What's more important than clean air and water?" Raymond asked.

"I'm on your side but I just got off paper, so I couldn't register. I'll have to see about getting my voting rights restored."

"You mean you can't vote if you've been in jail?" Beverly asked.

"Not if you're still in the system. I'm taking Aunt Belle and Mr. Ben to the polls, though. And I told her

I'd take anyone else she knows that needs a ride. Carolyn, I have a lot of free time. I can help you with Aunt Belle."

"Why so much free time?" Beverly asked. "I thought Portia was taking up all of your time. Should I be getting my wedding wardrobe ready?"

"They haven't been dating that long," Raymond said as he helped himself to another slice of caramel cake.

"It's been three months. Women over thirty don't like to spend much time kicking it. Either you're serious or you're not," Beverly said. "I can't count the number of clients who have wasted years on a guy thinking it was leading to something, only to break up and watch him marry his next girlfriend within a matter of months."

"If it's meant to be a little extra time won't matter," I said.

"This from the woman who met and married her husband in nine months," Beverly said.

"She didn't marry someone she just met. Derrick practically grew up at our house," Raymond said.

"That was a million years ago," Beverly said, as she cut a slice of cake. "People change a lot over all that time. You did the right thing. Make him commit or move on."

That sounded like the smart thing to do, but now I'm not so sure. I feel like an outsider in this house and buying our new home keeps getting pushed further and further away. I've given up trying to talk to him about my feelings. He takes everything as a personal rejection, and I haven't forgotten that he tore my blazer. Did I miss his temper, intolerance, and jealousy or did the dimple, sweet promises and caramel brown skin blind me to this flaw? I'm not saying I regret getting married and I know Derrick loves me. But why do we seem to disagree about everything?

"Carl, you never answered the question," Beverly said.

"Actually, Portia and I aren't seeing each other anymore. But I'm sure she's registered and will vote."

"I hate to hear that," Beverly said. "You two seemed like a perfect couple."

"Portia's a great girl, but I need to get myself together first. Maybe once that happens, I can think about getting serious. I'm working on a few things to get my finances in order. Hopefully she'll be patient and when and if it happens, we'll be as happy as Carolyn and Derrick."

CECELIA

"My husband truly has a split personality. He can be so sweet and loving. He is the life of the party and funnier than anyone on television. He is a good provider and an officer in our church. But when he drinks he becomes mean."

"And you didn't see any of this before you married," the counselor asked.

"No. He was my son's football coach. He was tough on the field, but I figured that was just football. The first time I saw any meanness was when he knocked my son down after a practice, saying he wasn't trying hard enough. We had only been married a month and of course I was furious. He said I was too soft and it took a man to raise a man. I thought maybe that's what boys needed."

"So when did he begin to abuse you?" the counselor asked.

"The first time he hit me was when I came in from a birthday happy hour for one of the girls at work. He met me at the door, asked where I had been and slapped me before I could answer. I had told him I was going to be late, but he had been drinking and forgot. I know when that happened I should have left, but it was so gradual. It started with name calling, then yelling in my face and one thing graduated to the next."

Hmmm. That fool would have flunked the first time he laid a hand on my son, Cecelia thought. *I can't believe these women are this weak. We could save a lot of time if this counselor would just tell these women to get a backbone.* These stories always made the women in the circle cry and everyone was passing around a box of tissue. Cecelia didn't cry. It just made her mad. Mad at the women for having no backbone and mad at herself for ending up here. Carolyn's condo had sold and Cecelia had spent the money she had set aside for first and last month's rent at the casino. Now. she was officially homeless.

She knew it was a mistake when she pulled into the casino parking lot. But that Sunday had been one of her worst days on the job. Sunday afternoons were usually slow, but two shooting victims were admitted within ninety minutes of each other. She was usually able to remain detached, but that day had been different. The first boy was the same age as her son and was also named Michael. The second boy was only fourteen and came in with a bullet in his neck. He made it through a four hour surgery and was in ICU but then went into cardiac arrest and died. His mother's wail sounded like her insides were coming out. Cecelia sat with her. There was nothing she could say, so she didn't try to patronize her. She just let her cry and held her until her husband came. When the woman's blood pressure shot up she had to be admitted. By the time Cecelia left, she sat in her car for thirty minutes in a daze. She got chilled and came out of her stupor, as she hadn't even put on her coat. Every now and then the life and death nature of her job got to her. Not that she didn't care about all of her patients. But to be effective, you couldn't get emotionally tied to them. Although, sometimes it was hard to remember that rule.

She knew the Chicago murder statistics. Black folks were outraged at reports of black boys shot by whites or police, but where were the protests about the boys killing each other? Those numbers were epidemic and she had seen boys as young as eight shot by rival gang members and babies shot by stray bullets. Where did this disregard for life come from? People touted money, studies, and politicians as the solution. All she knew is they admitted a gunshot victim almost daily. The police didn't even come take a report anymore unless the person died.

As soon as she put on her coat, she called her son, but he was getting ready for school and couldn't talk long. She just wanted to hear his voice. Cecelia missed seeing him every day. The condo was convenient to the hospital, but was almost an hour away from her son so she couldn't just stop over whenever she thought about him. But she was glad he was there. She and Michael had argued for years about moving out of the city. Michael said leaving was part of the problem and they needed to stay. Cecelia said she wasn't trying to save the whole race – just her family. One day Junior came home with a black eye, torn jacket, and no shoes. He said some boys jumped him in the bathroom at school, said he 'talked white,' and took his new Jordans. Michael was furious and wanted his son to identify the boys so they could press charges. Cecelia said nothing, but went to the school the next day and withdrew her children. She kept them home for a week while she looked for another house. She told Michael he could stay with his people or be with his family, but she was not staying any longer. Michael agreed to rent out the house and they bought a house out in Glenview. The seventy-five minute commute was worth it not to have to worry about gangs and drive-bys. They rented their old house for a while, then she moved back in after the divorce. She stayed in the house a few months before letting it go into foreclosure. How ironic that Michael was now the one in the suburbs and she was living in the city.

Without Gabriel to share the details of her shift, she found herself in a familiar place. The clinking and ringing of the machines and the busy paisley pattern in the carpet dulled her senses and within fifteen minutes her breathing slowed and her headache subsided. She planned to go to the buffet, get breakfast, run home to change, then head back to the hospital. She was surprised to see no eggs or pancakes on the buffet. When she asked the waitress about it, she told her they stopped serving breakfast at eleven thirty. It was just past noon, and she was supposed to be at work at one o'clock.

She went to the ladies room, splashed water on her face, washed under her arms, rinsed her mouth, then rushed to the hospital. She worked a double shift then went to her casino hotel room to take a bath and get the last of her things. She had found an apartment, but still hadn't gathered together all she needed for the security deposit, and first and last month's rent. The manager was holding it for her and she had planned to move at the end of the month. There was a gap between when she had to vacate the condo and when she would have the money for her apartment. She had used all her comp nights at the casino and still had six days before she could move in her apartment. She went through her bags and pulled some items she could take to the consignment shop. One benefit of buying designer clothes was that she could get money for them. She dropped off some clothes and picked up one hundred eighty dollars from items she had left last month. That money had to last until payday. She sat in the parking lot an hour, unsure of her next move. She could use it all and pay for a room at the casino, or she could go find her favorite machine and try to double the money. She could have called Carolyn or one of her brothers but she was too embarrassed to ask for help. She knew their help would come with a lecture and she didn't want to hear it. This was just a rough patch and she'd be okay with her next paycheck. She went back to the hospital and went to the chapel to nap before going back to work. As she passed the bulletin board in the cafeteria, a flyer caught her eye. The employee assistance group had a contract with an abused women's shelter. She recognized the neighborhood and knew there were nice houses over there, so she had made up a story and headed to the shelter.

They welcomed her, no questions asked. They were so caring, she almost felt guilty being there under false pretenses and vowed to send a donation when she got her finances straightened out. The only thing she had to do was help in the kitchen every other day and attend daily counseling sessions. They didn't make everyone talk so she didn't have to come up with a story and no one asked her any questions. She was seen as one of the lucky ones. She didn't have small children and she had a good job. Some of these women made minimum wage, or had no job at all. Where were these women's families, Cecelia often wondered. Carolyn had dated a boy in college that hit her a couple times. Cecelia told her brothers and all four of them drove to campus, jumped on the dude and left. That was the only time Carl had ever missed a game. Carolyn didn't have any more problems. Unfortunately, many women's stories didn't end as well as Carolyn's had.

This was her twenty-second day here. She had had two roommates. One went back to her boyfriend and the other moved to Texas with her sister. Cecelia could have left after one week, when she got paid, but decided to stay two more weeks so she had enough money to get her things out of storage. At least Gabriel wasn't here to see her predicament. Her apartment was ready and all of this would be a memory by the time he got back. She was making her rounds to say good-bye to the evening staff. Most of them would be gone when she left in the morning.

"You've been pretty quiet, but we're still going to miss you," the counselor said as she hugged Cecelia. "The girls have learned a lot from you."

"But I feel like I didn't really contribute anything," Cecelia said.

"You have. Your quiet strength is a testimony of action. They see you taking care of business and vowed to do the same. And the information about the hospital training program was really helpful. Many times women don't leave because they can't afford to. We all know it's usually who you know that makes the difference in getting a job. Two of the women have a second interview scheduled."

"The hospital is always short staffed. There's a lot of paperwork, but I'm confident they'll get hired."

"Take care of yourself. I wish you the best and hope we helped you."

"You have, and don't take this personally, but I hope I don't see you again," Cecelia said with a smile.

"At least not under these circumstances," the counselor replied.

Quiet strength – if they only knew, Cecelia thought as she went back to gather her belongings. She had called human resources several times to be sure they pulled the ladies applications. At least she helped in some way. They had definitely helped her. She still didn't understand why a woman would stay with someone who abused her. No one in her family would take that mess. No one in her family would be hiding out in a shelter either. *How could I have been so stupid?* She thought. She had gone astray, but like Scarlett in *Gone With the Wind,* she would never be homeless again. She had gone to the bank today when she got paid and put her apartment rent on auto debit. If she didn't have a dime, at least she'd have a roof over her head. She had cleaned a lot of stuff out of her storage unit and sold it. After being with these women for almost a month, she realized she didn't need so much stuff. Then she called all the casinos where she had a line of credit and closed them. Her credit was so messed up, she knew they would never reopen them. From now on, she would go back to the changes she had adopted last year. She would leave her credit and debit cards at home, and limit her casino visits to Triple Play Thursdays. She had a one hundred dollar free play coupon left that expired in two days. She needed to use it, and once she used that, she'd be done. She had learned her lesson. After all, she had already been homeless and broke. How much worse could it get?

"When you get what you want, you don't want what you get..."

Irving Berlin

Chapter 10
AFTER YOU GET WHAT YOU WANT, YOU DON'T WANT IT

"You paid a lot of money for this little BW car, didn't you, Chubby?" C.W. asked.

"It's called BMW, Daddy," I said. "It was a birthday present to myself for turning forty."

"I don't see what the big deal is. Give me a Cadillac any day. Plus, you'll be keeping jobs in this country," C.W. said as he turned his head back and forth. "Trying to nap in this little car has given me a crook in my neck."

We're headed to Little Rock and should have been there by now. Traffic slowdowns on this freeway are almost as bad as in Chicago. At least up there if you run into a problem you can take another route. Down here you're stuck, unless you want to take a two lane highway and stop in a bunch of small towns. We finally passed the last construction cone and I changed lanes and increased my speed to eighty-five miles per hour.

We've got thirty minutes to get downtown so I can file the CARE injunction against U.S. Energy for failing to register as a lobbyist. The state's lobbying ordinance defines a lobbyist as anyone employed to communicate with government officials to influence their action. It's a long shot but it's worth a try. We have thirty days left to file, but I don't want to wait. Every day we wait is like letting the dynamite get closer to the end of the fuse, so I took a vacation day to make the drive, although I didn't tell Derrick.

I had planned to leave earlier, but I had to search for an electrician to fix issues the inspector found in my condo. Cece said she would do it, but didn't. I tried to get the best price but that was taking too long, so I just picked the next one that popped up on my internet search. Then I spent more time than I anticipated at Aunt Belle's. Her home-care aide called and asked if I would come over. This is the third one she's had in two months. Either they don't wash the dishes good enough, or they're stealing, or they can't cook. I spent hours completing paperwork to sign her up for the Dwight County Seniors Meals on Wheels program. Then Carl told me, he saw unopened trays in the garbage when he would take the garbage out. She said she wouldn't feed that slop to her dog. I know it's not the home cooked meals she's used to, but seems like it would be better than nothing. But of course, the alternative isn't nothing. I've been cooking extra on the weekends and packaging food in to-go containers for the week. Carl says he'll help me with her. But how did she become my responsibility? I know her son died and her grandchildren don't live close, but still... I try to be sympathetic. That could be me one day. I don't have any children. Who will care for me when I get old? I just hope I remember to be more cooperative.

By the time I resolved Aunt Belle's drama (she was livid that the worker swept her feet with the broom - a bad luck omen - time to look for home-care aide number four), my plan for a leisurely drive with Daddy was history and this day turned out to be just as hectic as any other day. I'm going to get home even later than if I had gone to work, which only confirms Derrick's claim that CARE is too time-consuming. My husband and I are in an uneasy truce. There have been no more harsh words, but we've each drawn our line in the sand. He claimed he had a cold and slept on the couch the last two nights. The couch gives him backaches, but if he wants to be stubborn, so be it. I can't sit by and let Daddy's legacy be ruined.

I'm always amazed when I see tax returns for young couples with six figure salaries, capital gains, and Schedule D income. Of course there are no pictures, so I can't swear that they're all white, but I'm ninety-nine point nine percent certain they are. They have trusts and inheritances, and even if they aren't wealthy, at least they don't start from zero like black folks always seem to. My parents worked hard so my generation and those after us had a little head start. They sent us to college and invested in our businesses. Mama may not have been in the field, but she was just as important to Daddy's success as fertilizer and good weather. I can't let their hard work be for nothing. I've given in to Derrick on just about everything else. I know marriage is about compromise, but it's his turn to compromise.

"I see we're almost there," C.W. said. "Emma wants me to stop at a GNC and get her vitamins."

"She's got you doing honey-dos and you're not even married yet."

"If I had known this wedding was going to be such a big production, I would have tried harder to talk her out of it. Seems silly to me, going through all of that at our age, but if that's what she wants..."

"I'm just glad you found someone to make you happy."

"I'm relieved to hear you say that. I know your sisters don't feel that way. They think I'm trying to replace your mother and that could never happen."

"I'll admit I felt that way too. But now that I'm here, I can see how happy she makes you. It's nice to have someone to spend your days and nights with. Everyone grieves differently, and just because you're living the rest of your life and not spending it shut up in the house wearing black, doesn't mean you didn't love Mama."

"I'm still grieving. Losing Lois was like losing my right hand. But for some reason, I'm still here. If it had been up to me, it would have been the other way around. I don't understand why the Lord took your mother and not me. Maybe because she was so good, he wanted her closer to Him."

"I never thought of it that way."

"It's the only way I could make myself go on. I don't know how much longer I have, but Emma really helped me and I don't have time to be courting."

"Well, don't worry about my sisters. They'll come around."

"You'll all understand one day. We have to live life to the fullest. Tomorrow is not promised."

"You're right and that's what I want to talk to you about."

"What's on your mind?"

"Have you discussed a prenuptial agreement with Miss Emma?"

"What's that?"

"It's a legal document that outlines what happens to your assets if something happens to you."

"I already have a will. Paul helped me set up a trust to hold the land. I already put forty acres in timber. That portion will start generating income in about eight years, and you'll all get one or two royalty payments a year. I did it after that family reunion when y'all acted a fool, thinking I was ready to kick the bucket. Everything is in order."

"But it will be different when you have a wife, a new wife. Some things she will have a right to just because she is your wife. I'm not trying to be morbid, but I'm sure your wishes will be different for Miss Emma than what you would have left Mama. She has children too, and it's possible they could end up with a right to your land. Since you accumulated all of this prior to marrying her, a judge would probably uphold your children's rights but if you had a prenuptial agreement, there would be no need for lawyers and judges. It's just another form of insurance to make sure your wishes are carried out."

"Emma has her own stuff. She has no interest in the farm."

"Human behavior is hard to predict. You can't be sure of that."

"So you're saying I should have her sign something before we get married that says she doesn't want any of my stuff?"

"Something like that."

"No wonder marriages don't last these days. We've talked about all of that and I wouldn't marry her if I didn't think I could trust her. We even discussed burial plots. She's done pretty well for herself and you don't see her handing me no papers to sign. This is a marriage, not a business deal."

"But you need to think of it as a business deal. Remember all the money Halle Berry and Sherri Shepherd had to pay?"

"Those folks are all celebrities with lots more money than I have. Did you and Derrick do one of these prenoopal things?"

"No."

"Then how are you going to tell me to do something you didn't do?"

"It's different with us. There are no children involved and other than our retirement plans, there aren't any other assets."

"Umm. Folks always trying to tell somebody else to do something. I guess I'll just take my chances that Emma isn't a gold digger after my loot."

"But Daddy—"

"Look, I already have a will. I'm through talking about this nonsense. Let's change the subject. Have you heard from Cece lately? She had talked about coming down here awhile back, but she hasn't called lately.

"Now that you mention it, I haven't talked to her in a couple weeks. I need to call her," I said as I exited the freeway. "We're going to be cutting it close, so I won't try to find a parking space. I'm just going to hop out in front of the courthouse. I have to go to the third floor and get my documents time stamped then I'll be right back. Drive around the block a few times if you see police. We'll stop at the GNC near the mall on the way back. Maybe we can get something to eat too. I haven't been to Olive Garden in ages."

"I love spending time with you, baby girl, but I need to get on back to Eden. Me and Emma like to watch the baseball game of the week. Derrick probably wants you home, too."

"I'm not so sure. Between me and you, I'm not sure getting married was such a good idea."

"We all feel like that from time to time. Look at Raymond and Geneva." Eden seemed to have resurrected my brother's marriage. He took family leave from his job at the bank and came to Eden to help Mama take care of Daddy after his stroke. While he was down here, his bank merged with another bank and he was offered a buyout. He and Geneva were on the verge of divorce anyway, so he took the buyout and moved to Eden. Absence really did make the heart grow fonder, and they reconciled. He moved back to Chicago for a little while, but couldn't find a job. He bragged so much about the benefits of living in Eden that he moved his family down here. If Geneva, the epitome of city girl, can adjust to Eden, maybe I just haven't tried hard enough.

"But we should still be in our honeymoon stage. Instead, we're arguing every day."

"It takes time to get used to living with someone. Your little differences will work themselves out."

"This is more serious than leaving socks on the floor or leaving the toilet seat up. For one thing, he doesn't think I should be working with you against the oil and gas companies. He doesn't understand I'm just helping my family."

"Well, he is your family now. If he feels that way, you should have just stayed out of it. Raymond could have found another lawyer. I wish I had known this before we came up here."

"The lawsuit isn't the only issue."

"Chubby, marriage is for better or worse. You just have to work through these things. Derrick is a good man. He's smart, works hard, brings his money home, and doesn't lay up with other women."

"Now you sound like Mama."

"You know she was generally right. As long as he doesn't drink too much or put his hands on you, you can work it out."

That was the last thing I wanted to hear.

CARL

"That was a pretty good breakfast son," C.W. said as he pushed his chair back from the table. "I never did learn to cook."

"They had the toughest, saltiest bacon and nastiest powdered eggs in the world at Cummins. When I first got there, I refused to eat it and just drank coffee for breakfast. But working in the field was strenuous so I forced myself to eat so I wouldn't get light-headed. I vowed when I got out, that I would eat a good breakfast every day," Carl said. Cummins was a working farm with sixteen thousand acres of cash crops like cotton, rice, and corn. Guards on mounted horses watched their every move. He felt like a slave with an overseer. He had grown up on a farm and couldn't wait to leave. To end up on a prison farm was like being punished twice. After six months, someone found out he was a plumber and they assigned him to the building maintenance team. He had more freedom and the guards let him smoke and make calls on their cell phone.

"Your mama believed in a good breakfast. Sometimes it's still hard to believe she's gone."

"Fifty years is a long time. People don't hardly even get married anymore, let alone stay together fifty years. What was the secret?"

"No secret, like everything else in life, it took commitment and hard work. To be successful in anything from losing weight to playing basketball, you got to be committed to it and you got to work hard."

"I guess I worked hard and was committed to having a lot of women. I respected you, but thought your life was really lame. Now I see you had the best."

"There were times I wanted to leave and times she wanted me to leave, but I guess those times never happened at the same time. I was living back and forth between here and Detroit, and Lois and I had been courting off and on. I was getting ready to go back when Aunt Belle told me I was making a big mistake and that Lois was a keeper. She told me Earle Weaver was sniffing around and if I didn't step up she might not be there the next time I called."

"You mean Mr. Weaver that owned the cleaners could have been my daddy?"

"No. I wasn't hardly going to let that happen. The only thing that was going to keep Lois from me was death. We had a good life," C.W. said as he turned his head.

"I admire the way you've kept going. I know it hasn't been easy."

"I just remember she's in a better place. I'm glad you got to spend time with her before she passed. Maybe that's why you couldn't really find a job before then. She took it hard when Charles died. Then Brenda and the grandkids moved away. Nothing I said or did cheered her up. Then you came home and she was her old self. The man upstairs wanted Lois to have that time with you. I know it's all part of a master plan, but I don't think I could have stayed here without your mama and without Charles next door, if you hadn't been here."

"I felt bad being a grown man and having to live with my parents. It's good to know you didn't mind me being here. I remember you always said we had eighteen years to get out of your house."

"That was just to get you motivated to learn to take care of yourself. You know you always have a home here if you need it."

"I had planned on being gone by now. Hopefully something will come up before you get married. I don't want to cramp the newlywed's style."

"Don't worry about it. This house was home to nine people at one time. It can handle three. I'm going to meet Carolyn at the attorney's office," C.W. said, as he stood. "They want me to sign some papers. This drilling mess is starting to wear on me. I was hoping you'd consider what I suggested to you about working here, but maybe I should just sell out. Take the money like everybody else, and get a house uptown, or move into Emma's house."

"It's your decision, Dad. Don't let those big companies bully you, but don't let Raymond pressure you either."

"I won't. You've got company," C.W. said as he raised the shade in the front room.

"Who is it?"

"I don't know. Someone in a gray GMC." C.W. stepped on the porch and waved. "Good to see you. Go on in the house."

"Daddy, who do we know with a gray---" Carl said as he entered the living room, pulling a t-shirt over his head. "Oh, hello, Portia."

"Not exactly the greeting I was looking for," she said as she entered the house.

"I didn't mean anything by it. You just caught me off guard."

"That's the only way I was going to catch you. You haven't returned any of my calls or texts."

"I've been a little busy."

"Oh. I heard you were taking people to Memphis. I was hoping you'd have time to take me to work next week. I can get a ride home. My car is in the shop. They promised me it would be ready today, but they had to order some part. I drove Daddy's truck last week, but he has doctor's appointments next week and needs it."

"No problem. I can take you," Carl said.

"I'll pay you and buy the gas."

"I know I don't have a big office job like you, but you don't have to pay me. I wouldn't say I would do it, if I couldn't pay for it."

"I didn't say anything about a job. That never concerned me. I knew you were too smart not to land something else."

"Smart doesn't seem to matter when you have a record."

"So is that why you stopped calling?"

"To be honest, yes. What do I look like, can't even keep a job flipping burgers trying to talk to you who just got a promotion?"

"Your job wasn't important to me."

"You say that now, but I know how this movie ends. I figured we could skip all that drama."

"So all that stuff about not wanting to be tied down wasn't true?"

"Let's not rehash all of that," Carl said.

"You're right. But it would have been nice to know the real reason. I was depressed for weeks thinking that you felt like being with me was being tied down. But if you let the Burger Barn dictate your life, then you're not the man I thought you were."

"It's easy for you to be judgmental; you didn't fill out hundreds of applications. You don't know what it's like for people to dismiss you without even giving you a chance or to need your father to get you a job."

Phyllis R. Dixon

"It seemed to work for Donald Trump and Ted Turner, but you're right, no need in rehashing all that now. But as a friend, you say that you can give me a ride on Monday?"

"Sure. And to make you feel better, you can pay."

Portia walked toward the front door. "Thanks again," she said. "I'll see you Monday."

Carl stood on the porch and watched her get in the truck and drive off. He lit a cigarette, but quickly put it out when he saw his father coming up the driveway. "I forgot my Seed and Feed coupon," C.W. said as he stepped out of the truck. "Since I'll be uptown, figured I'd run a couple errands. I saw Portia Ann pass me up the road. That was a quick visit."

"She just stopped by to ask for a ride next week."

C.W. shook his head as he walked in the house. "You may have had a lot of girlfriends, but you don't know much about women. That girl ain't come all the way over here for no ride."

"What do you mean?" Carl asked.

"You can figure it out. I'll just tell you like Aunt Belle told me about your mama. She's a keeper. And one more thing, you need to quit smoking."

Carl knew his father was right. He thought about Portia all the time, and had even deleted her number so he wouldn't be tempted to call her. But all he had was bills and problems. He didn't even have his own place. He didn't lack female company, but with her it was different, and he didn't want to be the man she settled for.

CECELIA

Cecelia had spent her day getting ready for Gabriel. His father was making progress, but Gabriel hadn't

224

wanted to leave Florida until he was sure his parents could make it on their own. His instructors were flexible and he had kept up with his classes online. He was returning to Chicago to do an oral presentation and he would arrive in the morning. Since moving to her apartment a few weeks ago, she had lived among boxes and suitcases. Most of her things were in storage, and the apartment was filled primarily with things Carolyn hadn't taken to Arkansas. Gabriel's visit was incentive for her to clean and personalize the apartment. This morning she put up new curtains and arranged her pictures on the wall. For once, she was going to take both of her off days. She was looking forward to his return like a teen girl waiting for prom. She had missed Gabriel. She wouldn't call it love, but she felt a strong like. She had one last errand on her list, making a quick stop at the storage unit on her way to work. She planned to wait and get her things out of storage at the end of the month, but she wanted to get her good china for Gabriel's visit. The china set was the only thing she had taken after her mother died, and this dinner with Gabriel would be the first time she used it.

Cecelia pulled in front of her storage unit and left her car running while she hopped out. Her fingers got cold as she fumbled with the lock. The calendar said spring, but Chicago weather made its own rules. She rubbed her hands together, then got back in her car and drove around to the office. The clerk was on the phone and finally opened the partition when Cecelia switched from polite taps to hard knocks.

"Something is wrong with the lock. My key keeps getting stuck," Cecelia said as she handed her key and identification to the clerk.

The clerk took her license and went to the back room. "Miss Brown, you have a past due balance," she announced when she returned.

"I know. I have it right here," Cecelia said as she counted out two hundred dollars. "That should get me almost current. I'll pay the balance next week. Now can you see about my key?"

The clerk disappeared to the back room again. Cecelia glanced at her watch then tapped on the glass partition. "Excuse me. I'm in a hurry. What's taking so long?"

The clerk reappeared and seemed to be walking even slower. "Your contract was terminated and the unit has been re-rented."

"What does that mean?"

"It means your unit was classified as abandoned due to nonpayment."

"But I just paid you."

"I know, but the deadline was two weeks ago. Actually you were forty-five days past due."

"Okay, I'm current now. Can you see about my key?"

"That key has been de-activated and the unit released," the clerk said.

"So where is my stuff?"

"We have a vendor that we sell abandoned contents to and they haul it away."

"Wait a minute, are you telling me my things aren't here?"

"We sent several notices to the address we had on file."

"I moved, but you had my phone number. You always manage to contact me when money is due. So where are my things?"

"As I said, we have a company that buys contents from abandoned units."

"I didn't *abandon* my unit. What is this company's number? I need to contact them. The things I want will be of no value to anyone else. They can't make any money off of them. What is their number?"

"I'll have to go look it up," the clerk said as she went to the back room again. After what seemed like an eternity, the clerk returned.

"I called my manager. He said we can't give out that information, but I can tell you that stuff is probably gone. We auction off the whole unit and they take what they want. Whatever they leave we give to Goodwill, then we have a company go in and clean out the unit."

"This is absurd. You can't just auction off a person's stuff. This isn't some reality show. My children's baby pictures and my mother's dishes were in there."

"I'm sorry. There's nothing I can do."

"Then give me my money back."

"I can't do that either."

"You can't keep my money and sell my stuff. I need to speak to your manager."

"I'm the only one here."

"Then give me a number. This is ridiculous."

The clerk disappeared to the back room. She returned five minutes later and said, "I called the office and they said it's in the contract."

"I don't give a damn about a contract. Why am I talking to you? Give me your manager's number."

"You can call our 1-800 customer service number."

"I don't want to talk to a machine. You can't do this," Cecelia yelled, then turned around to see a security guard coming in the door.

"We're going to have to ask you to leave, Ma'am," he said as he grabbed her elbow.

"Do not touch me. I am not some illiterate vagrant. I will leave on my own. But you haven't seen the last of me. What you have done is illegal and I will sue," Cecelia said as she walked out and slammed the door. She got in her car, turned the ignition, then broke down in tears. How could this be happening? She had enough designer clothes in the unit to start her own boutique, but she was most upset about her personal things. She had tons of pictures and home movie film she had planned to convert to digital files. And her mother's china – the only material item she had left, was gone.

She looked up when the security guard tapped on her window. "Are you alright, Miss?"

What a stupid question, she thought. But he was just doing his job. It wasn't his fault. She usually found someone else to blame for her predicament. But this time she had no one to blame but herself. *Why hadn't she brought the payment?* She knew why. She had taken the money to the casino. She had been up eight hundred dollars and knew she should have left. But she stayed and gave most of it back. *Why do I keep doing this?* She really hadn't been too concerned at the time. She had set a limit like they tell you and gone in with two hundred dollars. When that was gone, she got up and left. She had called and left a message that she would bring the payment in this week. *Nothing I can do now,* she thought as she glanced at her watch.

She made it to the hospital, locked her coat and purse in her locker, then rushed to her floor. As she went to the nurse's station, her coworker handed her the telephone.

"Miss Brown, please come to human resources."

"Now?"

"Yes."

Cecelia pasted on a smile then made the trip to the human resources office in the annex. As she passed the cafeteria, her stomach growled and she remembered she hadn't eaten.

"Miss Brown, here is the Second Notice of Policy Infraction we discussed a few weeks ago."

"What is this?"

"You were late today. When we last met, you had a ninety-day probation period to avoid a more serious action. That included no unexcused absences or tardies. You are being placed on unpaid leave."

"I was on my way to work, but had a personal emergency."

"Unless it was a verifiable illness or accident, it's an unexcused absence. Do you have a doctor's excuse or accident report?"

"No, but I'm just thirty minutes late, and I always work more than forty hours."

"This is a hospital. We are responsible for people's lives and must have a dependable staff."

"So when it's in the hospital's favor, that's fine. But when it's not, tough luck. How long is the leave?"

"Ninety days."

"Ninety days? Is there someone I can appeal to?"

"No. Those were the conditions you agreed to when you signed your performance improvement plan. I suggest you contact the employee assistance number. They offer free counseling and may be able to help you."

Unless they could counsel her on how to track down whoever had the stuff from her storage unit, she didn't want to talk to anyone. This lady probably dealt with all kinds of functioning alcoholics and addicts, but she wasn't like them.

Cecelia left human resources and went directly to the parking lot. She had some items in her desk, but didn't want to see the nurses on her floor. They were probably the ones that sold her out in the first place. As many times as she had given up her off days and worked for them, or covered for them when husbands, boyfriends, supervisors called, who was there when she needed a favor? She then noticed she had missed a phone call and text from Gabriel. The hospital was like a little city and the news about her status was probably already public knowledge. How would she ever face them or Gabriel? And how would she make it ninety days with no pay?

BEVERLY

A benefit of no longer being in the Anthony business, is mornings like this. I slept with my window cracked, something Anthony would never allow. He was taught that sleeping with windows open let in sickness. He said he wasn't superstitious but why take the risk. There were window units in the kitchen and in my parent's bedroom, but my parents were stingy about using them. They preferred to open our windows whenever the weather allowed. Memphis morning air isn't the same as Eden, but I'll take it. There's a light breeze coming in and I can faintly hear birds chirping in the distance. One of the neighbors has already fired up their grill, and the smell makes me long for some of Daddy's ribs. I thought about going downstairs to take a slab out of the freezer, but like an athlete the day after the big game, I'm too sore to move. My neck is stiff and my wrists still tingle. *Too bad every weekend can't be like this*, I thought as I searched through my nightstand drawer for my wristband.

Yesterday the salon was super-busy. Customers we hadn't seen in months called for an appointment and we had several walk-ins. Seems like everybody came out of hibernation to get their hair done for Mother's Day. Even Mark called several times to check on me. I had feigned a stomach ache the weekend we were supposed to go to the jazz festival. He has been on an extended east coast stretch, and his runs haven't brought him to Memphis lately, but he did send flowers. Everyone was kind, knowing I recently lost my mother.

But we were so busy, my mind stayed focused on the job at hand. We didn't close until eight o'clock. Everyone paid their booth rent and even the soda machine sold out. And not a moment too soon. The extension I got on the light bill expires this week. I was dreading having to ask Anthony for the money, so yesterday's rush was right on time.

It's been a while since I've been in the salon for Mother's Day weekend. The last few years I spent this weekend with Mama. Even though it was Mother's Day, she spent the days before preparing and wouldn't let us take her out to dinner. She said she wanted to fix what her children liked, and her present was just having us there. The Saturday before Mother's Day was the Spring Tea, sponsored by the Ladies Auxiliary of Friendship Missionary Baptist Church. I always spent Mother's Day in Eden, but hadn't gone to the tea since I was grown. The year before she died, Mama was the Chair and I went to support her. When I was growing up, those events seemed long and boring. This time, I actually enjoyed it and promised to join her every year. It was a promise I didn't get a chance to keep. Now

Phyllis R. Dixon

Mother's Day is like Valentine's Day for someone getting over a lost love, but I'm making progress. I stayed in bed two weeks after Mama's funeral. Then I progressed to getting depressed on Fridays, the day she died and the day of the funeral. Then I progressed to the fifteenth of the month, the date she died. Just like a newborn's life is initially measured in weeks, then months, then years, I commemorated Mama's passing in stages. Tomorrow will be my second Mother's Day without her. Seems like everyone left at the same time. Mama is gone, Tony is fighting a crazy war, and Anthony is history. But I can't afford to drown my sorrows in my pillow. I need to work. I just got a notice that I have to start making payments on the loan I took out for Tony's tuition, since he's not in school. I used to teach at the cosmetology school, but they're cutting back too, so they didn't renew my contract. My insurance went up, even though the accident wasn't my fault, and I still haven't gotten my settlement. Anthony may have been a rogue, but he did take care of home. Between his job, barbering on the weekends, and picking up side contracting jobs, he paid the bulk of the bills and my money was for extras. He was always good for a hundred dollars walking around money, and he kept my gas tank full.

The grief counselor said holidays will never be the same and you have to create new traditions. But what else can you do on a day to honor your mother, when your mother is gone? Mark said this would be a good time for me to meet his mother, but I told him no. I know I wouldn't want to spend Mother's Day with Tony and some new girlfriend. Carolyn will be entertaining her mother-in-law. She invited, actually pleaded with me to come visit. But as much as I dread being alone, I don't want to do that either. I presume Cecelia is

232

working – haven't heard from her lately. Raymond will be with his own family, and Carl and Daddy are spending the day with Aunt Belle. Everyone seems to be coping just fine. I know they all miss Mama, but as the oldest girl, I feel our bond was the closest. While the others were away building their lives, I was seventy-five minutes away. We talked almost every day and I went to Eden at least once a week, but I was usually in a rush. The shop was busy, or I needed to get back to do something for Anthony or Tony.

How ironic, now I have plenty of time but Mama is gone, and Daddy has become a man about town. I don't have to rush back to the salon because business has been terrible. I used to turn away walk-ins and most of my customers had standing appointments. But so many of them have cut back, that I've started handing out business cards to solicit new business. My best barber said he's not making enough money and cut back to weekends so he could get a full time job. They say Wall Street is reaching new highs, but that boom has not trickled down to my neighborhood. Also, lots of folks are going to natural hair styles. They come in for a cut or color, but those visits are much less frequent than when they had a perm.

But it's too pretty a day to be sad. Even though Mama's not here, I still have lots to be thankful for. Aunt Belle's accident could have been much worse, so why not celebrate with her? Uncle Nap was her only child and he died a few years ago. Daddy and Carl said they were going to look in on her but neither said anything about food. I've got lasagna in the freezer, her favorite dish. Adding garlic bread, green beans and a salad won't take long, and I'll stop at the grocery store and buy a cake.

I took a shower, let the water mix with my tears, and had myself a real good cry. *Now, I'm through with that. I'm not the first person to lose a parent. If they can make it, I can too.* I packed an overnight bag. Just as I finished ironing my sundress, my phone rang.

"Happy Mother's Day, Mom."

"It is now that I've heard from you," I said.

"I can't talk long, but wanted you to know I was thinking about you. Got to go."

"All right. Be safe, baby. I love you." I was happy and sad at the same time and said a prayer that the angels would continue to watch over my baby. I finished dressing and was on my way out the door when my phone rang. This time it was Cecelia.

"Hey there. I thought you would be working today," I said.

"I'm off today. I know you always spent the day with Mama and thought you may need a little cheering up. How are you?" Cecelia asked.

"I'm okay. A little sad, but okay."

"Well, I'm going to have a few days off work and wanted to know if I can come visit you."

"Of course. When?"

"The kids are taking me to dinner this afternoon. I thought I'd catch the ten o'clock Megabus and I'll be there in the morning."

"The Megabus?"

"I'm trying to save money these days."

"You certainly have gone from one extreme to the other. I was thinking about staying over in Eden, but I'll come back if you're coming. Is everything ok?"

"Yeah. It's a spur of the moment decision."

"Then I'll see you tomorrow. Are you sure you're ok?" I asked.

"Yes, I'm fine. See you in the morning."

I heard her, but didn't believe her.

CAROLYN

"We need to talk," I said as soon as my husband walked in the house.

"What happened to, 'Hey, baby? Good to see you dear? How was your day honey?'" Derrick asked as he closed the door behind him and put his keys on the table. "I should have known something was wrong when I saw your car in the driveway this early."

"I didn't mean to bum-rush you, but it won't wait and I don't know how to sugar coat it."

"Okay, Carolyn, what is it?"

"I'm working with CARE on the fracking lawsuit. The judge approved an injunction that I wrote and filed. It will be in the paper tomorrow."

"So that's it? I don't get a vote?"

"I know how you feel about this but—"

"But you're doing it anyway. I thought you said you were so busy at work? "

"I am, but this is personal now. Turns out Brenda signed the leases after Charles passed. We thought she got a lot of insurance money, but it was money from the leases on Charles' land. They can't drill on Daddy's land, but it's so close, they may as well be. I've done a lot of research and it's criminal what these companies are doing. Fracking is causing water contamination and water pollution everywhere it's used. They won't reveal what chemicals they are using, but we do know the toxins cause cancers and all kinds of neurological diseases, especially in small children. I can't sit by and do nothing."

"I understand you feel ties to your family; I get that. Helping Carl out of a sham arrest is one thing, but going against big corporations and city leaders is another. You're not the only lawyer in the family. Tell them to ask your brother."

"You know Paul is out of the country," I said.

"Eden may be a small town, but we do have the internet and email. Raymond can contact him anytime."

"I hope Paul will help, but that still doesn't mean I sit by and do nothing."

"Well, you've made your decision, now here's mine. Fracking brings jobs and money. This is one of the poorest counties in one of the poorest states in the country. I've worked here twenty years helping people get the most from their land. There was a time when that meant showing them how to irrigate and what pesticides to use. Now it means helping them make decisions about their land. Those leases pay anywhere from five hundred to three thousand dollars a month, plus royalties. You're asking these folks to walk away from a lot of money. And if you and Raymond are so concerned about saving the world, gas is cleaner and more secure than relying on foreign energy sources. So I say, 'drill, baby, drill'. But it's not my decision, yours or Raymond's. People have to do what's best for them. And you need to do what's best for us. I can think of ten other things that would be a better use of your time, and as my wife, I forbid you to pursue this lawsuit. "

"Did you say *forbid*?" I asked as I stood.

"You heard me."

"I did but I can't believe it. I was not asking your permission."

"That's the problem with a lot of things around here," Derrick said.

"I thought you were my husband, not my father," I said as I grabbed my purse and phone. "Actually, my father doesn't even act like this."

"Where do you think you're going?" Derrick said as he grabbed my arm.

"Let me go."

"I'm tired of you acting like what I say doesn't matter. Your allegiance is supposed to be to me, not your brother, or your job."

"And I'm tired of you acting like King Derrick. Let me go."

"So you can go running to your family and tell them how mean and unreasonable I am? Just because I want my wife to put our marriage first?"

"It's not much of a marriage if you have to impose your will on every issue."

"That's because you seem to take everyone else's side on any issue that comes up. Most women would be glad to have a man that wants to take care of them. How could you even consider jeopardizing my job?"

"You're hurting me," I said as I tried to twist free. "What happened to your promise not to ever hurt me again?"

"The same thing that happened to your promise to love, cherish, and obey. Sit your ass down," Derrick said and shoved me into the recliner. I tripped and knocked my computer and the porcelain ashtray to the floor as I fell back to the couch.

"My mother's ashtray," I screamed. "Look what you've done."

"I'm sorry," he said as he picked up the pieces. "Luckily it's in big chunks, I'll put it back together."

"Don't touch it. Put it down," I said as I grabbed the pieces from him.

Phyllis R. Dixon

"Baby, I know how much this means to you. We'll fix it," he said as he reached for my hand.

"Get away from me."

"You'll see, it will be as good as new. Look, your hand is bleeding. Let me get a towel."

"Leave me alone," I shouted as I struggled to stand and fell back down.

"Just stay there," Derrick said. "I'll bring you a warm towel right away. It will be as good as new. You'll see," he said as he took my purse, phone, and keys.

"First you forbid me to do anything. Now you take my purse and keys. Am I being held prisoner?"

"Of course not. But I know you're upset and your hand is injured. It's not wise to drive in your condition. I would never forgive myself if something happened to you. I'll just hold on to these until you calm down. Let me get some ice for your hand. Everything will be fine. You'll see."

How could Mama, Steve Harvey, and the Bible be wrong? I waited to give up the cookie. When I considered moving in with Derrick, Mama talked me out of it. He courted me in a way no man had. He showed me his credit report and his background check was clean. I had the passwords to his computer, email, and phone. He paid for my tickets to come see him, paid for my phone upgrade so we could do FaceTime and bought me a computer to leave at home so I wouldn't have to worry about doing Skype on my work computer. I can sign onto his bank accounts, even though I haven't given him signing privileges on mine. I was as cautious as can be. So why am I now sitting here searching for an extra set of keys and longing for my single life?

The littlest thing seems to set him off and this subservient role doesn't fit me well. I'm tired of holding

238

my tongue and tiptoeing around what's supposed to be my home. Mama managed to let Daddy think he was in control for fifty years, and still get her way. I don't remember them even raising their voices and I know he never laid a hand on her. Beverly can fight better than most men, and had a drama filled marriage with Anthony, but getting pushed around wasn't one of her problems. Michael rarely even raised his voice to Cecelia, let alone put a hand on her. I never knew the private details of my brother's relationships, but I would bet money, abuse was not part of it. But am I being abused? Technically, Derrick has never hit me. He brings his money home and is faithful. Maybe he was right. Have I been single too long? Are these the compromises women make to sustain their families?

The signs were there. While we were dating, he called and texted several times a day. He sent sweet e-cards, thoughtful gifts and insisted I call him as soon as I got home from work. If I worked late, I had to call him to tell him. I thought that was his way of showing he was fully committed, even though it was a long-distance relationship. On one of my visits, I had to finish some reports for work. Derrick had a tantrum and swept the papers off the coffee table. I knew that was over the top, but he explained it away by saying he just wanted us to spend time together. He was extremely jealous, but again, I thought it was cute that he cared that much. He had already apologized, and even Daddy said I shouldn't work on the lawsuit. But deep down, I know no apology can excuse his behavior today. And if Daddy knew the real Derrick, I wouldn't have to worry about being a battered wife, I'd be a widow.

I braved the scary site that was his desk and looked through his desk drawers for super glue to piece the ashtray together. I didn't find glue, but did notice an envelope at the bottom of one of the drawers. I was going to ignore it like I did all the other old bills and statements I had waded through, but the return address caught my eye. The envelope was from the Pulaski County Chancery Court. This court didn't handle traffic citations. I held the envelope for a few minutes before opening it. I broke out in a sweat as I read the words on the page. Derrick had a record. He was convicted of a Class A misdemeanor six years ago; aggravated assault, battery and criminal mischief. The plaintiff was Karen Jones, Derrick's old girlfriend. There was also a certificate for attendance at anger management classes, a receipt for twelve hundred dollars and a notice that the conviction was expunged from his record. That's why nothing showed up when Cecelia did the background check. I slowly sat on the couch. My dream come true had turned into a nightmare. Now what?

"Well, ain't no need in coming back. That's the end and that's that."

Pearl Woods

Chapter 11
THAT DID IT

Now I know how seemingly normal people end up in jail. Folks will be whispering, *"Did you see Beverly in 'Beauticians Behind Bars'? Not yet, girl. I taped it but haven't watched it. Has she ever said what happened? No one knows. She just snapped and attacked Anthony with her curling iron. What a shame."*
I can't remember ever being this mad at anyone. Even the doctor's diagnosis didn't make me this mad. Then I was more mad at myself than at Anthony. When I told him to get tested, he had the nerve to insinuate that it was my white boyfriend, as he refers to Mark. I knew that wasn't possible, but didn't argue. I don't know if he ever went to the doctor and I don't care. As far as I'm concerned, his thing can shrivel up and fall off. It just reconfirms that our marriage is over and any smidgeon of feeling I had left for him has left the building. I was sad because a part of my life had ended. But in a way it's been liberating. I feel like I have official permission to move on with my life. We agreed to mediation to save money, and had been cordial during the first two sessions. *I should have known he was up to something,* I thought as I fanned myself.

I waved my hand over the sensor so the toilet would flush then exited the stall. I had retreated to the ladies room for a self-imposed time out to keep from catching a case as the young folks say. I sat in the stall long enough to make sure he was out of the parking lot. I had been shocked to get served with an amended divorce petition three weeks ago. We had already agreed during mediation that he would keep the rent houses and I would keep the salon and the house. We only had one mandated session left. Now he wanted to change the deal.

Anthony called the next day to apologize, and said his attorney told him the papers wouldn't be served until Friday and he had planned to come tell me in person before then. He said he was applying for the houses to be in the Section 8 program and some repairs were needed to bring the houses to code. He was getting a loan for the repairs and the titles needed to be in his name alone. He said he told the loan officer that I would sign a quit claim deed, but there were some other legal issues and they would need my signature and financial statements from the salon. His attorney advised him a divorce would be a cleaner process.

Sandra definitely knew her stuff. She warned me at the start to be prepared for a few curve balls. "Beverly, I know you think you guys have things worked out, and that's great if you do, but it's usually never as simple as it sounds," she said.

"Our son is grown and we've already agreed how to split our assets. I don't see what else there is to settle. I think that attorney is just trying to get more money out of Anthony."

"What about health insurance?"

"Yes, I have health insurance," I said. "I'm on Anthony's — okay, that is something I hadn't considered. I guess I'll need to look into getting a policy. I was thinking about getting coverage for the salon anyway."

"And what about taxes?"

"We've always filed jointly," I said.

"If you keep the salon, and give up the houses, you'll lose your passive losses. The income will be on your tax return and the losses will be on his. So your taxes will go up and his will go down."

"Okay, so that's something else I didn't think of. But none of that sounds earth shattering. I'm sure we can work all that out."

"Hopefully you're right. Just don't be surprised if something else comes up."

I would have bet my last dollar that I was right. And I would have lost. My first sign that something was up was that Anthony changed lawyers for the second mediation. He walked in with a white man I had never seen before. The next sign was when Anthony postponed our last mediation appointment at the last minute. I had no word from him until I got served.

As soon as we were all seated, Anthony's attorney skipped the pleasantries and got right to the point. "My client would like to amend the original petition," he said as he slid some papers in front of me.

"And surely you don't expect my client to sign something we have not had a chance to review," Sandra said as she picked up the papers.

"They have already agreed that Mrs. Townsend will keep the salon. However, upon further review, the salon is more profitable than the rental properties, so we would like Mrs. Townsend to buy out her husband's portion of the salon."

"What?" I said. "You want me to pay you?"

"No, we simply want Mr. Townsend to have his rightful portion of the business that you both built. Of course, if you don't want to buy him out, you can sell the business and split the proceeds."

"You're kidding, right? Anthony, what kind of mess is this?" I asked. "You didn't know a flat iron from a hot comb. I was doing touch ups and roller sets for years before you even thought about getting a barber's license, and now—"

"Let me handle this," my attorney said. "Obviously, we have not had a chance to review your proposal. Have you placed a value on the business?"

"We've had an accountant review the bank statements and Oasis generates almost two hundred thousand dollars in gross revenue and product sales annually. Those type of service businesses are valued at an average multiple of three times pretax income plus inventory. So we're in the neighborhood of six hundred thousand, which would mean three hundred thousand for my client. Then there is the property itself, so we think a value of four hundred thousand dollars would be in the ballpark."

"Are you crazy? You may as well ask for fifty million, because you're not getting either one," I said.

"My client would entertain spousal support if you prefer not to sell the business and don't have the assets to pay him outright."

"Our son is twenty-one," I said.

"Spousal support is different from child support," Sandra said. "It's Tennessee's version of alimony."

"Now I know you're crazy. You screw every Keisha, Jane, and Jill in Memphis, sue me for divorce, and expect me to pay you?"

"My client—"

"Your client can speak for himself," I said. "I thought you didn't like white folks all up in your business."

"I'd like clarification on paragraph seven b on page five," Sandra asked.

"There is a pending accident settlement that my client is entitled to half of."

"I'm the one that was hurt and couldn't work," I said. "And I'm the one that's now stuck with a car note. This can't be fair," I said as I turned to Sandra.

"Fair is when you go to get cotton candy and ride the roller coaster. This is real life," Sandra said.

"We know it is everyone's desire for this to be as quick and drama-free as possible. So my client has been more than fair in the property distribution. To speed up the process, we will forego the discovery process."

"No, I don't think so," Sandra said. "We will file a motion for discovery and a response once we have had a chance to review your petition. And what is this on page eight?"

"It is my client's understanding that Mrs. Townsend has an interest in a trust that holds land in Arkansas with pending royalty payments—"

"Oh, hell to the no," I said as I stood and grabbed my purse. "My family kept that land despite the KKK, boll weevil, depression, Jim Crow, and fracking. If you think you're going to get your gold digging, STD having, hands on a penny generated from it, you are sadly mistaken. Let's go."

Sandra exchanged business cards with Anthony's lawyer as they walked to the door. They seemed mighty friendly, and I wondered if I should have gotten another lawyer too. Maybe doing someone's hair for twenty years wasn't the best way to pick a lawyer.

Phyllis R. Dixon

"Sandra, I'm going to the ladies room. I'll meet you at the car."

"Beverly, wait," Anthony said as he tugged at my elbow.

"Unless you're going to tell me this was all some sick joke, there's nothing I want to hear you say."

"I just want you to know, I didn't want us to be like this. But I have to think about my future. Hopefully we can—"

"Anthony, kiss my ass."

So here I sit in the bathroom. I can feel the heat rising around my neck, but this isn't a hot flash. Now I understand how people can snap and hurt someone. But to quote Sophia, "He ain't worth it." I also understand how people sign something just to get it over with. But even if we had reached a settlement on the salon, the accident money and the rent houses, there is no way I will let him have one penny from my family's land. I cannot let the fruits of my father's toil and sacrifice be wasted on Anthony's sorry behind. Anthony had never expressed any interest in my family's property and I was caught off guard. They say there's a thin line between love and hate. I just crossed that line.

CAROLYN

It's only ten o'clock, but it is already hot and there is no breeze at all. I don't see how people can argue that there is no global warming. We are in the middle of a heat wave and technically it isn't even summer yet. If it had been any other day, and any other event, I would have stayed home. But today is Father's Day and we are gathering at Raymond's. Last year I came to Eden, even

246

though Derrick worried that it would be too emotional for me. But I felt we needed to support Daddy. It rained all day and the rain matched our mood. It had only been a few months since Mama's passing and despite our best efforts it wasn't a celebration without her. We were low key the rest of last year. Miss Emma invited Daddy over for Thanksgiving, and no one planned anything for Christmas or New Year's. We didn't get together for Easter either, and Aunt Belle announced that was enough of that. She told Raymond we were coming to his house for Father's Day. So here we are.

I saw smoke rising behind the house and followed the smoke signals, and my nose, to my brother's back yard. "Happy Father's Day," I said when I spotted him and Daddy hovering over a black metal barrel, cut in half that served as the grill. It is a replica of Daddy's grill and had belonged to Charles. That was old school, but Raymond also has a gas grill and a turkey smoker. The Washington men are serious about barbeque and consider themselves experts. Even Raymond made an exception and cooked pork on these occasions.

"Thanks, Carolyn," he said and took my bags of buns, condiments, and chips. "Just in time. The burgers and hot dogs are ready. Where's Derrick?"

"At church." Derrick is still in apology mode. He served me breakfast in bed, and said I could stay home and rest. My head, hand, and stomach ached, and I planned to stay home whether he said so or not. We had barely spoken in the last two weeks. I'm not mad. Well, maybe a little bit. I turned my life upside down for this man, but now he was showing me another side. Should I believe the sweet side or the angry side? I know I need to make a decision. Even not making a decision is making a decision. I still haven't confronted him about my discovery, but it will have to wait until another day. Today is a day to celebrate the men in my family. Raymond is the host. Carl's boys are in town and Daddy is the guest of honor. I won't let Derrick's drama ruin this day.

Daddy and Raymond were tending to the grill, and Carl and the boys were playing horse on the makeshift basketball court. Malcolm was winning, and had inherited his father's trash talk skills. Today is game seven of the finals. Raymond hooked up a TV on his deck. His team members were coming over later to watch the game. Eden High lost in the state tournament, but they gained so much during the journey, and they looked up to Raymond like a father.

After dinner, Raymond brought his laptop outside and surprised Daddy by Skyping with Paul and Cecelia's children. He kept trying to rush, thinking the cost was expensive, like long distance used to be. Once he realized there was no extra cost, we couldn't get him off. Paul carried the computer all over his house and showed us every room. Junior and Sheree didn't talk too much since Simone monopolized the time reciting her numbers and alphabet. Daddy, the proud great-grandfather, fawned over her as though she were spouting physics.

"This new stuff is really amazing. Who would have thought I could look at a screen and talk to folks in another country? I feel like a time traveler from a cartoon."

"Welcome to the twenty-first century, Daddy," I said.

"Emma has a computer and has been saying I should take classes at the library. I think I will. Maybe I'll even get a Picgram page."

"I don't know if the internet is ready for C.W. Washington," I said.

"I tell you what I'm ready for, some more dinner. That first plate was just the appetizer. Son, your barbeque is almost as good as mine," C.W. said as he stood.

"I learned from the best. Geneva is in the kitchen, she'll fix you a plate. Carolyn, since I have you here, can I get you to do one quick thing for me?" Raymond asked. "We have a CARE meeting on Tuesday and I made some last minute changes to the presentation and grant papers. Will you proofread them for me?"

"Okay. I'm going to go inside and print it. It's easier for me to read," I said as I took the computer inside, glad for an excuse to sit under the air conditioning for a while. "And remember, the meter is running." CARE's activities are starting to gain national attention and we're getting support from similar organizations in Texas and New York. We have even been awarded two grants from national environmental groups. My labors are bearing fruit, but I had been right to be concerned about the time CARE would consume. Until recently, I have been spending most of my evenings, and even some work time, on CARE related activities. I don't mind, it's a distraction from my marriage, or what's left of it.

"Here you are," Derrick said as he poked his head in the doorway. "I saw your car outside, but didn't see you in the yard."

"I didn't know you were here," I said, without looking up.

"Service ran long, then we had cake and punch in the fellowship hall for Father's Day. Everyone asked about you."

"I'm sure you told them a good story. You're good at covering up."

"A little bitchy, but at least you're talking to me. Look, I admit, I've made mistakes. I didn't realize I had to be perfect."

"I didn't expect perfection, but honesty would be welcome."

"This is not the time or place to discuss this. Let's go home," Derrick said.

"I don't feel like I have a home. Besides, I'm busy."

"See, that's half the problem. You are always too busy. Everything comes before our marriage."

"Right now it's not much of a marriage."

"Maybe you had unrealistic expectations. We're not big ballers like Jay-Z and Beyoncé, so we don't need a big mansion. And we're not Halle Berry and whoever her baby's daddy is. We don't need a baby at our age. Instead of focusing on what we don't have, why not enjoy what we do have? So let's enjoy the day and—"

"You're right. This is not the time or the place for this conversation. This is a day to celebrate my father," I said as I turned off the computer.

"I do love you, and I'll do whatever you want. Even though I disagree, if you want to move, we can find the biggest house between here and Memphis. I'll go to counseling. We'll be the only parents buying diapers and Depends, but we can have ten babies if you want. You've added so much to my life. A day like today reminds me of that. I never paid much attention to Father's Day, but being with you and your family has made me realize how much I've missed. Just let me make things up to you," he said as he reached for my hand.

I didn't extend my hand to meet his, but I didn't pull away either.

"Aww, ain't that sweet?" Carl said as he walked by on his way to the bathroom. "Do you guys need a 'do not disturb' sign?"

"To be continued," Derrick said as he gave me a quick kiss. "Let's go get something to eat."

Derrick went outside to catch the score and I stopped in the kitchen where my sisters were washing dishes. Cecelia had come to Memphis for a surprise visit three weeks ago. She told Beverly she needed a break. We didn't think that was the whole story since she had four suitcases and was vague about her plans to return to Chicago. But we decided to let her tell us in her own time. Beverly said she was glad for the company and was even learning to like Cecelia's meatless meals.

"I was wondering where you were," Beverly said. "You haven't signed the card."

"I was working on something for Raymond, and I needed a break from the heat."

"Well, I hope you're not getting ready to leave. We haven't given Daddy his surprise yet," Beverly said as she pulled a gift bag from under the sink. "Daddy is really going to be surprised."

"Oh yeah, don't I owe you some more money?" I asked as I took my wallet out of my pocket.

"You're good," Beverly said. "But Cecelia, I do need your money."

"You said Paul sent enough money to cover everything," Cecelia said.

"He did, but we all still need to contribute. The gift is from all of us. We'll just give Daddy the extra money."

"So that gold digger can get her hands on it? I don't think so," Cecelia said.

"Who are you to dictate what he does with his money?" Raymond said as he entered the kitchen. "Just like you give your money to those machines, Daddy can give his money to anyone or anything he pleases."

"We understand if you're a little short," I said. "I can put in for you."

"I can pay my share, thank you very much. I don't see why you all are so determined to let this woman keep using Daddy. What are we going to do about this?"

"About what?" Raymond asked.

"Daddy getting married. We can't let this happen," Cecelia said.

"There is no *we*," Raymond said. "It's not up to us. Daddy is happy. That's all that should matter."

"I can't believe you're all just going to sit by and say nothing. So much for loyalty," Cecelia said.

"Cecelia has a good point. It does seem like we're just tossing Mama's memory to the side," Beverly said.

"You haven't even given her a chance," Raymond said.

"A chance to do what – spend Daddy's money?" Cecelia said.

"I asked Daddy about a prenuptial agreement and he wouldn't even consider it," I said.

"So, if there's nothing you can do about it, just be happy for him," Raymond said.

"There is something we haven't talked about. People Daddy's age don't always make the best financial choices and there are avenues we can take to protect his interests," Cecelia said.

"There you go with that *we* again," Raymond said as he grabbed a beer out of the refrigerator.

"Are you talking about legal action?" Beverly asked.

"Carolyn's a lawyer. Aren't there legal avenues for situations like this?" Cecelia asked.

"I doubt if she wants to get in the middle of something like that," Derrick said as he walked across the room. "It's never a good idea for family members to —"

"What you're talking about is durable power of attorney," I said. "But it's usually used when people have Alzheimer's or other debilitating illnesses. Daddy hardly fits—"

"You're talking about having Daddy committed? You're the one that needs to be committed for even thinking such a thing," Raymond said. "We didn't take away your rights when you were throwing your money away and running around meeting other men."

"This is not the same thing, and not that it's any of your business, but I was not meeting other men."

"Just be honest. You're not worried about protecting Daddy's interests. Beverly saw the hospital notices and we know you've lost your job and you're broke. Looks like you're the one making poor choices," Raymond said.

"I did not lose my job. And Beverly, if you're going to snoop and tell my business, you need to at least get it straight."

"I wasn't snooping. I was looking for some papers my attorney needs for the divorce. It *is* my house."

"If you want me to leave, just say so. I'm looking out for all of us and I'm the one getting attacked. We want Daddy to live a long time, but what happens if he dies before Emma?"

"If you don't mind my saying so, Cecelia is right," Derrick said. "I handle all of my grandmother's affairs and we've discussed everything regarding her final wishes."

"This is different," Beverly said, rolling her eyes.

"Daddy didn't get where he is by being careless. I'm sure he'll update his will," Raymond said.

"Maybe he will and maybe he won't. Emma is talking him into a lot of things we didn't think he'd do. You talk about me gambling – that's a gamble," Cecelia said.

"Daddy has always taught us to protect the family legacy, but this is nothing we should decide based on a kitchen conversation," I said. "This is a holiday. Let's talk about this another time."

"This is the perfect time," Cecelia said. "We're all here."

"Maybe we should bring our concerns to him as a group," Beverly said. "None of us thinks any legal action is necessary, but I'm sure Mama would want him to consider his children, grandchildren, and great-grandchildren before taking such a big step. Miss Emma seems like a kind lady, but dollar signs do change people."

"Look who's here," Carl loudly announced as he accompanied Miss Emma into the kitchen.

"You didn't have to bring anything, but I'm not complaining," Raymond said as he rushed to relieve her of her bags. "This looks good."

"C.W. loves German chocolate cake," Emma said.

"Daddy is borderline diabetic. He shouldn't be eating German chocolate cake," Cecelia snapped.

"I made it with Splenda instead of sugar and I used sugar-free applesauce instead of butter. I'll bet you won't even be able to taste the difference."

"We're so glad you and your cake could make it," Carl said.

"Well, I overheard part of your conversation, and I'm not sure that's a true statement," Emma said. "I understand your concern. C.W. is blessed to have

254

children that care about him. I want you to know I love your father and I can't wait to be his wife."

"So you're glad our mother is dead?"

"Cecelia, hush," Beverly said.

"Of course not. Lois was a lovely person."

"We don't need you to tell us about our mother," Cecelia said. "Let's just cut to the chase. Daddy is a man, and like all the rest of them, he's letting his body rule his mind. You can seduce him with fake cakes and phony airs, but if you think you're going to get your hands on his money, you can forget it."

"I know that's coming from a place of love for your father, so I won't take it personally—"

"Oh, you can take it personally, or any way you want to," Cecelia said. "But I tell you what you're not going to take—"

"I cannot believe my ears," C.W. said as he entered the room. "I've been standing in the hall outside the bathroom and I don't know what's gotten into you. This was so hard to listen to, but once you started disrespecting Emma, I had to step in. I am so sorry you had to hear this. Let's go," he said as he gently touched her elbow.

"C.W. this is supposed to be your day. I don't want you to leave because of me. The last thing I want to do is come between you and your children."

"They aren't children. They are grown, and they were taught better than this," Daddy said as he grabbed Emma's hand. "Y'all act like I'm some senile old man with one foot in the grave. I'm going to live what time I got left the way I see fit and anybody don't like it – too bad."

"Daddy, it's just that we care about what happens to you," I said.

"I hope that's it, and not that you're counting my money."

"And for the record, I'm not counting his money either," Emma said. "I am not after your father's money, or land, and if he wants me to sign something, I will."

"Emma, honey, you don't have to explain yourself."

"Let me say this," Emma said. "I know I can't replace Lois and that's not my goal. But I do want us to be friends, and I think we will be if you give me a chance. We all want the same thing and that's for your father to be happy. C.W. is a wonderful man. Your mother took great care of him and will be a hard act to follow, but I'm honored to try. Nobody is more surprised than I am to be talking about getting married at this time in my life. Girls, if you think the pickings are slim now, wait until you get my age. The few single men out there are either looking for a home or a nurse."

"I didn't realize I was such a hot commodity. Maybe I shouldn't limit all of this to just one woman," C.W. said with a wink.

"In the words of Bill Withers, you're too much for one but not enough for two," Emma said. "Look, I'm going on home. C.W. you stay here. Enjoy your family. I have to get up early and go pack the last of my things in my classroom. Raymond, I'll see you at the staff meeting tomorrow."

"Well, I guess they told us," Raymond said, as C.W. walked Emma to her car.

"Time will tell," Cecelia said.

"Well, the mood for Father's Day has dissipated. I guess we'll be getting on home," Derrick said. "We both have early days tomorrow."

"I'm going to stay and help clean up so Beverly and Cecelia can get back to Memphis before dark," I said as I began loading the dishwasher.

"Cecelia, we know you mean well, but sometimes you need to just be quiet," Carl said, when Raymond came back in the house.

"I know you're not trying to say this is all my fault just because none of you have the nerve to speak your mind."

"Some would call that tact," I said. "As Mama used to say, it's not always what you say, but how you say it."

"Mama also said, 'God bless the child that's got his own'. I work with life and death situations and I'm trained not to waste time. I'm sorry if little Miss Emma's feelings got hurt, but you of all people know if things aren't in writing, it doesn't mean a thing."

"This isn't about Miss Emma's feelings," Raymond said. "But by insulting her, you insulted Daddy."

"I cannot believe you are ganging up on me. I'm looking out for all of us."

"Well, stop doing us favors," Carl said.

"I would think you would be the main one concerned about this train wreck since you're the one who'll be homeless."

"Carl will be fine. Stop trying to deflect your money woes on everybody else," Raymond said. "We're not stupid."

"You know what? I'm leaving. I'm tired of everybody blaming me for everything. Excuse me for being loyal," Cecelia said as she grabbed her purse and stormed out the door.

"Now we have two family members with hurt feelings," I said. "Should we go after her?"

"Let her stew," Beverly said. "She won't get far. I drove."

CECELIA

"So how long were you going to sit out here?" Beverly asked as she opened the car door.

"Luckily you didn't lock your door," Cecelia said. She was sitting inside the car playing a game on her phone. "Glad you finally came out. My battery is running low and these mosquitos are tearing me up."

Beverly loaded her ice chest of ribs, chicken, and turkey legs in the trunk, then got in the car and headed toward the highway.

"Why is Daddy being so stubborn?" Cecelia asked. "Emma said she would sign anything he asked her to."

"He's interpreting your position as trying to tell him what to do and he doesn't like it. He sees that as a sign of getting old and wants to show he can still make his own decisions. The argument isn't about money, it's about control."

"I see daytime TV teaches you a lot about relationships."

"Being a beautician is like being an unpaid therapist. I hear all kinds of stories. Most people aren't trying to hurt each other. There are two sides to every story, and the truth is usually in the middle."

"I don't know that there's a middle ground on Daddy getting married, but it bothers me for him to think I'm plotting against him. This is no way for us to end Father's Day. I want to talk to him."

"Call the house phone. He rarely answers the cell."

"No, I want to talk to him in person," Cecelia insisted.

"Now?"

"Yes. The shop is closed tomorrow and I'll drive back if you're tired."

"All right," Beverly said as she pulled over, checked for the state police, then made a U-turn heading back to Eden.

Cecelia couldn't understand why she was being made to be the bad guy. *Black folks are too emotional,* she thought. That's why we always come up on the short end of the stick when it comes to money. We try to be fair and logical and sentimental. Money has no soul or allegiance. Just like the slot machine will pay off to someone who's just sat down even though someone else fed it all night.

"It's been a long time since I've seen this highway at sunset," Cecelia said, as she let the window down. The sun was so big in the western sky, it looked fake. Corn was waist high and the road to her father's house looked the same as it always did. Unfortunately, everything was different. No more family trips down home with the kids. No more pulling up to see Mama and Daddy rocking on the porch. And no more of her mother's tight hugs. She knew she was right, and her mother would want her to look out for the family, but she didn't want to win her battle with Emma and lose her dad.

Beverly parked behind her father's truck and the sisters went to the porch. Cecelia pulled the screen door, but the hook was on. "We know he's in there, maybe he's sleep."

"Let's leave him a note," Beverly said.

"Wait, did you hear that?" Cecelia asked, and cocked her head to the side.

"It's probably the TV," Beverly said.

"No, it sounded like a moan or a cry," Cecelia said.

"I think I do hear something," Beverly said, as she started knocking.

"Maybe all this stress gave him a heart attack. Don't you have a key or something?"

"Not to the screen door, but the back door screen doesn't latch." Beverly dug her father's house key out of her purse and the sisters rushed to the back door. Beverly fumbled with the lock before opening the door.

"Daddy?" Cecelia shouted. "Do you have 911 service down here?" she asked Beverly, as they rushed through the house. They found the master bedroom door closed.

"Daddy, are you alright?" Beverly asked as they pushed the door open.

C.W. was standing next to the bed in his boxers. "What in the world are you girls doing?"

Beverly and Cecelia stood at the door with their mouths open, as they watched Miss Emma pull the seven hundred thread floral sheet to her chin.

CAROLYN

Geneva and I made quick work of the dishes. I had forgotten how much easier kitchen clean-up was when you have a dishwasher. "Do you think Daddy is really mad?" I asked Raymond as he walked me to my car.

"Yep."

"I'll call him and Miss Emma tomorrow and apologize. But I still feel like he needs to consider some of these things we were talking about, but it's not worth upsetting him. As far as the grant application, I did as much as I could, but I wish you would have asked me earlier. Some of the facts about the injunction aren't quite right. I would have included more information about upcoming events. Even the number of people at the meetings would be good to include. Grant donors like numbers."

"I didn't want to impose. I know you're busy," Raymond said.

"And since when has that stopped you?" I said as I playfully punched his arm.

"After I talked to Derrick—"

"What do you mean after you talked to Derrick?"

"He called and asked me to limit your CARE involvement. He told me about your pressures at work and you've been seeing a doctor—"

"He had no right to do that and you should have talked to me."

"Don't go getting all mad. He's just looking out for his wife. He's right to be concerned."

"Let me work on it some more tonight. I'll email it to you first thing in the morning."

"I appreciate it. We need every penny we can get, but I don't want my brother-in-law thinking I'm taking advantage of you."

"You let me worry about your brother-in-law."

Raymond had cooked way too much food and had sent us all home with plenty of barbeque. I brought enough home for Derrick and me to take for lunch. I planned to freeze some of the meat, but I had promised Raymond I would finish editing the CARE grant application. The humidity had wreaked havoc with my hair and I really needed to curl it if I was going to have any trace of a style tomorrow. I was wiped out and thought maybe I'd just get up two hours earlier and do my hair, put the meat in freezer bags, and complete the application in the morning.

"Hey, baby. I dozed off and didn't hear you drive up," Derrick said as I walked through the living room. "I put some wine in the ice bucket. I thought we'd take

Phyllis R. Dixon

a bath and get the barbeque smell off of us, then see where the night leads."

"I'm tired and I'm going to bed. I need to get up extra early to work on the CARE application before I go to work."

"You spent half your time today working on it and now you're going to get up before daybreak to work on it?"

"Maybe I wouldn't have had to spend Father's Day working on it if you hadn't told Raymond to limit my involvement."

"If you won't speak up for yourself, I will."

"I don't need you to speak up for me. I know what I want to do and what I can and can't handle. It was not your place to butt in."

"This is silly. Sometimes I think you just look for things to argue about. Now come over here," Derrick said as he patted the couch. "I've been missing you."

"Derrick, you can't be serious."

"I figured since we were talking again, we could get back to loving again."

"Well you figured wrong. And the fact that you don't get why I'm upset about you talking to Raymond behind my back is even more evidence that we have a problem."

"I'll tell you what the problem is. I'm tired of you acting like I'm Chris Brown and Ike Turner rolled into one. And another thing, when I say it's time to go, you should come with me. It's like you look for an opportunity to make me look bad. You need to get over yourself and start acting like my wife."

All sorts of snappy responses were rolling through my mind, but I was tired. *Maybe I should just fake it. He'll be satisfied and fall asleep, then I can get some rest*, I thought as I took the CARE folders out of my

262

bag. I had arranged the surveys in order, so all I had to do in the morning was fill in the spreadsheet.

Derrick walked over to the table and swept all the papers on the floor. "Let's go to bed."

"What are you doing?" I yelled and bent over to start picking up the papers.

"You must think I'm stupid. You're making excuses not to be with me because you're seeing someone else."

"I am not seeing anyone. Although you certainly make it tempting," I said as I stacked and sorted the papers.

"What the hell is that supposed to mean?" Derrick said as he slammed the table, causing the lamp to fall to the floor. "Look at me when I'm talking to you. I can't believe you're acting like this because I tried to help you."

"Help or control?" I asked. "And you're yelling and knocking over stuff like King Kong. You cannot talk to me like that."

"It's better to yell about it than to pout for weeks like you do. At least I get it out and over with. What happened to our promise not to go to bed angry?"

"What about your promise to be honest? I know about Karen Jones."

"I told you about her a long time ago."

"You didn't tell me you were charged with assault."

"That was a farce and the judge was a woman. She had her mind made up before I even opened my mouth. You keep bringing up stuff that has nothing to do with us. I think you're just looking for excuses," he said as he grabbed my arm so tight it felt like his thumb would bore a hole in my bone.

"Get away from me," I shouted and twisted out of his grasp. He grabbed my collar from behind and snatched me backwards. The buttons on my blouse ripped, and I was practically choking as he pulled my top dragging me across the room. My gagging turned into vomiting and I think it scared him.

"Jesus, are you alright?" he asked. "Let me get you some water."

As he walked to the kitchen, I threw a stapler at him. Derrick ducked, and the stapler broke the ceiling fan light, then fell and shattered the glass coffee table.

"I can't stay here," I said in what sound I could muster from my throat.

"I don't know why you make things so difficult. Let's just go to bed and things will look better in the morning," Derrick said. "I'll run you a bath."

"The only thing I'm going to see in the morning is another bruise on my arm."

CARL

Raymond was giving Carl a ride home since Carlton had his license and Carl let him take his car to a cousin's house to play video games. But he needed to drop some more CARE papers off at Carolyn's house first.

"Here's the envelope. I'll text her and let her know you're coming to the door," Raymond said, as he handed the package to his brother.

Carl walked to his sister's front door, but slowed his gait the closer he got, then turned around. He went to the driver's side and motioned for Raymond to roll down his window. "They're having an argument."

"Talk about awkward. I guess we can just leave the envelope on the step and I'll text her back and let her know you left it outside."

"They were all lovey-dovey at your house," Carl said. "I wonder what happened."

"Who knows? I told her something Derrick told me. I hope she didn't start fussing about that. It's hard to satisfy women. They want to be all independent but they want you to pamper them at the same time."

Carl headed back to the front porch, but again slowed down, then returned to the car. "I heard more hollering and it sounded like something breaking."

"You said they were lovey-dovey earlier. Maybe they're getting their freak on," Raymond said.

"You know I mind my own business, but I don't think we should leave."

"You've been watching too much daytime TV," Raymond said as he turned off the car. "I'm sure everything is fine. Let's both go ring the doorbell."

CAROLYN

We both jumped when we heard knocking at the door.

"Carolyn, are you all right?"

"It's Raymond," I said, as I peeked through the blinds. "And Carl."

"Just great," Derrick said. "I'll get it. Hey guys, this isn't a good time," Derrick said as he opened the door just enough to talk through.

"Carolyn said she was going to finish the application tonight, and I found some additional information that might help her," Raymond said.

"Okay, I'll give it to her."

"I'd like to give it to her myself," Raymond said.

"Like I said, this isn't a good time."

Phyllis R. Dixon

"We heard," Carl said. "We'd like to talk to her a minute. Just want to make sure everything is okay."

"I don't mean to be rude, but your sister—"

Carl kicked the door and the chain came off, knocking Derrick off balance. "Man, you can't bust into my house like this."

"Carolyn, what's going on?" Raymond asked as he looked around.

"You need to leave my house," Derrick said. "And one of you is going to pay for that door."

"We'll leave, but we're not leaving her here," Carl said.

"Carolyn, are you all right?" Raymond asked. "If you want us to mind our own business and leave we will. But you know you don't have to stay here."

"I never wanted this," I said. I tried to close my shirt with tears running down my face. My neck and arm were throbbing, but the tears were more from humiliation than pain.

"If your whining ass had listened to me in the first place, none of this would have happened," Derrick said.

"I don't know what goes on in your house," Raymond said as he stepped over the broken coffee table toward me. "But I can't let you talk to my sister like that."

"Your sister is my wife, and I'll talk to my damn wife in my damn house any damn way I please." We all turned around when we heard footsteps on the porch. "Now who's at the damn door?" Derrick said.

"It's Rick. Is everything all right in there? We got a call about a disturbance." As the police officer entered the room, he stepped over a lamp. "Your neighbors said two guys broke in."

"This is my sister's house," Raymond said. "You can see she's upset. It's a good thing we were here

266

before he did anything else to her. He needs to be arrested."

"Rick, this is just a misunderstanding. You know things happen between married people. Me and my wife are in our own home. I'm sorry the neighbors were disturbed, and I'm willing not to press charges against them for breaking in my house."

"Press charges against us? We're not the ones—"

"Look, I'm sorry you heard what you heard. I didn't know we had an audience, but I'll ask you again to please leave."

"We're not going anywhere without our sister," Carl said.

"My wife is fine. Officer, you see what I'm dealing with."

"If you're not going to arrest him, I'm not leaving," Raymond said.

"Ray, I like your family. But right now, what I see is that you and your brother unlawfully entered this man's home. His door is busted and he's asked you to leave. I can't arrest him for arguing with his wife, unless she says something. Did your husband assault you?"

"Well, tell him," Raymond said.

"Carolyn, we heard you," Carl said softly. "Don't be afraid. We'll make sure you're okay."

"That sounds like a threat to me," Derrick said. "With your record, you need to be careful what you say."

"I got your record if you put your hands on my sister again."

"Sounds like another threat. With witnesses too. Not very smart."

"Well, what do you have to say? Who do you want me to arrest?"

Phyllis R. Dixon

I feel like I'm dreaming, make that having a nightmare. My head is spinning, and it feels like what little is left in my stomach wants to come out. Maya Angelou said, when someone shows you who they are, believe them. I'm finally a believer, but do I really want my husband to go to jail or have a record? This time it will stick. Eden is a small town and everyone will know. He might even lose his job. I can't do that to the father of my child.

"They call it stormy Monday, But Tuesday's just as bad."
                                                    T Bone Walker

Chapter 12
STORMY MONDAY

Some off day. Monday is supposed to be my day to run a few errands, then rest. But I didn't sleep well, and woke up so hot I felt like the sheets had just come out of the oven. It's not a flash. The air conditioner isn't working. It's running, but not blowing cool air. I didn't know the company that Anthony usually calls, so I spent half the morning calling around trying to find a repairman. I mentioned it to Mark when he called and he called a friend who came within thirty minutes. He diagnosed the problem, but can't get the part until tomorrow, so I hung out at the shop all day. I had three walk-ins, a lady and her daughters, then I did Cecelia's hair. I'm pooped. To discourage any more walk-ins, I closed the blinds. Just as I was about to turn the blinds on the last window, Carolyn walked up.

"I was texting you as I walked to your door, but noticed you over here."

"Is this a professional visit or are you just hanging out?"

"If you have time, I'd like my hair done," Carolyn said. "But if not, I'll just visit a while – unless you have something going on."

"Nothing going on but the rent, as they say. Your hair was looking a little shabby yesterday. That's bad advertising for me. Come on and get in my chair. What are we having done today?"

"I want my hair cut."

"You don't need a trim."

"I don't mean trim. I mean cut. Maybe like Halle Berry's."

"Carolyn, you can't be serious. Your hair hasn't been this healthy in decades and it's really growing. Just because you're mad at Derrick, don't take it out on your hair."

"Now what makes you think I'm mad at Derrick?"

"First of all, it's a Monday, not your regular hair appointment day. Then I see your phone lighting up and you not answering it. Now you want to cut your hair because you know Derrick likes it and it's your way of asserting your independence. It's passive aggressive behavior and a symbol of making a change. "

"You should have been a psychiatrist," Carolyn said.

"Sometimes I feel like one. You're mad today. Tomorrow you make up."

"I doubt it. I am beyond mad."

"Okay, so you make him work a little harder. But whenever you do make up, you can't paste the hair back. I've seen too many cases of cut hair remorse. Just think about it. If you still want it cut, I'll do it next time. How about we go with a different color instead of cutting it? "

"Sure," Carolyn said.

"Let's go with a honey brunette. I've always said you should go lighter."

"Fine," Carolyn said.

"Since we're doing color, why don't you take this top off? I don't want to get anything on it. Want me to get you a short sleeve shirt?"

"No thanks. It'll be okay," Carolyn said as she rubbed her arm.

"So do you want to talk about it?" I asked.

"Not really, but I do need a favor."

"Name it."

"I'd like to stay here a few days."

"Oh, you got some big project at work?"

"No. I just need a place to stay."

"You know I'll help any way I can. When are you talking about coming?"

"Today. I have my bags in the car. If it's a problem, I understand. I know Cecelia is staying with you. Where is she anyway?" Carolyn asked.

"She's been having problems with her phone and went to see if it can be fixed. Then she was going to pick up catfish dinners."

"Wow, she must be having a midlife crisis. She always lectured me about fried food. And I can remember when she would just go get a new phone. That could just be a cover for her to go to the casino."

"I'm not keeping tabs on her, but I don't think she's into gambling like she was. She seems very different."

"So, how is she?" Carolyn asked. "We didn't really get to talk yesterday."

"She seems okay. At first I thought she was just coming for a visit. But she hasn't said anything about going home, and she came with lots of baggage. She just sits around all day. I think maybe she lost her job. Something else – I found a passport application on the dresser."

"Maybe she needs some more official identification. She doesn't have any money to be taking an exotic vacation. And as bad as they need nurses, I don't see her losing her job. She's a good nurse. She's probably just burned out and needs a break," Carolyn said.

"So that's her problem, what's yours?" I asked.

"What makes you ask?"

"Carolyn, you show up on a Monday then announce you don't want to go home. Doesn't take a genius to figure that one out. You don't have to talk about it if you don't want to."

"Have you talked to Raymond or Carl today?" Carolyn asked.

"No, why?"

"It's a long story."

"Well, tell it when you get ready. In the meantime, it will be fun for all of us to be together. I'm just glad I'm here for you guys. Whenever I needed some space, I'd tell Anthony I needed to go help Mama with something. I'd spend a few days with her rocking on that porch, and that was enough to recharge my batteries. Sometimes you just need to get away a few days."

"I wish it were that simple. Actually I may need to stay more than a few days. I think we're getting a divorce."

"Carolyn, no. What in the world happened?" Is there another woman or something?"

"No, unless you count his grandmother."

"Well, what in the world could it be? That man is devoted to you."

"Beverly, did Anthony ever put his hands on you?"

"I know you're not saying he hit you," I said as I spun the chair around so I could face her.

"Not really, but—"

"Carolyn, what are you doing here?" Cecelia said as she walked in the door. "If I had known you were here I would have ordered three dinners."

"We'll talk later," I whispered as I led Carolyn to the shampoo bowl.

"Cece, I'm going to be away a few days and I really need you to go stay in Eden for a while," Carolyn said.

"What's going on?" Cecelia asked. "Nothing's happened to Daddy has it?"

"No. It's not Daddy, it's Aunt Belle. I've been checking on her almost every day and taking her meals. She's fiercely independent, and won't admit she needs help, but someone needs to keep tabs on her."

"Oh no. That's not the job for me. I love Aunt Belle, but we would not get along if I had to be her caretaker."

"So join the club. She fires every aide that goes over there. She can't fire family. I just thought with you being a nurse and being off work..."

"As hard as you worked to get assigned down here, now they're going to ship you off someplace? Why don't you just tell them you can't go? You already took a downgrade, what more can they do?" Cecelia asked.

"Why don't you just think about someone other than yourself for a change?" Carolyn asked. "Beverly said you're not doing anything all day."

"First, you're reading my mail, now you're talking about me behind my back?"

"I told you yesterday I was just looking for a document. If you don't want me to see something, in *my* house, then you need to move it. It isn't a hotel," I said.

"Fine. I don't plan to be here much longer anyway."

"Timeout," Sharon said as she walked in. "I forgot to bring my towels with me on Saturday, and didn't realize it until I went to do my washing. I'll just get my towels and you girls can continue with your loving family gathering."

"Sharon, who's that with you?" I asked.

Just then a man rushed in and shoved Sharon to the floor, then pointed a gun at me. "Nobody move," he shouted.

Carolyn screamed.

"Shut up," he yelled. "Give me your purse. And you" he said pointing the gun at me, open the cash register.

"There's nothing in there," I said.

"Open it anyway, and give me your watch."

As I led him to the cash register, the front door slammed. "How many times have I told you to lock this door? Hey, what the hell is going on in here?"

The gunman turned around and Anthony lunged at him. "Run," Anthony shouted as he grabbed the man's arm. I ran to my station and opened my bottom drawer where I kept my peacemaker. I pulled the trigger, just like Daddy taught me.

Gunshots, shattered glass, and screams filled the air.

"I woke up this morning as the rooster crowed
Feeling brand new from head to toe...
I feel like a million dollars inside
Don't remember the last time that I cried.
I'm smiling. Smiling again."

Grady Champion

Chapter 13
I'M SMILIN' AGAIN

Seeing Daddy standing in front of the minister reminded me of my wedding last year when we stood on the beach, under an orchid covered arch, steps away from the Atlantic Ocean. Daddy probably hasn't been to two weddings in his lifetime, and now he's been in two in two years. Today was a perfect day for a wedding. The sun was shining brightly, so even though it's December, it's not cold. Daddy had on a grey tux and Miss Emma wore a cream colored suit with a faux fur collar. They looked like they belonged in the newlywed section of *Jet Magazine*.

"Carolyn, we've been looking all over for you," Cecelia said as she opened the door to the sanctuary. She and Beverly came in and sat on the pew behind me. "They're getting ready for their first dance, then they want us to gather for a picture."

"It was a lovely wedding. Fall was Mama's favorite time of year. She loved to can. I can see her sitting on the porch shelling pecans. Too bad she's not here to see this pretty day," Beverly said. "I guess that was a dumb thing to say."

"If Mother was here our father wouldn't have just gotten married," Cecelia said as she shook rice out of her hair.

"Although technically, he didn't get married today," I reminded her. Turns out he and Miss Emma got married in June. By getting married before she retired, she could add Daddy to her dental and vision plan. "Finding out they had already married was really a surprise."

"Daddy isn't the only one with surprises, Miss Island Girl. Here we were worried about your mental state and you're soaking up sun and sand in the Caribbean," Beverly said as she playfully tugged one of Cecelia's locs. "And I love your hair. Never pictured you as the locs type, but it looks good on you."

Cecelia had spent the last five months in Haiti with Gabriel. Like the FBI's most wanted, he tracked her down when she wouldn't answer his calls or texts and wasn't at the hospital. When she did finally speak with him, she told him all the embarrassing details, in what she thought would be their last conversation. Instead, she got a totally different reaction - he invited her to come to Haiti. His uncle had urged him to come to their homeland and gotten him a position with the Ministry of Health. Gabriel got her a job at a hospital and she lived with his cousin. The salary was a small stipend, but compared to most of the residents, she was rich. Even though millions of dollars had been pledged after the earthquake several years earlier, most of the money still had not made it to the residents, and medical facilities were stretched past their limits.

"When you see their living conditions, it makes you remember what's important. Taking time off for roller-sets and touch-ups seems silly when clean water and electricity aren't even assured. I did the big chop and it's grown a bunch already. Once I started with the locs, I surprised myself with how much I liked it."

"You're just full of surprises. Engaged to a doctor," I said.

"He's not a medical doctor. He's getting a Ph.D. in public health."

"Close enough," I said. "Maybe I need to go to Haiti and find me a man. I haven't had too much luck with these American men."

"Don't even think about taking my niece anywhere. I'm looking forward to spoiling her and taking care of her hair ," Beverly said.

"Maybe you should check the obituaries for widows. It worked for Emma," Cecelia said.

"You know that's not how they met. Daddy drove the school bus for her school, and they worked together for years," I said. "She's not so bad. She'll take good care of Daddy and it's what he wants. That's what counts."

"I see you've drunk the Kool-Aid too," Cecelia said. "But as long as Daddy is happy and she doesn't try to take advantage of him, I'll back off."

"I will say this. I don't know what that lady has, but Mama could never get Daddy in a suit, and Miss Emma got him to wear a tux. He looked like a distinguished professor," Beverly said. "Bought her a nice ring, too. I didn't know he had it in him."

"So what should we call her?" I asked as I fanned with the program.

"I can think of a few things," Cecelia said.

"Whether you like it or not, she's Daddy's wife, so be nice," Beverly said as she checked her phone. "I'll meet you for the picture. I need to get the charger out of the car. Anthony's wheelchair battery is running low."

BEVERLY

I love weddings. It's nice to see extended family and it not be a funeral. Maybe Anthony and I will renew our vows next year. Most people wait for the years ending in zero or five to celebrate. We had already started planning Mama and Daddy's fiftieth anniversary even though it was a few years away. Daddy was in a wedding today, but not to Mama. Just goes to show you can't predict what lies around the corner so it's best to live for today. People always say that, but we still take things, and people for granted.

Anthony was in intensive care for five days after the shooting. Then his medicine kept him pretty groggy the next few weeks. He's had two surgeries and has one more scheduled for March. He's finally able to get in and out of the wheelchair by himself. Aunt Belle's leg healed, so we put her hospital bed in the downstairs bedroom – so much for my exercise room. We added a ramp to the front door and installed a shower seat in the downstairs bathroom. The doctors say he could be on a walker this time next year and walking down the aisle would be a special way to commemorate his progress.

Daddy's wedding has been a welcome break since I don't have off days anymore. I fix breakfast then go to the salon. I come home to fix Anthony's lunch and start dinner. I don't take any customers after two. I come back to the house and we watch the crazy judge shows on TV. Three days a week, I take Anthony to therapy. Luckily, Grant agreed to return and run the salon for us, and I can focus on Anthony. It's a hassle to eat out with the wheelchair, so we eat most of our meals at home. He's on a restricted diet and cooking dinner requires more planning. After dinner, we play marathon gin rummy sessions.

I wanted him to slow down his running around, but not like this. Of course, my sisters think I'm crazy for taking him back. But when I saw his body fall to the floor, and blood squirting everywhere, I forgot about the divorce, lawyers, and everything else. I crossed back over that line. You'd think they would be grateful to him for saving our lives. If he hadn't taken that bullet, who knows what would have happened? And what kind of person would I be if I deserted him in his time of need? Maybe it took something drastic for us to get back together and realize we're meant to be together. Even Money is back home. Anthony has always had a dog, and when we went to the animal shelter to get a puppy, we saw Money. We were both ecstatic. Tony's deployment ends next month and he's going to be stationed in Millington, right outside Memphis. So I'm getting my family back, and I don't care what my sisters think. Anthony has given me more than my share of the blues, but he's my husband. We said for better or worse, in sickness and in health. I'm sure he would do the same for me.

CAROLYN

Daddy complained about Miss Emma's preparations for a wedding reception – said they were too old for such a fuss. He was so nervous this morning when I helped him tie his bowtie. I couldn't get him to eat a bite. But he looks to be having more fun than anyone. He's wearing out the dance floor, and shows no sign of missing his usual afternoon nap. Raymond is taking the newlyweds to Hot Springs for their honeymoon. It will seem strange to go back to the house tonight and Daddy not be there. I was just getting used to living back at home, but it's time to move on.

I've been living like a vagabond the last few months. Derrick stayed with Mother Roberts a couple weeks and let me stay in the house until I "cooled off" as he put it. When he came back, I moved in with Daddy and Carl, or should I just say Daddy, since Carl is either working or with Portia. Daddy said I can stay as long as I like, but the commute is getting to be draining, especially now that it's dark in the morning and dark when I get off work.

Beverly wants me to come stay with her, but the baby and I need our own place. She's too judgmental about Derrick. She even arranged an intervention, when she found out Derrick and I were seeing each other. I was furious and told everyone to stay out of my business. How could we work out our problems if we couldn't see each other and talk about them (of course we were doing more than talking). But I've watched enough *Lifetime* TV to know the signs, and talking wasn't going to make the problem go away.

Why didn't I walk away at the first sign? The same reason people smoke cigarettes and know they're bad for your health, or text and drive. Everyone thinks they are the exception to the rule. Just like an alcoholic or drug addict doesn't get out of control with their first drink, pill, or smoke, it's a gradual process. It starts with a raised voice, a push, or grab. They aren't abusive all the time and usually the good times outweigh the bad, at least in the beginning. By the time things get bad, you're ashamed and embarrassed. You believe somehow you are partly to blame, and it can be intoxicating to think an otherwise rational person, loves you so much they lose control. Beverly told me story after story of some of her customers. One of them was shot when she tried to leave. Even Cecelia seemed to know a lot about domestic violence. She called it battered woman syndrome. I hadn't considered myself a battered woman. I didn't have a black eye or teeth knocked out. I wasn't some poor uneducated woman with low self-esteem. Cecelia said all income levels were victims and quoted shocking statistics. She talked about domestic violence being generational, and what message would I be sending my daughter if I stayed? She almost sounded like a counselor.

What really opened my eyes was Aunt Belle's story. She said one of her almost husbands was extremely jealous, and she took that for love, but it was really just insecurity. When she was a background singer at Stax, she was supposed to go to Los Angeles to film the Wattstax concert. Her boyfriend slapped her and her face and lip swelled. She could have tried makeup or made an excuse and gone anyway, but she didn't. She never forgave him. She had spent almost twenty years singing in small clubs in and around Memphis and always felt like she missed her big break, since the other ladies did release a record. It wasn't a big hit, but who knows, if she had been on it maybe it would have been. She said you shouldn't have to suppress your goals and desires to please someone else. I thought about how I had rearranged my life and made the ultimate sacrifice, washing dishes by hand. I realized nothing would ever be enough. It's been six months, and time has a way of dimming the memory. I don't ever want my memory of Derrick's rage and my fear to dim, so I carry the button from the blazer he tore in my wallet as a reminder.

Just like I didn't question Beverly's decision to stay with Anthony, not to her face anyway, I don't want to hear her constantly badmouth Derrick. I know our marriage is over, but he's still going to be a father and we need to find a way to parent together. Besides, Anthony has never been one of my favorite people, so I don't want to be under the same roof with him, even if he is in a wheelchair.

Nothing has quite turned out as I expected. I did get my man, for a little while anyway. I got my promotion and I'm going to be a mother – all things that I asked for. I could have done without the blues that came along with my requests, but in the words of the old spiritual, I wouldn't take nothing for my journey now."

Memphis will be the best of both worlds. It has southern hospitality and all (well make that most) of the amenities of a big city, minus the subzero temperatures. It's December and I'm wearing open toed shoes. I laugh when my coworkers complain about the cold temperatures and having to turn their heat on. I like my new department and since I have not worked with these people day in and day out for years, it's actually been easier to be a supervisor here. I'll be close enough to Eden that I can see Daddy and my brothers often, but not enough for us to get on each other's nerves.

And speaking of my brothers, who would have predicted Raymond as a county alderman? The incumbent candidate got caught in a Little Rock hotel with a woman other than his wife, and at the last minute, an independent coalition asked Raymond to run. I think they thought they were just making a symbolic statement, but they didn't know my brother. He hustled in those six weeks and shocked everyone by winning. He says he's going to try making change from the inside. It's not a full time job, so he's still teaching – for now. But this could be the start of a new career. Didn't someone else go into politics after being a community organizer?

Carl now has more work than ever. He got the contract to transport dialysis patients and hired Perry to drive three days a week. The police dropped the charges against Perry due to a technicality and he promised Carl he would be legit. We weren't too thrilled with that choice, but I guess if family won't take a chance on you, who will? That leaves Carl time to help run the farm. Daddy says he's retiring and Carl will be taking over. Miss Emma says Carl better learn quick because she has other plans for our father.

I've spent thousands of dollars on vacations, spas, and shopping sprees trying to unwind and find peace, while waiting for my "real" life to start. Time to take my life off hold and push play. No more waiting to be asked to dance – so I'm heading to the dance floor. They just finished the electric slide and Aunt Belle is leading the wobble line. I see an empty spot right on the front row.

Reading Group and Resource Guide

The questions and discussion topics that follow are intended to enrich your discussion of Phyllis R. Dixon's, *Down Home Blues.*

Questions for Discussion

1. All marriages face challenges, and both parties must make an effort to work things out, when difficulties arise. Since Derrick is willing to get help, is Carolyn being premature in ending her marriage? Are some offenses unforgiveable?

2. Carl is a fictional character, but his struggle is real. Depending on which study you cite, approximately two thousand men and women are released from state or federal custody each day, and two-thirds of them will be rearrested within three years. What can be done to turn these statistics around? Why do you think Carl was successful in rebuilding his life? Once a person "pays their debt to society" should there still be consequences?

3. Discrimination in employment is illegal, but what about the employer's rights? As co-owner of The Oasis, doesn't Anthony have a right to hire and fire as he sees fit?

4. Do you think people in the "south" are different, or are people basically the same everywhere?

5. Do you believe in prenuptial agreements? If you need a prenuptial agreement, should you be marrying that person?

6. What do you predict for Beverly and Anthony's future?

7. Hydraulic fracturing, or "fracking," is a process where drillers blast millions of gallons of chemically treated water into the ground to extract gas from hard-to-reach deposits deep in the earth. Thanks to improved technology, drilling for these deposits is now profitable. The environmental impact is controversial, but what is certain, is that fracking provides good paying jobs and increased tax revenues for some communities. It's easy to say residents should forego current income and consider long term costs to the environment. But what would you do if you were offered money for the right to drill on your property?

8. Caregiving for Aunt Belle seemed to fall in Carolyn's lap. If you were Carolyn, would you have handled this differently?

9. Cecelia is an example of someone who gives one hundred ten percent to their career, but their personal life suffers. Is it possible to have it all?

10. Were Carl and Raymond right to bust into Carolyn's house? What can you do if you suspect someone is in an abusive relationship?

Sources of Help and Information

Pros and Cons of Fracking
www.foodandwaterwatch.org
www2.epa.gov/hydraulicfracturing
www.energyfromshale.org

Domestic Violence Resources
www.ncadv.org
www.domesticshelters.org
www.thehotline.org

Advocacy and Resources for Ex-Offenders
www.sentencingproject.org
www.helpforfelons.org
www.csgjusticecenter.org

It goes without saying that you must read *The New Jim Crow–Mass Incarceration in the Age of Colorblindness* by Michelle Alexander.

About the Author

Phyllis R. Dixon is the author of the novel *Forty Acres*, *Let the Brother Go If...* and a contributing author to *Chicken Soup for the African American Woman's Soul*. She is a graduate of the University of Wisconsin–Milwaukee and resides in Memphis, Tennessee.

You can visit her at www.PhyllisDixon.com

CPSIA information can be obtained at www.ICGtesting.com
Printed in the USA
LVOW08s2239120116

470290LV00008BA/736/P